Shadow of the Marula Tree

Tess Jackson

Published by Green Shutter Books Ltd 2018

Copyright © Tess Jackson 2018

The right of Tess Jackson to be identified as the author of this work has been asserted by the author in accordance with the Copyright, Designs and Patents Act 1988.

The story contained within this book is a work of fiction. Names and characters are the product of the author's imagination and any resemblance to actual persons, living or dead, is entirely coincidental.

All rights reserved. No part of this book may be reproduced, stored in a retrieval system, or transmitted in any form or by any means, electronic, electrostatic, magnetic tape, mechanical, photocopying, recording or otherwise, without the written permission of the publishers: Green Shutter Books Ltd, Greenacres, St Ouen, Jersey, JE3 2DA

www.GreenShutterBooks.com

Dedication

To the talented writer Deborah Carr, for the encouragement she gave me, insisting I could write a book.

She is my inspiration.

Acknowledgements

This book is a work of fiction inspired by my love of animals and many visits to the bush over the years I've lived in South Africa. Any mistakes I have made in the book are unintentional and my own.

I would like to thank those of my friends whose names I have borrowed for some of my characters, as well as the following people who have helped me during the writing of this novel:

To Rachael Troy, for being my beta reader.

Richard Garland for his knowledge on the birds and trees, without whose help I would have spent many more hours carrying out research.

Deb Finlay for her much appreciated editing and Helen Baggott for proofreading this book.

To my husband Garry, and the rest of my family, for believing in my ability to finish this novel.

Chapter One

Kay Anderson woke with a shock, as the fuselage began to shudder when the light aircraft landed with a thump on the grassy runway of the Impangela Muzi Lodge airstrip. The handsome young pilot who had only been introduced to her as Andrew, turned and gave her a wink, as the plane taxied towards the end of the runway. It was too late to change her mind now, even if she wanted to. She looked at her white knuckles as she gripped her hands together to stop the trembling.

'Sorry to wake you, miss. Looks like a perfect day for your arrival. Hope all goes well for you with this lot,' he said with a wave of his hand towards the distant thatch dwellings.

'Thank you.' Kay yawned.

'Made good time, too. It's only eleven o'clock. We had the wind on our tail. You chose the right time of year to start a job in these parts. March starts to cool down and the animals move around much more during the day.'

'That's exactly why I said I would start now and get to know the area before the Easter guests arrived,' Kay explained.

She felt a bubble of excitement as she looked out at the dense bush, where she knew the animals would be grazing. This was to be her home for the foreseeable future, and she couldn't wait to meet her manager and all the staff. It was going to be a big challenge. One she couldn't wait to tackle. Her spirits rose as the pilot announced she could leave the plane and go to the awaiting car that would make the short journey to the lodge. As she was the only passenger, the cases were taken out by the driver of the car.

The chauffeur greeted the pilot and then introduced himself to Kay.

'Hi Kay, I'm your driver, Sam.' He shook her hand as he looked her up and down. 'My good fortune to collect you. We don't get to see much glamour in these parts,' he said, smiling.

She just had time to wave goodbye to the pilot as the little plane was turning ready for take-off, and collection of passengers who stayed at the different lodges in the Sabie Sands area.

'As you know,' Sam said, starting the car, 'we're situated close to the Kruger National Park, in Mpumalanga district. Welcome to northern South Africa.'

Kay smiled. 'Thank you.'

They drove through thick bush as they left the airstrip, where Kay spotted just the heads of three giraffes reaching up to leaves on the high branches of trees. She breathed deeply, enjoying the smells of dry grass and animals as the light breeze entered her open window. As they drove, the land opened up and as if on cue a large lone lion ambled out of some trees and walked in front of their vehicle.

Sam slammed on brakes and Kay braced herself against the dashboard. 'Sorry about that, he's a regular on the airstrip. Thinks it belongs to him, because he's been in this area for years.' He laughed. 'Apparently, he was run out of his pride by another younger stronger male.'

'Once I've settled in and got my bearings, I'm going to take photos of that magnificent lion,' she said. 'I think I'll do a painting of him for my grandmother. She loves lions.'

'Are you an artist?' Sam asked.

'Yes, I'm an art teacher and lecturer. It was my job back in Durban.'

'What made you come to be a ranger?' he asked. 'It's a tough job after the one you've left.'

'It's a long story,' she smiled. 'I'll tell you about it sometime.'

'Look over there,' he said pointing towards the dam.

She gazed in the direction of the huge expanse of water surrounded by bush and marvelled at the thorn trees dotted along the banks. 'Where's the water source that's filling it?'

'It's an underground spring,' he said. 'And over there are the staff quarters, just before the lodge comes into view,' Sam explained, as she looked towards the lodge.

A large sign in big black letters said, *Impangela Muzi*. Kay recalled someone telling her that the name meant the house of the guinea fowl and wondered if there were any about. She noticed an arrow pointing towards a very impressive building that took her breath away with its huge thatched entrance enhanced by stone pillars on either side. Her eyes followed the stone pathway leading to the entrance, where staff stood at the ready to help guests with luggage. Kay listened as the hornbills squawked loudly and incessantly to each other from their perch in the thorn trees that surrounded the entrance.

'What a racket those birds make,' the driver said with a laugh.

'I guess it's one of the things I'll have to get used to, having forgotten how loudly they squawk. Thanks so much for collecting me and making me feel so welcome. Will I see you around?' Kay asked, as the car came to a stop. She was impressed by the way Sam leaped out and rushed to open her door and held out his hand to help her out of the car. She stood for a moment as the warm breeze wrapped itself around her toned body and looked with excitement at this amazing building that immediately made her feel as if she'd arrived home.

'I'm not often around, but I sure hope to bump into you,' he replied with a twinkle in his eye.

Kay looked around, while the driver took her case and laptop bag out of the car and carried it to where a porter was waiting by a deserted reception desk.

'I'll say cheers for now, and leave you to get settled in. Just ring the bell and someone will come to look after you,' Sam said, as he turned to leave.

Kay waved him goodbye and rang the bell. When nobody arrived, she walked through to the covered veranda that overlooked a long low building with six chalets surrounding it. All the roofing was made of thatch. She noted doors that opened out onto covered verandas with stone steps onto the grass. A couple of guests were sitting on their balconies, looking through binoculars watching young elephants with their mothers. Kay laughed as she watched the babies falling about as they squealed and played in the dam which the chalets overlooked.

Further along she spotted a large swimming pool with twelve lounger chairs covered with brightly coloured towels and cushions on each of them. Sun umbrellas finished off the scene. Close by was an enormous marula tree, the branches leaning over and casting long shadows across the grass, and a table with its matching benches on either side.

A feeling of tranquillity descended on her as if she was arriving home after a traumatic time. The smell of dry grasses and the sound of snorting wildebeest made her feel relaxed and happy for the first time since she had left Durban.

Hearing a noise, she turned towards the lodge. A tiny blonde-haired woman of about twenty rushed out of the building towards her. Hair in a ponytail, dressed in khaki shorts and shirt, her lace-up boots and thick socks finished off the ensemble. Kay knew she would soon be wearing the same uniform. A young Shangaan man smiled and nodded a greeting as he lifted her case from where Sam had left it, waiting while she shook hands with the woman.

'Welcome to Impangela Muzi, Kay, we've been expecting you. Come and have some refreshments. Did you have a good journey?' she asked. 'I'm Alice van Rooyen, Ed's secretary. He apologises for not being here to greet you but will be back after lunch. I'll get Nozi, our porter, to take you to your quarters once I've shown you around.'

'Thanks, Alice,' said Kay, following the girl into the lodge. 'I can't wait to meet Ed, although I was warned that he wasn't very happy having a woman ranger.'

Alice gave Kay a strange look, before replying. 'He's your typical alpha male,' she said, narrowing her eyes. 'Don't let him bully you.' She lowered her voice. 'He's a great guy to work for, but then I'm just his lackey.'

She had a musical laugh, Kay thought. A member of staff brought her a drink. Kay thanked him and took the glass of orange juice. She closed her eyes momentarily relishing the ice-cold drink as it hit the back of her throat.

'Whatever made you want to be a ranger, Kay?' Alice asked. 'It's one of the hardest jobs to qualify for. Hours are long, and we get some horrendous guests at times. Big perks of course, as you get given amazing gifts.' She glanced around her, before lowering her voice and adding, 'One of our rangers was given an expensive camera by a couple, as well as a huge tip when they left.'

'Really?' Kay was not sure how she would deal with extravagant gifts and suspected they would make her feel a bit awkward.

'Hell, Kay, you could be a model with your long legs and that silky chestnut hair. You look more glamorous than most of the guests. So, what brings you here? Do tell.'

'It's a long story, Alice. I'll tell you about it when we have more time.' Kay put her glass down on the nearest table. 'May I look around now? I have heard so much about this place. I'm intrigued to see if it stands up to my expectations.'

'Right, follow me. Let's start in the kitchens and then lounges. We've just upgraded all the chalets and moved the boma to the other side of the kitchen for easier access when it's a braai night. Handy if the rains come and our guests can get back to the lodge quickly,' Alice said. 'The old one was just too far away to be managed with ease.' Alice led the way to the kitchens.

Kay took in her surroundings and marvelled to herself how thrilled she felt to be there at last. She liked Alice enormously and felt she might have a friend in her. She was beginning to think she probably needed one in this mainly male business.

Having finished the tour, Alice led Kay to the table under the marula tree, where the staff had laid out a light lunch. Two squawking brightly coloured hornbill birds sat on the branches, looking down at the girls as they sat. A herd of elephants were lazily making their way towards the large dam at the far end of the grounds and Kay sat enchanted, watching them.

'I think we'd better get on with lunch before the big boss gets here, Kay, if you don't mind. He'll expect us to be waiting in his office at two o'clock,' Alice said looking at her watch. 'He won't be pleased if he finds staff having lunch under his favourite marula tree. We're not guests and our dining room is behind the kitchen. However, when Ed's away we sometimes have lunch here under this great tree.'

'It's wonderful,' Kay said.

'I think so too. The elephants used to come and eat the

berries in the old days, but now there's a low electric wire at the edge of the camp to keep them out. Apart from being dangerous they do such a lot of damage and have been known to try and knock the tree down to reach the top berries.' Alice said. 'They get drunk on them, hence the Amarula liqueur. I'm sorry, Kay; I forgot you know all this, having passed your exams to become a ranger. I love telling our guests the story,' Alice added with a nervous giggle.

Lunch consisted of homemade health breads, salads and an assortment of cold meats and cheeses. Kay especially enjoyed the mixed fruit salad with cream and ice cream that followed. Choices of fruit drinks, tea or coffee with truffles made the meal complete.

Finishing in plenty of time, they made their way to the office. It was large and bright and from the bay window had a view of the dam. Whoever sat at the mahogany desk had an uninterrupted view of any animal going past. A smaller desk was tucked away in a corner with a high-backed red leather chair. A couple sat at a coffee table and chatted quietly.

Standing with his back to the room, as he looked out of the window, was a very tall broad-shouldered man with reddish blonde hair that curled on the collar of his safari shirt. He turned as they waited by the door, making a point of looking at his flash designer watch.

'Well at least you're punctual,' he growled in a deep baritone voice. 'I expected someone older, and preferably a male.' Cold grey eyes glared from Kay to Alice. 'I will see you later, Alice,' he said in a dismissive voice. Alice smiled reassuringly at Kay.

'I'll catch up with you later, Kay, and take you to your lodgings,' she added. 'By the way this is our boss, Edward Blake. He's not as fierce as he'd like us to believe,' she said over her shoulder, making a hurried escape.

'Very nice to meet you, Edward,' Kay said. 'Even though it seems you're not at all happy with my gender. Are there no other women rangers in the park?'

'You're a great deal younger than I expected. Which probably means you'll have issues with some of the male rangers and guests.' His expression softened. 'This is no business for the likes of you. It's hard enough for the men. I need people with stamina to cope with long hours as well as being able to identify the animals, birds and trees. It's not all about the big five you know.' His voice was getting louder as he became angrier. 'Why the hell do women want to become rangers? It's a job for men.'

Kay was furious. She felt her eyes filling up. How dare he treat her this way? Alice was right. He was so chauvinistic and unbelievably patronising. It reaffirmed her determination to do the job she was very qualified to do. She was not going to let Edward Blake get away with this attitude. She needed to defend herself immediately.

Holding her hands together to stop them from shaking, Kay took a deep breath. 'I'm sorry my age and gender disappoint you, Mr Blake, but I'll have you know that I passed my exams with higher marks than the men in my class.' He opened his mouth to say something, but she said, 'I am fully aware how to treat guests and conduct myself in the manner that is expected of me. I have driven all sorts of vehicles while on the course, and am a crack shot, should I be required to save a life.' She knew she was ranting, but was unable to stop from adding, 'Furthermore, I have spent most of my summer holidays in the bush with my parents and brothers while growing up. I knew the names of most species long before I decided to become a ranger. Finally, it is none of your business why I've chosen this profession. Now, if you've quite finished, I'd like to go and unpack.' Kay knew she would burst into tears if she said another word. She was irritated having to look up at this arrogant man towering above her. She turned to leave.

'Calm down, woman, I have no doubts about your qualifications, or your ability to look after yourself, having just got a taste of it myself. What you don't seem to realise is that I'm responsible for you rangers and trackers, and we have had some unpleasant incidents with poachers in this area. It makes me bloody sick to think a woman could end up in an unsavoury situation. I've read your file. What are you, twenty-seven?'

Kay nodded, wondering what he was getting at.

'Sit at Alice's desk while I go through your work schedule.' He sat down at the big desk, shaking his head. 'And for pity's sake call me Ed. We don't stand on ceremony here; we're one big happy family.'

'You could have fooled me,' Kay said, smiling for the first time, noticing how those cold grey eyes had taken on a warmer hue.

A bakkie came to a screaming halt outside the office door in a cloud of dust. Out jumped a tall, suntanned man in the khaki uniform, his thick black hair standing at all angles. Without knocking he rushed into the office, stopping short when he caught sight of Kay.

'What?' Ed said, jumping to his feet.

'They need you over the far ridge. Poachers. One of our guys has been hurt. I radioed Ben to go get him and take him to the hospital, but he wants to talk to you first. Not sure how bad it is, but he's losing a lot of blood.'

'The animal?'

'The rhino is hurt but got away, so it'll be dangerous. We must find it, not sure which sex it was. You're the best one to dart it so that we can check it out.' He took a deep breath. 'Sorry, you must be Kay? Bad day to arrive,' he said. 'I'm Frank Warren.' He shook her hand before turning back to his boss.

'Who's hurt and how bad is it?' Ed growled, as he moved towards the door.

'Tom, and he's got a bullet in his shoulder. Dexter's with him trying to keep him still, but you know what Tom's like. Wants to get after the buggers. Dexter's giving him first aid, I gather,' replied Frank.

Ed took his radio from his belt and called Dexter. 'I want Tom taken to hospital and that's an order!' Ed shouted. 'No, tell him I'm leaving now with Frank. We should be there in half an hour. Leave Zumbe there with a rifle and I'll pick him up. He may find tracks and follow those bastards.' He slammed his hand down on his desk in fury.

'Sorry, Kay, I'll have to catch you later,' Ed said. He reached the door and bellowed for Alice. She must have heard the commotion, because she arrived at the office within seconds. 'Take care of Kay, will you?' Ed said. 'Stay by your radio in case I need you.'

He and Frank ran outside. Kay watched from the window as they leapt onto the bakkie and raced out of camp.

'Wow, nothing like being thrown in at the deep end,' Alice said, smiling at Kay.

'Now I realise why Ed is concerned about having a woman ranger working here. Let's face it, Alice, does it matter? I'll be doing the same job, but hopefully this isn't the norm, is it?' Kay asked.

'No, we haven't had any incidents for a few months now. The poachers have been hitting Kruger Park mostly, but every now and then they come to the Sabie Sands to try their luck. They set traps for the smaller animals like the duikers and young waterbuck, impala and klipspringers,' Alice said sounding sad. 'Come, let me show you where you're going to live. I'll be right next door, so that's great. The manageress of the restaurant is the other side of our chalet and shares with the waitresses. They have three rooms within their chalet. The men's quarters are at the other camp, so they have to drive home after work. You and I will be able to walk though. Ed has his own house down in the valley, a short drive away.'

'When are the next lot of guests due to arrive?' Kay asked. 'I think Ed was about to tell me when I would get to go out with one of the other rangers, when all hell broke loose,' Kay said with a sigh.

'Tomorrow. We have a group of tourists arriving at

lunchtime. Usually they come and have a light lunch and then go on a three-thirty drive, back at seven, dinner at eight. You'll be able to meet the rangers tonight and then know who is on duty with that group of people.' Alice linked arms with Kay as they walked across the lawn to the group of staff rooms. 'The porter has put your case in the room,' she added.

After taking her time unpacking and a leisurely shower, Kay changed into the new uniform that had been ordered for her and was awaiting in her wardrobe. Then, standing at the window enjoying the scenery, she wondered if the men had found the injured rhino, and if they got Tom to the hospital in time.

She knew March was a lovely time to start her new job, because the summer rains were over and the insects she hated were not so bad. She had been taking a course of antimalarial pills, so hopefully she would be immune. One of the girls on her course wanted to be a ranger, but having lived in this area for years, had contracted malaria three times. Kay recalled the doctor telling the girl that she had to either stay on the pills or leave the area. Luckily, she was going to work for a safari lodge near Cape Town and didn't have malaria in that part of the country.

Gazing across to the dam, memories flooded back to a happier time, when she was young and would spend days swimming and boating in the dam on her uncle's farm just outside Komatipoort. Kay dragged her mind back to the present, as the memories were too painful to contemplate. Realising this is exactly where she was meant to be, it was her chance to make a new life for herself. Ed Blake was not going to break her resolve. She knew she could do this job and would just have to prove it to him and other members of the staff. Kay realised that the men obviously thought a woman couldn't be as good a ranger as any of them. She would just have to prove them all wrong.

Then checking herself in the long mirror, she felt happy with her reflection. Tall at five ten, her long legs looked better with the tan after her time on the Durban beaches. She loved the new uniform of the rangers and felt she looked the part in the khaki shorts and shirt. She liked the sensible boots with the required cotton socks. Kay tied her long dark chestnut hair into a ponytail. As she noticed the fine lines around her amber eyes as she smiled into the mirror. She was a little on the thin side, but after all the preparation for this job, her body was firmer and stronger than it had ever been.

She picked up her bag, torch and the fleece with the work logo on it. The evenings turned cold at this time of year, and she guessed it would be late when she returned to her room. Making sure the screen and door were firmly closed, she made her way towards the main lounge where Alice had arranged to meet her.

Entering the lodge, Kay made her way to the lounge. Alice was sitting with another girl who, like Alice, was fair haired, cut in the latest fashion of the short bob. Pretty too, thought Kay as she stood to greet her, and realised she was tall like her.

'Kay, meet Sally Pope. Sally runs the beauty spa at the other lodge. She is besotted with our boss, hence her presence here tonight. Unfortunately for Sally, his lordship is out hunting a rhino.' She pretended to whisper. 'She was not pleased when I told her she had wasted her time visiting our camp.'

'Shut up, Alice, everyone has the hots for the boss. Pity he's so up his own derriere and only notices us if we do something wrong. Hello, Kay, good to meet you,' Sally said, smiling at Kay. 'Let's go to the bar. I need a bit of sustenance having come all this way. What do you drink, Kay?' Sally asked, leading the way into the cosy cocktail bar.

'A glass of dry white wine would be great. I'm so pleased to meet another female in this place. Such a domination of the male species,' Kay said with a smile.

'You ain't seen nothing yet, wait till you meet the whole team. How many have we, Sally?' Alice asked.

'You know better than me, Alice. You do the correlation of all the rangers and trackers. I'm not sure any more, what with the new contingent of extra people.' Sally thought for a moment. 'Do you mean just this lodge, or the main lodge as well?'

Alice laughed, as she ordered a gin and tonic from the barman. She turned to Kay. 'I reckon we have three dishy guys, Ed, Tom and Frank, attached to this lodge. The others are from the main lodge, and there's no woman ranger over there. I've got my eye on one of the new recruits though. You can take a good look at him at the meeting in the morning, but I saw him first,' Alice laughed. 'That's if Ed gets back in time to hold a meeting. Why that look, Kay?'

Kay apologised. 'I'm here to learn the ropes so count me

out in the men department. I'm just not interested in getting involved with any man,' Kay said.

It didn't go unnoticed by Kay that the two girls gave each other a knowing smile.

'You aren't the first girl to say that,' Sally said, 'and probably won't be the last. I bet my bottom dollar you'll have an affair at the very least while you live here. It gets pretty lonely when we only get time off every three months.'

'Yes, and you've been trying to get our boss to notice you since the day you arrived,' Alice teased Sally.

'Anyway, Kay, I'm sure you'll enjoy working here and it's really great to have a girl as a ranger. Hope you give those guys a run for their money and bag the best guests when it's your duty days.' Alice took a sip of her drink. 'And watch out for Frank, he's a real charmer with the women. He's also a top ranger. His tracker Zumbe is excellent, but very aloof, but don't take that personally.'

The next hour flew by as the girls enjoyed each other's company. Kay listened as they enlightened her about some of the affairs that had taken place over the last year with some of the rangers and guests. Sally told her to watch out for certain male guests who arrived without their wives and thought it the norm to proposition single women. She admitted that she had indeed had a couple of affairs with men who had come to the spa for treatments.

Kay tried not to show her surprise and kept a fixed smile on her face.

'There was one in particular,' Sally continued. 'He returned every three months. He's a businessman from America and spoils me with gifts.' She admitted that he was in love with her and she certainly had feelings for him. He was engaged to a high-powered girl whose father owned the company he worked for, and because she was the only child, it had been made clear that he would take over once the father retired. It meant being married to the daughter, so if he wanted to keep his job, nothing could come of their affair.

Kay watched as a very hard expression crossed the girl's face but vanished in a flash. Could she have imagined it? Hurriedly she changed the subject. 'I thought it was against the rules for any staff to become involved. I presumed that also applied to guests,' Kay said.

'You're right about the staff, Kay, but nobody said we couldn't get involved with the guests. The thing is, never get caught or it could lead to trouble. If it got out or caused a scandal, we'd be for the chop,' Sally whispered.

'Let's eat, shall we?' Alice said, picking up her drink and making her way to the dining room. 'The food is to die for here,' she laughed.

Having seated themselves at a table by the window, they watched animals moving towards to dam for their evening swim or drink. Kay studied the set menu. She felt happy to have these interesting and friendly girls where she was to spend her time for the foreseeable future.

The waitress arrived promptly with their first course of prawns in a peri-peri sauce. Kay enjoyed the fillet steak, French fries and salad. The girls refused puddings but ended the evening with Irish coffees and petit fours.

'I wonder how that chap is that got shot,' Kay mentioned, looking at Alice.

'Hell, I hope he's going to be sorted out at the hospital, it's miles away from where he was attacked. Thank goodness Ed's gone to see what's up. The poor buggers will be exhausted when they get back. I think I'll ask chef to keep a plate of food for them all.' Alice got up and made her way to the kitchen.

Kay tried to hide a yawn, but Sally saw her and raised her eyebrows.

'I'm not surprised you're tired, Kay. Getting up early to catch your flight, and then meeting the handsome boss, not to mention your introduction to the dramas we've had here today. I'm also shattered. I have had four treatments from seven this morning. One lady was a right pain. I really battled with her because she kept fidgeting and I had to stop, which made me loose the rhythm of my massage. Silly cow has so much money and she is so obnoxious whenever she visits, and that's often,' Sally moaned.

They were interrupted by the guard informing Sally that her driver was waiting to take her back to her lodge. Alice returned, and the three girls gave each other a hug and promised to stand together against the male population at the camps. Alice did a little dance of joy making them laugh. Kay felt she had made two good friends.

Before Sally left, Alice and Kay promised to keep her up to date with all the news, once the men got back.

It was ten o'clock and still no sign of Ed and the others. Kay announced that she was tired and thought she should get some sleep.

'I want to be fresh for the meeting tomorrow morning,'

she said as she and Alice went with the security guard to their rooms. They wished each other goodnight. 'Thank you for a brilliant day,' Kay said, 'and for introducing me to Sally.'

As Kay drifted off to sleep, she heard the roar of the lions in the distance, as they called to each other. She was looking forward to waking up to the next day of her new life, determined not to let past heartbreak hinder her new-found happiness. The day had turned out better than she could have hoped for.

Chapter Two

Ed, Frank, and the tracker had been making for the area where the poachers were last seen. Ed's main concern, was the injured Tom, who could be bleeding and near to death by now. Ed cut across tracks and roads driving at speed, around hairpin bends, missing elephants and other animals that on a normal day would have been a bonus to see. Ed concentrated hard as he was driving much faster than he normally would in the bush. Frank was frantically radioing Tom as Ed drove, trying to locate exactly where he was. Thanks to Tom being able to tell them his exact location, they arrived just over half an hour later. Dexter, who had trained as a first-aid specialist, was attending to Tom who looked much the worst for wear. He was propped up against an old tree stump.

'How's he doing? Bloody hell, man, that's some slug you've got there,' Ed said as he jumped from the vehicle and looked down at Tom's ashen face.

'There were three of them, Ed, all with rifles and handguns. If it weren't for Dexter, I'd be a goner. He shot the poacher just as he shot me. I can't believe the chap managed to get away,' he panted slightly. 'Dexter definitely wounded the one chap, but his mates dragged him to their bakkie before he could take another shot,' Tom said with a voice getting weaker as he spoke.

Ed turned to Zumbi and asked him for his version. He replied in his native Shangaan. Unlike the others, Ed spoke it fluently. Unbeknown to everyone else, Zumbi explained that he had his suspicions about the ambush being an inside job, as the poachers knew exactly where the animals were. Ed asked him to meet him later for further talks. He needed to know more.

'Right, Dexter, get going to the hospital. Looks like Tom needs urgent attention. We're off to locate the wounded rhino before it causes problems. Did you remember the darting kit, Frank?' Ed asked as he helped Dexter pick Tom up. As gently as possible they put the injured man on the back seat of Dexter's people carrier. 'You'll be able to drive Tom to the hospital?' Ed asked Dexter.

'Sure, I'm good. Be there as quickly as possible. I don't like the look of Tom. He's lost one hell of a lot of blood. He'll need a transfusion,' he added.

'Good man,' Ed said as his ranger revved the engine and took off in a cloud of dust.

'Let's get out of here, mate,' Ed said, running to his four-by-four and jumping in just as Frank did.

They spent hours searching for the wounded animal, radioing all the rangers from neighbouring lodges, who were out with their clients. He reminded them to be vigilant and not approach the wounded animal should they make contact with it. Instructions went around to all personnel on the adjoining camps and lodges. Everyone in the Sabie area was on the lookout, with instructions to contact Ed immediately if they located the injured rhino.

When the two men returned to camp, it was one-thirty the following morning. Nobody had seen the injured beast. Any hope of finding and darting it to remove the bullet before it was too late, was turning out to be an impossible task. No one could find the injured animal in the dark. They would have to wait until morning to continue their search.

Ed, having dropped the others off at the lodge, drove to his own cottage in the valley. He showered and fell onto his bed. He couldn't sleep. All he could think about was the new ranger Kay Anderson and her uncanny resemblance to his late wife Claire. His eyes stung with unshed tears, as he recalled their short, but blissful married life. He had managed to put their marriage at the back of his mind by keeping busy. Now this girl had broken open his wounded mind by her very existence.

Finally, he slept, but dreamt of Kay and Claire merging into one. It seemed he had just closed his eyes when he was woken by a call from the tracker giving him an update about the rhino's whereabouts. Dressing at lightning speed he picked up his rifle and handgun and grabbing an apple from the pottery bowl on his kitchen table, he ran out to his four-by-four.

Frank was waiting for him as he reached his office.

'You look like hell. Looks like you haven't slept at all,' Ed said giving him a quizzical look.

'I had a problem sleeping, but I did get some shut eye once the roaring lions moved away,' Frank moaned. 'You're a great one to talk, you look like you've aged ten years.'

Ed was not taken in by Frank's expansive smile, or his explanation. Something more was going on with him than met the eye, but Ed did not have time to worry about that now. He had more pressing matters to attend to.

'Let's get some coffee and get out of here,' Ed said as they made their way to the kitchens where staff were already busily preparing breakfasts.

'Have you heard anything more about the poachers?' Ed asked.

'No news, but the trackers have been out for the past hour or so trying to pick up the scent again. Ben will radio us once we move away from camp, and let us know if they've found them,' Frank replied.

Ed couldn't help feeling that something was amiss. His gut feeling had never let him down before, but this time he couldn't put his finger on what was bothering him. He put it down to lack of sleep.

The sound of a ranger's bakkie arriving in a cloud of dust brought him back to the present. Dexter leapt out and hurried towards them.

'Morning, guys. What a night. Ben called me soon after I fell asleep. He located the wounded animal and we managed to sedate her and take a look at her injuries. Bloody horrendous I'm afraid. There was nothing we could do to save her, so sadly it was euthanasia.'

Ed banged his hand on the table with a thud, making the

coffee cups jump. 'We have to catch those bastard poachers, Dexter. I want you to round up all spare locals who want to make some cash. Once we've done our drives with guests today, we'll head out to try and catch this bunch. For some reason they seem to be getting inside info on all the animals.'

'Surely you don't suspect one of our staff could be in cahoots with the poachers?' Dexter asked, frowning.

Ed ran his long fingers through his hair, his thoughts racing. He was feeling on edge. Something was getting out of hand, so close to home, but he couldn't put his finger on what it was. He was missing something.

His thoughts turned to Kay, who he wished had been the man he needed, not a stunning brunette. He hated the responsibility of having a woman ranger, knowing it would cause problems between his other rangers and at least one of the trackers. They could cause trouble for Kay, should they have to work with her. Another thing he would have to be very aware of when matching her with a tracker.

'Penny for them, Ed?' Frank said, interrupting his train of thought.

Before Ed could reply, he heard Kay's voice as she greeted the staff. She was followed by a group of guests, all excited to be going on the early drive.

'You chaps carry on. I have a meeting over at main lodge. The big boss is arriving and wants to catch up on the poaching situation. I need to let him know about the burning programme I've planned over on the west side of camp, so I'll see you later.'

Ed walked over to where Kay was helping herself to

coffee. He was aware of her stiffening as he approached, but when she looked at him her smile was warm. Her amber eyes seemed to see right into his soul. One dark brow lifted fractionally as she studied his face.

'Good morning, Kay, I hope you slept well?'

'Hi, and yes I did, thank you.'

'You can get Alice to give you the map of the area we're able to traverse and I'm sure she'll be able to answer any other questions you might have while I'm away this morning. I'll be back at lunchtime, so we'll meet up then,' Ed said before turning and walking away.

Ed was already aware as he drove out of camp that this new woman ranger was going to disrupt his entire world. There was no doubt in his mind that it was going to become a battle of wills between him and his new member of staff. He could tell from the way she spoke and looked at him. Being used to women fawning over him, he was very aware that Kay regarded him quite differently. It amused him just a little to find out how their relationship would progress. Of one thing he was certain, she would follow orders and treat him with respect, or she'd be out. He wasn't taking any aggro from this woman.

As it happened, Ed spent the entire day at meetings at the main camp. He phoned Alice and asked her to tell Kay he could only catch up with her the following day. She was to familiarise herself with the camp and relax. Alice agreed to introduce her to any members of staff that came by and hadn't already met her.

Aware that Alice was delighted to have another woman

on the staff, and how well the two girls had taken to each other, made him a little less nervous. He had Alice to pass on any unpleasant tasks to Kay, should he have a need to do so, he thought.

By the time Ed returned to camp late in the day, he didn't bother to go and join guests for drinks, but simply checked his mail in the office. Having replied to emails and made a few notes, he went back to his cottage, hoping to catch up on some well needed sleep.

Chapter Three

Kay's alarm went off at five-thirty. Light streamed through her windows, as she stretched leisurely. She could hear snorting and heavy footsteps, so leapt out of bed, picked up her binoculars and rushed to the window. To her delight a family of elephants and a herd of wildebeest were already at the dam.

Pulling on her dressing gown, she opened the door to the veranda and made herself comfortable on one of the chairs. Her binoculars were being used to full effect magnifying the sight of the elephant calves cavorting in the mud, while their mothers showered themselves and rolled in the mud. Further along, wildebeest drank their fill while snorting and bashing the ground with their hooves.

The meeting with Ed was at seven-thirty, so sitting on the veranda she allowed herself another few minutes before returning to dress. Kay put sun cream over her exposed skin and sprayed herself with mosquito repellent. It was imperative that she didn't catch malaria, or in fact get sunstroke. It was one of the things drummed into her while taking part in her course. So many first-timers at the bush camp suffered these things because they had no idea how easy it was to forget important preparations each day. Late or not, Kay was told, you do not leave the room before first preparing for duty.

A loud knocking on her door brought her back to the present.

'Wake up, meeting at six-thirty. The boss wants everyone there without delay,' the duty guard shouted from the hallway.

'Thanks, I shan't be long,' Kay replied, dressing quickly and adding a minimum amount of make-up.

Her foundation had a factor fifteen which she reckoned would help over the sun cream already applied. Her new peak cap fitted perfectly over her ponytail, then the jacket with the lodge logo on it. She would need it if she was going out with one of the other rangers who would be showing her the ropes. Ed had told her she would have a couple of weeks being someone's assistant before taking over and finding her own way around the bush.

Leaving her room, she bumped into a grumpy Alice.

'Bloody hell, all this rushing. I hate mornings, just not awake until I've had a strong cup of coffee,' Alice said by way of a greeting.

'Hello, Alice, lovely morning. I've been watching the animals down at the dam. Is this unusual to have the meeting brought forward?' Kay asked.

'It can only mean one thing. Ed's had a drama last night and he wants to fill us all in. I haven't been rushed into an early meeting for months. The last time was when one of the cheetah females was attacked by a lion and her back was ripped open. Ed decided against what would normally happen, which is to let nature take its course, because she had four cubs. He instructed the rangers to take food to her until she was well enough to hunt again. Poor thing had hidden her cubs away, but thankfully one of the trackers found them.' Alice sighed. 'She was close to death due to the loss of blood. Ed darted her and had the vet stitch her up. Then they returned her to the cubs. It took a couple of months before she could hunt again. A tracker guarded them during the day, until another took over the nightshift.'

'How traumatic.' Kay tried not to picture the poor injured cheetah.

'It was. The hyena surrounded them one night and the tracker had to radio for help.'

'What a story. I hope it's not something like that that we'll hear about this morning. Did the mother and cubs survive?' Kay asked.

'She's fine now,' Alice reassured her. 'If only you could have been here. It was wonderful to see how quickly she recovered. She seemed to realise she was being cared for, because she stayed in our area until her cubs left her. Visitors were thrilled to see her and the cubs, unaware what had been going on. It's totally against anything I've heard of before or since.'

They walked up the pathway to the office. Kay saw that other members of staff were heading the same way as her and Alice. She wondered if they were also going to the meeting with Ed.

Alice lowered her voice, adding, 'Then again, our boss is a law unto himself. Nobody tells him what to do. He's been in this job since he was a teenager. From what I've heard, his father was one of the best managers, rangers and trackers.'

Kay was not surprised to hear what Alice was telling her. She listened as Alice stopped walking and continued to speak.

'He was shot by poachers a few years ago.'

Kay gasped, horrified.

'I know, so sad. Ed's distraught mum moved to Cape Town. You might meet her, she often visits. They ran one of the other lodges in the park. That's why Ed is so passionate about catching poachers.'

'I can understand that,' Kay admitted.

'Trouble is, he wants to kill them all.'

Alice checked her watch. 'Well, here we are; we'll know soon enough what this meeting's about,' she said, leading the way into the already crowded lounge where one of the staff was pouring coffee from the breakfast counter. Baskets of homemade muffins and biscuits sat ready for all present.

'Thanks for getting here so quickly, everyone.' Ed looked directly at Kay with a mutinous look on his face. He rubbed his hand over his eyes and ran his fingers through his untidy hair.

He looked like he hadn't slept, she thought, with a feeling of sympathy.

'I'm sorry to get you all here so early but as Frank and I haven't had much sleep, I felt it makes sense to inform you all what went down last night before guests arrive.' He poured some coffee and took a drink. 'We didn't manage to find the injured animal, but I had a call just after five this morning from one of the trackers from the other side of the concession,' he said.

Kay tried to picture which area he meant that was still in the area the rangers were allowed to traverse with their visitors.

'He spotted the rhino that had now collapsed from her injuries. She's lost a lot of blood.' He sighed heavily, adding, 'Unfortunately, he had no choice but to put her out of her misery, as the bastards had hacked off her horn.' The attendees made their shock known. 'The poachers must have found her once we gave up our search. However, the tracker did find her young calf standing by her body.'

'What happened to the calf?' Kay asked, concerned.

'He was darted,' Ed said. 'Then taken to the sanctuary for orphans just outside Kruger.'

'How's Tom?' Alice asked. 'I can't believe he was shot. Is he doing okay in hospital? Is he going to be alright?'

'Hell, Alice, give a guy a chance to finish,' Ed snapped. Alice pulled a face. 'Fine. If you must know, Dexter got Tom to hospital in Nelspruit. He'd lost a lot of blood, so had to be given a few pints. Look, you can get hold of the matron for me and let us know how he's doing,' Ed added.

'Yes, of course,' Alice said.

'Remind them it's workman's compensation, will you?' he added. 'Tell them to email the forms right away, and then you can fill them in. I'll be back later to sign them.'

'If you're finished here, I'll go,' she said.

'Yes. Now I'm going to make some calls and I'll meet you all back here for breakfast in an hour. Alice, I want the guest list for today's arrivals when you've made that call.'

He waited for the others to start leaving the room and indicated for Kay to wait.

'You'll be driving with me,' Ed said, 'so you can learn the ropes as quickly as possible. We've got a full house from now to the end of the month and there's no time for anyone to take leave for the next few weeks, unless there's a family emergency.'

Ed left the room and Kay could not miss the shock on the faces of all the remaining staff.

Frank looked across the office at Kay. He rolled his tired eyes heavenward before giving her a smile. He sidled up to her. 'Not the best day to start work, but you'll be in good hands with Ed. I was hoping to be given the job of teaching you the routes and all the other info, but I guess it's the privilege of the boss to take the prettiest girl out,' Frank said with a grimace.

Kay studied Frank. He was not as tall as Ed and had black hair and warm brown eyes framed by long lashes that any girl would be proud of. He was just the sort of man she fell for, but she warned herself that he reminded her too much of the man who had broken her heart. She felt a knot in her stomach as she noticed Frank's resemblance to Harry, her lost love. She smiled at him, feeling her resolve not to get involved or get her heart broken again wane. As he turned away, he grabbed her hand and gave it a squeeze. Their eyes met, and Frank gave her a slow wink causing Kay's heart to flutter.

'Kay, stop daydreaming and come and chill before breakfast is served,' Alice said, interrupting their intimacy. She watched Frank walk out of the office.

'Shall we get our binoculars and watch the dam?' Kay asked. 'I love the peace and serenity of just sitting sometimes.'

'Sure, let's,' Alice agreed. 'Once our next guests arrive there's no peace to be had. They can be so demanding.'

Kay turned to look out of the window. 'Alice, a waterbuck and her young are coming to the dam.' Alice followed an excited Kay as she led the way out towards the balcony chairs.

'If we get something to eat we can bring it out here and watch. I'm starving,' grumbled Alice, as she turned towards the dining room.

Kay followed, and while Alice chatted to some of the staff, Kay returned to the veranda to gaze at the magnificent vista. No sooner had she sat down, when Frank appeared. He stood over her and stared at her making her feel very disconcerted.

'Have I got a smudge on my nose or something?' she asked.

'No, beautiful lady, I'm just wondering why a gorgeous girl like you would want to hide away in a place like this, when you have the world at your feet? Having had a sneaky peek at your personnel file, I see you're an art teacher from Durban. Makes a man wonder,' Frank said.

'Actually, this is exactly where I wish to be, Frank. I have spent so much of my childhood with my family camping and doing safari trips. I am taking time out from city life and work so that I can spend a couple of years as a ranger. Does that answer your question?'

'Sure thing, whatever you say.' Frank gave a shrug before turning and walking away.

Kay was pleased that Alice had arrived with her breakfast. She sat down and glared after him. 'What did he want? And why was he frowning like that as he left you?' Alice asked.

'I'm not sure what he wanted or why he's so interested in why I wanted to become a ranger for that matter,' Kay said a little exasperated.

'I'll have to eat this and get to the office,' Alice said. 'Ed will have my guts for garters if I don't hurry.'

They finished their food and having drunk a refill of coffee each, Alice rushed off to do some work. Kay sat with her notepad and pen making a small drawing of the animals at the dam, with a few white clouds drifting over the cobalt sky. She was only sorry the smells of the grass and animals could not be captured on her pad. She decided to keep her drawings as a reference for larger pictures later.

'Time to get back to work,' a deep baritone voice said right behind her, making Kay jump.

'Sorry, I didn't mean to startle you,' Ed said, peering over her shoulder. 'What's that you're drawing?' he asked.

Kay hastily closed her pad and stood up feeling somewhat at a disadvantage. She felt like a naughty child who had been caught misbehaving. Looking up into amused grey eyes, she could feel herself blushing.

'Relax, I'm only joking. That elephant I caught a glimpse of looked pretty good from my viewpoint though,' Ed added, giving her one of his rare smiles.

Kay was surprised how his face changed when he smiled. Strong and handsome in a rugged sort of way, her brain registered. As he was smiling, she noticed his lips reveal a set of the most perfect teeth. Lifting her eyes to his she was aware his smile reached his eyes, as they locked with hers. There was a tightening in the pit of her stomach and she felt his eyes boring into her. A shadow crossed his face and he looked away. Kay felt as if she had missed something.

'I'll catch you later, when you've finished here. Meet me in my office and we'll get you some maps and other info that Alice is sorting out for you,' Ed said, over his shoulder while he walked away.

Kay watched as he marched off with his shoulders rigid. She couldn't understand what the hell had made his mood change from friendly to sullen. Her brow creased into a deep frown, wondering how on earth she would cope with a boss whose moods changed like night and day within moments. Picking up her pad and binoculars, she made her way to the office, in the hope of finding Alice.

'Hi Kay, that was well timed,' Alice said. 'I've got all your info ready. The boss is on the warpath today. He said you'll be taking time out with him this week as he has some important guests from main lodge. He feels it will be a good initiation for you to see how tiresome they can be,' she pulled a face. 'This lot come every year and only want Ed. All very flattering, but it has its drawbacks as they tend to become very familiar and start demanding what they want to see, instead of just enjoying the vista and whatever beasts they come across. You'll probably want to pack up and leave after a week of this irritating lot,' Alice laughed.

'May I ask you something, Alice, without it going any further?'

'Of course, fire away.'

'Well, when Ed came over to chat while I was doing a little sketching of the dam and elephants after breakfast, he was in quite a good mood and joked with me. Then when I started to relax with him, his mood changed completely. He stomped off in what I can only describe as irritation,' Kay said looking puzzled. 'Do you think I could have said anything to upset him, or is he always this way?'

'You do surprise me, Kay, because he's usually lovely. If things get out of hand in any way, like poachers or our Tom getting shot, well that's another matter. All the time I've worked for him, he's been balanced and charming. I know he can have a fiery temper, but that's not what you're asking is it?' Alice thought for a moment. 'Maybe it's because you're a beautiful woman and a ranger at that. He might find it difficult to know how to handle you, with his being used to men and he's like all the guys here, very chauvinistic. So sorry, my friend, I have no idea what ails the man. Maybe he fancies you and can't cope.' Alice giggled. 'Whatever it is he'll get over himself,' she added.

A week later, Kay sat on her veranda with her binoculars enjoying the peace of the dawn, with only the sound of the hornbills calling each other and animals munching grass close by. It was her favourite time of day, before everyone was up. Her thoughts turned to the past week. Ed had taken her out with his guests on all his game drives. She remembered how she had sat next to him at the front of the four-by-four vehicle as the tracker sat on the seat in front of the bonnet of the vehicle. She had learnt so much from listening and watching. She could now find her way around the reserve, providing she kept to the tracks. Ed and the other rangers knew every inch of the place and would traverse across rivers and donga to reach an area where one of the big five had been spotted.

Ed was amazingly patient with his guests, she'd observed. They asked the most basic questions and never stopped demanding to see the big five. His only complaint was that he hadn't been able to find a leopard for this party who had flown in from Cape Town. Being local and having been to the lodge on a regular basis they were extremely spoilt and had always seen the leopard on each visit, they kept saying. Kay thought she would scream if they asked one more time, but Ed seemed oblivious.

On one occasion, while stopping for sundowners in a clearing by the river, Kay had photographed the red of the setting sun as it turned into a shower of gold. She and the rest of Ed's party had watched as it sank behind the distant mountain and trees, as the sky darkened into a charcoal haze. That was the signal to pack up and get into the vehicle. In order to make herself useful and not least to try and impress her boss, Kay had helped Tsepho, Ed's tracker, to serve the drinks and snacks. They carried the refreshments in wicker baskets held in the box attached to the back of the people carrier. Ed's guests had been such fun to spend time with. Even Ed himself had joined in and appeared a different person to the man she was used to when he was in his office.

Kay was sorry her time with him had come to an end, as now she would be on her own with just Ben her allocated tracker. He seemed to accept her, whereas some of the African staff refused to look at her unless of course Ed was around. Ben had been brought up in a very different community. He had gone to university, so was much more accepting of women. He also spoke perfect English and wasn't bothered by her lack of other languages. Her confidence had improved enormously, due to being congratulated by the guests, on how great she was for having spotted the animals or birds they had sought on many occasions. Even Ed had been impressed, she recalled, having put his hand on her knee several times and giving it a squeeze.

Kay sighed when she heard the early morning rap on her door. No need to check the time, as the porters were instructed by Ed to do the rounds at six sharp. Kay was the first one to be called as she was the ranger. Stretching her long legs, she thought about her job as she gathered her things together and entered her room. Having studied all the workings of what Ed said and did during her week of initiation, she had made it a habit to return to her room every evening and make copious notes. Then would file them in a folder which she took with her every day on the drives, just in case someone asked her a question he had forgotten the answer to.

Although Ed was still aloof and abrasive at times, he had gone out of his way to teach her the ropes. On her last day, Ed took her aside when they returned to camp. He complimented her by telling her how proud he had been and knew she would do well. However, from now on she would be expected to find her way around and know what to say and how to handle the guests.

She was nervous about the week ahead but had a Sunday off before she started work again. Kay was planning to visit Hazy View, to stock up on more shirts, casual wear and face creams. Alice had told her they had a huge shopping mall there, where you could buy everything imaginable.

Kay remembered that she had yet to send a letter to her adored grandmother Kathryn, who everyone knew as Kate Anderson. She felt guilty aware her grandmother would be waiting with baited breath to hear all Kay's news.

Gran had brought her up since she was twelve years old, after her parents and brothers had been killed in a light aircraft when it crashed into a mountain on their way to Harare. She should have been with them as it was a family holiday. At the time of departure Kay had been unwell with a throat infection and their doctor had advised that she be left at home as flying could acerbate the infection. Cry as she might, the family left without her for their safari trip with friends who owned a tobacco farm near Bulawayo.

Kay had struggled to get over their deaths. Having such a wonderful grandmother who she had been named after, had helped her to heal. Her childhood had sometimes been lonely without her sibling around, but her grandmother made her interact with other children, which was something she now appreciated. Fortunately, she had other aunts, uncles and cousins who had helped.

It had been her grandmother's idea that Kay take the route of studying to become a ranger and leave her art teaching for just a year or so, to get her away from Durban and Harry.

Late one afternoon Kay went to the office, to find Alice sorting out the list of new guest arrivals for the following day and giving the wine waiter his list of wines to be offered to guests.

'Only imported champagnes were to be paid for as extras, otherwise all drinks were included in the bills,' Alice was explaining to the young man. She looked up and saw Kay.

'Hi, how was the viewing on your early drive? I thought of you this morning. Did the tracker help you find the cheetah? I couldn't believe the carry on from that lawyer chap last night. Insisting you find them a cheetah this morning,' Alice said.

'I had my usual tracker Ben Small with me this morning,' Kay said. 'My guest laughed when they learnt Ben's last name, especially as he's the size of a grizzly bear. I must say he makes me feel safe when we come across one of the predators.'

'Did they have a good time?' Alice asked, straightening the papers on the desk.

'When we stopped for our coffee break, they asked Ben

loads of questions, about where he grew up and lived. They were thrilled to see the family of hippo, especially the calf who was on the opposite bank playing in the mud.'

'Did you find a cheetah?' Alice repeated, just as Ed entered the office.

'What?' he barked.

They both jumped and turned towards him.

'I was just asking Kay if she found the cheetah for that lawyer chap. You know, the one who was a pain in the bum last night when he was pickled,' Alice explained.

'Well did you?' Ed asked.

Kay felt her cheeks growing red with irritation at the way Ed was looking at her, making her feel as if she had done something wrong.

She glared at him. 'Well, actually, no we didn't find a cheetah, but my tracker told them she had moved away from our camp area. I'm supposed to find one tomorrow morning as that group will be on the early drive,' Kay said.

'Did you radio the other rangers that were out? You must always keep in radio contact, so they keep you up with what they come across, and you inform them if you spot anything of interest. Remember what I taught you,' Ed added.

Desperate to get away from Ed's scrutiny, Kay picked up her lists from Alice and said goodbye. She was determined to prove herself to him and the others. She knew she was as good a ranger as any of the men, apart from Frank and Tom, who had been rangers for years. She and Frank were getting on so well, although she was a little concerned that he had made it so clear he would like more than friendship from her. She hoped she had made it equally as clear to him that she was only interested in working hard to learn the job. She wasn't ready to get involved in a relationship yet. Kay could not help feeling flattered by Frank's attention though, and that was enough for the time being.

Chapter Four

The following morning, Kay was on her second cup of coffee when her group of guests came staggering bleary-eyed into the lounge. The staff had laid out a pre-breakfast snack of biscuits and muffins, and pots of tea, coffee and milk ready for them to help themselves.

Looking at her watch, she noticed it was six-thirty. She clapped her hands loudly to be heard over the chattering. 'Right, guys, the sun is already up, so we must make a move, or we'll be late back for breakfast,' Kay announced.

There was a scurry as the group put down cups and collected their jackets, hats and binoculars. Kay was relieved to note that each of them looked as if they had plastered their faces and arms in sun lotion.

Alice always explained to new guests, when giving out their keys, that they needed to read the 'must do' list in their rooms. They had obviously done as requested. She also gave a talk about essentials to their comfort while out on a game drive and most importantly to protect themselves from the fierce sun during the day, and to cover up in the evening to avoid getting bitten by the mosquitoes. Kay recalled being told to wear light coloured clothes by day, dark by night for the first time and was pleased to note that it must also be the order of the day here too.

Kay realised that Ed would not be joining them, much to her relief, as she noticed he had a party of his own from the other lodge. He had just stopped by to check that all was well with her guests. She gave him a wave as she followed the others to the people carrier where, Ben, Kay's assigned tracker, was waiting with the iced bottles of water.

'Still or sparkling,' he asked as each person found a seat.

Leaving the lodge, Kay travelled across the dry riverbed leading towards to open space where she hoped to find the cheetah. While passing a dense wooded area, Ben put up his hand for her to stop. He placed his finger on his lips to warn the guests not to make a sound and pointed to a lone giraffe in the distance. Then he waved for Kay to go and look.

Kay changed direction and drove closer to see if there was a problem with the animal. When they got within a short distance from the giraffe, they could see she was in some distress. Out of her back end appeared to be a pair of little black feet. Kay was stunned to discover the giraffe was giving birth. She was delighted to be able to experience such a rare occurrence and be in the right place at the right time.

They sat watching the scene before them in stunned silence, the only sound coming from their group being clicking noises as they readied their cameras.

Mike, an American guest, videoed the birth. Kay doubted that any of the rangers had witnessed the birth of a giraffe, or any other animal for that matter, other than one in captivity. Not the same as seeing this in their natural habitat, she thought. The excitement on the vehicle was palpable. Everyone was too enthralled by the sight to speak.

Kay quietly explained that the female giraffe, when giving birth, goes away by herself to get on with it. 'Unfortunately,' she added, 'very often one of the predators get wind of this and just grabs the newborn as they enter the world.' The guests grimaced at the thought. 'This little chap has a long way to fall when he finally arrives.'

Not a word was said as they watched for what seemed like hours, although Kay noted it only took forty minutes.

Elaine, whose husband had not joined them that morning, got herself into a state, then bringing light relief as she made everyone giggle, when she kept whispering, 'Push, my girl, push.'

Kay was amused that Elaine kept up her encouragement the whole time the mother giraffe was trying to give birth.

Finally, with a great whoosh the baby giraffe fell to the ground. Cameras clicked as everyone tried to capture the actual arrival of the calf, and then they all waited while it tried to stand on the spindliest legs Kay had ever seen. It did so eventually and immediately began suckling milk from his mother.

Kay radioed every ranger in contact, telling them where they were and what was happening. She felt a bit mean not to have informed them earlier, but the giraffe would not have stayed, and was already in distress when her group had stopped.

Ed arrived first with a group of three couples, all looking

immaculate in obviously very expensive safari gear, unlike her guests from the Muzi. Kay couldn't help noticing a blonde had her hand on Ed's shoulder and leant forward to get a better look. She felt a knot of irritation in her chest and had to concentrate on not scowling at the woman.

Ed was staring at Kay as he came to a halt right next to her. Their eyes met, and she saw he had a huge grin on his face. Feeling a blush rising, and sensing he was aware of her irritation, Kay quickly started her engine, as he thanked her for letting him know about the sighting. His guests all greeted Kay and thanked her. More cameras clicked, as the now relaxed mother and her young, moved slowly away.

Another three vehicles came into view, Ed followed Kay as she turned and drove away. The rules were that no more than two lots of guests should be close to the animals at one time, so that they didn't crowd the animals in and distress them.

Kay lost sight of Ed as he went. She left with her group for the dam and stopped for morning coffee, tea and cool drinks to keep them going before returning later for their breakfast. The waitress had packed a variety of biscuits aware the guests would be peckish around eleven o'clock. There was the usual toilet break where the men went one way and the girls the other, all using thick bush to shield themselves from view. Just the one or two would not venture into the bush frightened of meeting a predator.

Everyone agreed it had been a most memorable morning. Her group admitted that they nearly missed the drive after a raucous night partying into the small hours and ending up having very little sleep. The drive continued until midday, but everyone couldn't stop talking about the fantastic experience of the giraffe giving birth.

Before her afternoon drive, and while all her guest where lazing around the pool or swimming, Kay took the opportunity to chat to Alice at the arbour by the pool.

'I hear there was great excitement this morning with your viewing a giraffe birth,' Alice said, looking envious.

'It was fantastic,' Kay said, still stunned by what she had been lucky enough to experience. 'I was so chuffed to be the one finding her. Well, it was thanks to Ben actually. He's got eyes of a hawk.'

'The boss was telling me how well you did. He was singing your praises to all who'd listen at the bar before lunch. Frank then took up the story, about how great it is to have you on the team,' Alice grinned at her. 'Well done to you, my friend, you're making a great impression.'

Kay let her loose hair fall forward to cover her face. The thought of the two men complimenting her was making her feel like a desirable woman. Something she hadn't felt for a very long time.

'I do believe you're blushing,' Alice teased.

'Blushing?' asked Ed appearing unexpectedly in front of the girls.

The women looked up at him. Kay was struck by his charisma for the first time. He looked into Kay's eyes with an intensity that took her breath away. She lowered hers first, but not before she had seen a puzzled expression cross his face, or had she imagined it?

'What did you say to her to make her blush Alice?' Ed asked looking at Kay.

'Not for men's ears. Girl talk,' she replied, with a secretive smile.

'I'm glad I found you, Kay,' he said, serious once again. 'I need a word. You might as well hear this, Alice. Frank just called in to say the newborn giraffe has been taken by young lions while he was checking on it at lunchtime. Poor man saw the kill.' He glanced around, and Kay presumed it was to check that none of the guests could hear what he was saying. She could feel tears welling up in her eyes and willed herself not to cry. 'He was pleased none of his guests were in the vehicle with him, especially having seen it just after its birth. Frank reckons it wasn't a well little chap and it was only a matter of time before one of the predators would take him out.'

Kay stood up, covering her mouth with her hands briefly, her eyes wide as she glared at the bearer of such horrible news. 'I can't bear it,' she cried, tears streaming down her face.

Ed grabbed her by her arms and shook her. 'Pull yourself together, woman, don't let the guests hear, or they'll all start wailing.' He sounded furious. 'After all your training, you should know better than to let this get to you. Go and sort yourself out immediately and come back for the afternoon drive when you've composed yourself.'

Kay shrugged him away, mortified by her reaction, and ran to her room. She wasted no time worrying about the altercation with her boss. She was irritated with him. She decided he was hateful and bombastic and knew his attitude had hurt her. She would just have to show him how much better she was than what he gave her credit for. Deep in thought, she jumped at a loud knock on her door.

'Can I come in, Kay?' Alice asked, opening the door and walking in. 'You alright? Don't take any notice of Ed, he's having a dreadful day. He's always ready to snap at whoever happens to be around at the time. They lost another rhino to poachers last night. That's probably why he seems to have less feeling for the loss of a newborn giraffe.'

'Sorry, Alice, I overreacted when he got cross. I really must be a little bit tougher, but he took me by surprise I guess, and I didn't have time to gather myself,' Kay replied.

'I'd better be off before he shouts for me, Alice added. 'I have to make copious lists for what they need in the kitchens. Dexter is off to Hazy View this afternoon to replenish the grocery supplies. See you later, and don't worry about Ed, he obviously is madly disturbed by your presence on the team and doesn't know how to cope with his feelings, poor bugger,' Alice said, opening the door, only to find Frank with his hand raised about to knock.

'Hello, Frank, are you looking for me?' Kay asked as he entered her room. Alice pulled a face behind his back and rolled her eyes at Kay.

'A little bird told me you were upset, so I'm here to check on you. You've been crying?' Frank said pulling Kay into his muscular arms. Without another word he began to kiss her, while his hands caressed her face. 'You're so perfect,' he murmured in her ear, as he pulled her so tightly against him she could hardly breathe.

Kay heard a moan, and realised it came from her. All the old feelings she had held for Harry came flooding back. She gazed into the deep brown eyes gazing down at her and realised with horror, she wanted them to be grey. She pushed Frank away.

'I'm sorry, Frank. I can't do this.'

'Relax, I know you wanted me as much as I need and want you. If that was a taste of what's to come, I'm happy to wait until you're ready.

Frank opened the door and, checking to make sure nobody was around, left.

Chapter Five

Kay rushed to the bathroom and looked at her flushed cheeks in the mirror. What the hell was the matter with her? Firstly, Ed had made her cry with news of the dead giraffe calf, and then wishing it was him kissing her instead of Frank. She really must get a grip, she thought. This job may be making her far too emotional.

Reapplying sun cream and a little mascara and lipstick, she was ready for the afternoon drive. She mustn't let her guests down by showing she was upset about anything, as they needed to be entertained and uplifted. They paid handsomely for the privilege. Remembering how hard she had worked to get the job of ranger in one of the top lodges in the Sabie Sands, she forced a smile on her face as she hurried to her vehicle, where all her group were waiting.

As she approached, Kay could hear Ben entertaining them with stories about his narrow escapes in the bush. He really was a great asset she decided, realising they were becoming a team to be reckoned with.

During the drive everyone was delighted when Ben found a rare sighting of the very shy black rhino mother and calf. They crossed the road making their way to the huge waterhole nearby.

'Tell us more about them, Kay. I've heard wild tales of the black rhino, and haven't ever managed to see one before,' Mike asked.

'Their sight is very poor, but their hearing is amazing. They can tell if something is approaching from one kilometre away. They are very dangerous and move with great speed, despite their heavy bodies,' Kay said, delighted to have the opportunity to spread her knowledge. 'All members of staff have profound respect for them and never venture too close. They have been known to charge a vehicle, especially when a rhino calf is around.

She parked a short distance away from the mother and calf, as her guests took photos and whispered to each other about the amazing luck they were having. A pungent smell filled their nostrils from the huge pile of dung close to where they were parked.

'Poo, what a stink,' laughed Glenda, holding her nose.

'Honey, that's so rude, we're in the bush, not Beverly Hills,' Mike admonished his wife.

'Right, I get the message, time to move on,' Kay told them amidst laughter.

Driving on for a few kilometres one of her guests spotted a family of five white rhinos. They were far more heavily populated and less nervy and again Kay explained to the group that everyone treated them with great respect. She stopped the vehicle while everyone took photos and commented amongst themselves.

Kay and Ben planned to stop and have drinks under a jackalberry tree, which hung over a large dam, housing a family of hippo. Everyone loved that time of day as the big red sun sank low in the sky and sent colours of yellow, red and pinks across the land, the trees standing out like charcoal drawings against the brilliance of the backdrop. As everyone got out to the vehicle, and looked across the vast expanse towards the mountains, a feeling of tranquillity descended on the party. Deep sighs and lots of oohing from her guests, made Kay realise she was incredibly lucky to be living in this amazing piece of paradise. They had time for drinks and snacks, before taking a leisurely drive back to the lodge.

Arriving back at camp, everyone thanked Kay and Ben profusely for a wonderful and exciting drive. All Kay's confidence was restored as Ed was in hearing distance by the bar. He caught her eye and gave her one of his rare smiles that transformed his rugged face.

Kay and all her group of guests went to the bar. Everyone started talking at once, telling Ed what they had seen and how clever a driver Kay was to be able to traverse across difficult terrain to get closer to the animals. They praised Ben's amazing gift of sight as they would have missed so much had it not been for him. He had even spotted a little chameleon in a thorn tree as they drove home in the dusk.

Frank joined them as he had also returned from his drive. His group had all gone to freshen up before dinner. He put a possessive arm around Kay's shoulders, as he pulled her against him.

'Hi gorgeous, thanks for all the info you sent through on

the radio. Great viewing, thanks to Ben. Well done, Ben.' They gave each other a high five with a load hand clap with his free hand.

Ed scowled from Kay to Frank's hand resting on her shoulder. He slammed his drink down with a bang and left the bar.

'What's bitten him?' Frank asked, watching Ed's retreating back.

Ben gave Kay a knowing look. She returned his look and wondered what he was thinking. He turned and left the bar as the guest gathered around Frank to listen to more of his stories.

Kay was grateful when Alice arrived and asked her if she could have a word.

'Come on!' Alice whispered. 'Guess who's turned up and is waiting for us in the lounge?'

Kay noticed Sally, looking like a million dollars.

'We'd better go and get tarted up,' Alice added, 'or we won't stand a chance with the guys at the party tonight.'

'What party? I haven't heard anything about a party. Are you sure, Alice?' Kay asked.

'Yes. Chef told me that a Canadian friend of Ed's and his wife are staying at the main lodge with their friend and sister. Sally told me we've all been invited as they're thinking of taking over this lodge and bringing friends from the States to experience our safaris. When I asked Ed about it just now, he confirmed it.' She lowered her voice. 'I gather they met when Ed visited Calgary last year. He was on a fishing trip with the owner of the lodges. Also, they were campaigning about saving the rhinos,' Alice explained. 'Obviously made a huge impact if the visitors we've had from Canada are anything to go by.'

'Wow that's brilliant. I can't believe we've been invited to the main lodge,' Kay said, surprised.

'I thought you should know as we don't have to wear bush gear, but our own choice of clothes.'

'That sounds great. What's Sally wearing? Shall I wear my designer frock that I bought in Durban?' Kay asked.

'That's a great idea. I'll go and glam myself up. I want to make sure Sally doesn't get all the attention, which will be a first. She's wearing a stunning brown lace mini showing off those amazing legs of hers to perfection,' Alice replied, as both girls laughed.

'You're quite sure about this Alice? The party, that is?'

'I'm sure. Charles wants Ed's friends to meet all the staff and guests. Sally's one of the designated drivers for our guests.'

'Why would they want to meet all of us from the Muzi?' Kay asked looking puzzled.

'I just happened to hear our boss talking to his friends on the phone,' Alice said trying to look innocent. 'Sounded to me as if they want to take over this place for a few months each year. Organising through their company and inviting people from the USA to sample life in the African bush. That's why they need to check us out. You'll be one of the main rangers looking after them. I also happened to hear Ed singing your praises, and no I'm not telling you what he said,' Alice teased.

'You can be such a cow,' Kay laughed.

The sound of a bell made the girls look towards the bar where Ed, having returned unnoticed by them, was standing. He was signalling at Ben to stop the ringing.

'Hi everyone, it is my pleasure to let you know that we have all been invited across to the main lodge for dinner,' Ed began. 'After which, an invitation had been extended to you all to a party being hosted by very good friends of mine from Canada. Sally will be escorting our guests from here, and Ben and I will drive our staff. If you could all now, please get a move on and be back here within the hour. Sorry for the short notice.' Ed finished and locked eyes with Kay.

'Wow, you were right, Alice. We've only got an hour and I look a fright. Come on let's go.'

Kay put down her glass and followed Alice who was already rushing towards to exit.

'How am I going to be tall, thin and beautiful in an hour?' Alice wailed, as Kay caught her up, laughing.

'I'll meet you back in the lounge,' Kay said. 'Or give me a shout when you're ready, whatever is easiest.'

'Sally will still be preening herself no doubt. Let's give her some competition for once. She's so full of herself, it's nauseating,' Alice moaned as she walked into her bedroom and slammed the door behind her.

Kay was used to getting ready quickly, showering and washing her hair in minutes. She chose a short designer frock that had been her one big extravagance before leaving Durban. Burnt orange was her favourite colour; her grandmother had always told her it showed off her dark hair and hazel eyes. It had been Harry's favourite, too. She had had so many compliments when she wore it the last time, and he had been so proud of her. Memories of happiness and pain flooded back. Kay slumped onto the edge of her bed and thought of what her life should have been. How had it come to this, she thought catching sight of her reflection in the mirror? She should never have brought this reminder of Harry with her, it was a stupid idea. Kay sighed. Unfortunately, she had not thought to bring anything else smart enough to wear for the party.

She hated to admit it but hoped Ed would find her more attractive if she wore something sophisticated. She knew she would look much more her age and hoped he would realise she was a woman and not the young girl he treated her like.

Giving herself a mental slap, she hurriedly dried her hair, letting it fall onto her bare shoulders and over her breasts. Make-up applied, she rummaged through her jewellery to find the right piece to complement her frock. She chose a set of amber beads and earrings that had once belonged to her mother. Kay then gave herself a spray of perfume. It was Harry's favourite and he had bought it for her on their second date. Every time she wore it, she felt happy.

Her hair cascaded onto her shoulders in thick waves as she ran the brush through it one more time. Dark brown eyeliner and a touch of golden eye shadow, helped make her amber eyes sparkle. Coral lipstick and black mascara added the finishing touch. Taking a final look in the mirror, Kay felt satisfied that she had done all she could to look her best.

Her skin had turned a golden brown from her time at the lodge. She was aware that her tall firm body and long toned legs, was so much more attractive than when she had arrived at the lodge. This is how she wanted her grandmother to see her, unlike when she had left Durban and all the drama she had put the poor woman through before getting this job. This was no time to dwell on the past, she decided.

Realizing she was showing off more of her cleavage than she was comfortable with, she began looking for a safety pin, to bring the material over her chest closer together. She was startled by a loud knock on the door that was immediately flung open by Alice, wearing a black and white dress that finished above her knees. She had long silver chains around her neck and silver earrings, as big as bracelets, dangling from her ears. Over her arm was a little white jacket.

'You gave me a fright,' Kay said, continuing to open all the drawers on the dressing table.

'What are you looking for?' Alice asked.

'I think my cleavage is far to revealing, so I need a pin,' Kay moaned.

'Shit, Kay, I'd give anything to look like you. That's an amazing colour on you, too. As for the cleavage, if you've got it flaunt it, girl.' Alice laughed looking at her own modest chest. 'I've a good mind to stay behind and sulk.'

Kay stopped her search and stared at Alice. 'You look stunning. I, on the other hand, would give anything to look as pretty and petite as you.' Alice tapped her foot on the floor impatiently. 'Okay, you win,' Kay said, trying not to get flustered. 'I just need some shoes and I'm ready,' Kay said over her shoulder as she grabbed a pair of brown wedge open-toed sandals from her wardrobe and slipped them onto her feet. Picking up a matching shoulder bag, and a tan and gold pashmina she followed Alice out of the room.

'Finally,' Alice groaned, giving Kay a wink.

Although she was feeling nervous, Kay was also excited and looking forward to the evening. It felt good knowing she looked her best and was wearing something flattering instead of the required uniform of a ranger.

The girls chatted and laughed as they made their way back to the lounge. They could hear by the howls of laughter that the guests and other members of staff were arriving.

'Everyone seems to be in a great mood for a party,' Sally said, greeting Kay and Alice. 'My, you two certainly clean up well,' she added sarcastically.

'Thanks, I think,' Alice retorted with a frown. 'You don't look too bad yourself.'

'Right, everyone, time to go,' Ed's voice boomed above the noise. 'Please make your way to your vehicle's driver.'

'See you later,' Sally shouted, hurriedly leaving the lounge, followed by Frank and Ben.

Ed stood, with a list in his hand, telling the guests who they would be travelling with. When Kay and Alice reached him, he just stared at them for a moment, with a look of amazement on his face.

'My, you two look stunning,' he said. 'You're driving with me. Everyone else has been allocated,' he added, not looking at Kay and focusing on the exit.

'Bloody hell, Kay, did you see how awkward Ed looked

then?' Alice giggled in a whisper as they followed him out of the building.

'Shush, he'll hear you.' Kay gave Alice a playful slap on her arm. She had noticed but didn't want to admit it.

'We'll let them go ahead, or their dust will cover us,' Ed said as he reached his private car. One of you can sit in the front with me. Kay?'

'We are honoured to be driving with you in this fab car,' Alice remarked.

'Well I can't have you in an open vehicle when you look so glamorous, can I?'

'Can't imagine how Sally will look when she arrives at the camp,' Alice said quietly. 'Mind you, she lives there so she can at least freshen up.'

Kay thought that Ed looked very handsome in his white shirt. It did wonders for his tan and still wet hair curling over the collar of his shirt. She thought of all the times she had been in his company, and how he made her feel.

'Am I boring you?' Ed's voice interrupted her thoughts.

'Sorry, I was miles away. What were you saying?' Kay asked, embarrassed.

'I was asking you and Alice if you'd like to join me for dinner? I have a table booked for eight, and there are my five friends from Canada, so I took the liberty of including you two, if you want to join us, that is? My friends want to meet you both.' He raked one hand through his drying hair. 'In the strictest of confidence, they intend spending a lot of time at the lodge and will be bringing in other guests from Canada and the States. They want you to do the bookings and correspondence, Alice, and you, Kay, they want as their personal ranger.'

'Seriously?' Alice asked from her back seat.

Kay was just as surprised but kept quiet, waiting for Ed to continue telling them the rest.

'They'll pay you both as you will be directly answerable to them. We'll see how it goes tonight and if you all get on. Personalities have to gel, or it can't work.'

Kay nestled into the luxurious seat, crossing her legs and tried to relax. It was going to be a very interesting evening, she thought, if Ed's conversation was anything to go by.

Ed seemed to be about to say something, but after glancing at Alice in the mirror, obviously changed his mind. Kay stole a glance at Alice, who raised her eyebrows in question. Kay smiled back at her and let the moment pass. The drive continued in silence.

As they approached the main lodge, they could see what looked like fairy lights hanging from all the indigenous trees. Candles twinkled as they got closer, and the place was a hive of activity. Even the herd of elephants had wandered close to camp and stood as if watching a show. There was a low electric wire around all the camps, to keep elephants from wandering in and destroying trees and furniture, in fact even cars if they took a mind to it.

Ed parked at the back where he had an allocated parking space. The pathway was uneven, so he made a point of holding their hands while helping the girls out of his car. Kay was amazed at the electric current that shot up her arm when his skin connected with hers. She pulled away, noticing a knowing look cross Ed's face. She wondered if he had that effect on all the women he touched. Why did that give her a feeling of annoyance? she mused.

Ed led the way to where all the excitement was taking place. Kay looked in wonder at this amazing lodge deep in the Sabie Sands. The moon was full, so the light was enabling them to see the wildebeest, zebra and waterbuck, way down at the river that looked like a gunmetal grey ribbon running through the trees. A distant roar of a lion just finished off the picture for her.

'Did you hear that?' Alice said, in a nervous voice.

'He's miles away. Stop worrying for goodness' sake, Alice, you'll make our guests nervous if they hear a local being scared,' Ed said laughing.

The head waiter was pouring champagne for everyone as they arrived. 'Your guests have gone through to the dining room with their champagne, Mr Ed,' he whispered.

'Thanks, Able, we'll do the same,' Ed replied, as he handed Kay and Alice a glass of the pale golden liquid.

He then led the way into the dining room, after checking the seating plan inside the large double doors. 'Good, we're near the doors leading onto the balcony. It can get very stuffy when crowded in here,' he added.

Kay followed slowly, taking in the opulence of the decor, which was so unlike the smaller lodge she worked for. As she glanced around, she noticed some of the people looking their way, at her in fact, which made her feel somewhat ill at ease. Gathering herself, she looked to where Ed and Alice had joined a group sitting at one of the tables. Loud laughter greeted her as she joined them.

She loved the sound of their Canadian accent. Ed was greeted by a firm slap on the back from a good looking blonde man in his early forties, who had leapt to his feet on their arrival. Kay couldn't get over how green his eyes were as they looked her up and down over Ed's shoulder. A dazzling smile showed off a perfect set of teeth.

Ed smiled broadly as he turned to introduce the girls.

'Kay, Alice, meet my old friend Charles and his wife Mandy Reynolds. Mandy's a model.'

Kay thought Mandy was very attractive. She studied the woman's long blonde hair and huge blue eyes. She was wearing a midnight blue mini dress which was slashed to the waist. Leaving very little to the imagination, as she jumped to her feet and took first Alice and then Kay in a firm handshake.

Ed smiled at the next couple who immediately stood up. The fair-haired, brown-eyed man towered above Ed with his wife, a tiny woman, with large hazel eyes and long red curls that bobbed around as she gave Ed a beaming smile.

'This is Paul and Trisha Allen,' Ed said. 'They are both artists, and friends of Mandy. You'll have a lot in common with them I'm sure, Kay, being of a likeminded artistic talent,' Ed added giving her a wink. 'Which only leaves Caryn. She's Charles's little sister. We couldn't do without her expertise in the hospitality industry.' Ed pulled out a chair for Kay as Caryn leapt to her feet and moved towards him. Meanwhile Charles was pulling out a chair for Alice.

Kay watched as Caryn wrapped herself around Ed giving

him air kisses. She looked stunning in an emerald green catsuit, with a high front and a very low back, which Kay noticed had Ed's hands firmly planted on it. Despite herself, Kay was fascinated by the woman's strawberry-blonde hair and brown eyes, although she was extremely thin to the point of looking undernourished. Feeling slightly overwhelmed, Kay was very pleased she hadn't found that pin after all. Alice gave Kay an amused look as if she was reading her mind.

After another glass of champagne everyone seemed more relaxed. The live band began to play. The five-course meal was excellent, the Canadian guests agreed, and Kay questioned if they would expect the same if they stayed at Impangela Muzi. As her thoughts wandered, she realised Paul was staring at her, and as their eyes locked she noticed he had eyes the colour of milk chocolate. He was smiling at her, giving her a flutter of anticipation. About what, she wasn't sure, but the evening was proving to be interesting.

'Have to say, this is the most amazing food and company you've laid on, Ed. If your lodge can produce this sort of thing, then our plans could work out very well indeed.

'Your South African wines really are great,' Mandy said, taking a sip from her recently filled glass.

'When are you guys going to book the other camp, and organise those tours we've been talking about?' Paul looked from one to the other, as his eyes lingered longer on Kay's.

'Ed and I have just got a few more things to discuss, like price, so Mandy can get on with the organisation and booking,' Charles answered.

'Edward, I want you to take us out on the drives,' Caryn said, fluttering her eyes at Ed.

'Sorry but that's not going to happen, I'm afraid,' he said. 'Kay will be assigned to whoever is on your tours. Alice will organise bookings. These girls are the most capable members of my staff. You'll be very lucky if they agree with the proposal we intend putting to them. Kay never disappoints with her knowledge and expertise in the bush. Her tracker Ben is also one of the best,' Ed said in a matter-of-fact tone.

'I'm sorry if I've offended you,' Caryn gushed. 'To make up, I'm booking the first dance with you, Ed.'

Kay felt her hackles rising, her jealousy mounting alarmingly. She needed to get her emotions under control. It wouldn't do to let anyone realise how she felt. She noticed Alice watching her from across the table.

'I'm so sorry. For what it's worth, Caryn usually puts her foot in it,' Charles said, looking mortified by his sister's behaviour. 'She doesn't mean it maliciously though.'

Everyone laughed, as Alice looked across at Kay and pulled a face.

'This is my favourite, lemon merengue pie,' Trish said, obviously intent on changing the subject, as she looked at the young waitress serving them.

'Mine too,' came a chorus, which set them all laughing.

As the dinner finished, so the music changed tempo and the lights were dimmed. Several couples made their way to the dance floor. Ed was dragged onto the floor by Caryn, while Charles and Mandy joined them, leaving Alice and Kay with Paul and Trisha. Paul couldn't keep his eyes off

Kay and she was starting to get irritated with his blatant staring. Suddenly she felt hands on her shoulders.

'Hi gorgeous, I've come to collect my dance,' Frank said, taking Kay by the hand and pulling her into his arms. As if on cue, Dexter arrived at the table and asked Alice to dance. Paul and Trisha got up to follow.

Frank was an excellent dancer and Kay relaxed into his solid embrace, as he held her close and whispered sweet nothings in her ear. Over his shoulder she watched Ed dancing very closely with Caryn. Her stomach knotted with irritation.

'What's the matter?' Frank asked, as he looked at her.

'Nothing, why do you ask?'

'You suddenly stiffened in my arms, just then. I wondered if you were okay, you were so relaxed a moment before. I don't mean to offend you. You surely know I'm falling for you by now?'

Stunned, Kay's feet faltered. 'Sorry?'

'Not that you've given me much hope, but I intend changing your mind.'

'Frank, please don't.' Kay tried to pull back, but he was stronger than her and had his hand pressing firmly against her back, so she was unable too free herself.

'Hi, you two, time to change partners,' Ed pulled Kay away from Frank's hold as he expertly exchanged her for Caryn, pushing her into Frank's arms. Kay thought she heard Frank cursing, as Ed expertly danced her away into the crowd.

'Thank you for rescuing me,' Kay whispered.

'What the hell was going on there? I could see he was holding you against your wishes. He's a strong bastard and a little too forward, if you ask me.' Ed scowled.

'Charles won't stand for Frank taking advantage of his sister. She's obviously had too much champagne. Now you, on the other hand, have not. I certainly cannot be accused of taking advantage of the most beautiful woman in the room, if I ask her to have a nightcap with me later?' Ed looked imploringly at Kay with raised eyebrows in question.

'Are you serious, Ed? I thought it was against the code of conduct to fraternise with your staff?' Kay giggled up at him, with a delight she couldn't hide even if she'd wanted to.

The dance ended. Everyone was leaving the floor, just as Ed bent towards Kay and very quietly told her he would hopefully see her later. She followed him back to the table as if walking on air, to find Caryn's chair empty.

'Thought Sis was with you, Ed?' Charles asked.

'She was, but then we changed partners and Frank is probably still chatting to her. There they are, on the balcony getting some fresh air,' Ed added, indicating the balcony to Charles.

'I think I'll join them. Don't like the way that Frank is pawing her. He seemed very drunk when I saw him earlier, as is my sister. Bad combination, mate,' Charles said to Ed as he got up and made his way towards them.

'Dexter is such a great dancer,' Alice announced, as if trying to lighten the atmosphere that suddenly seemed to engulf the table. Everyone watched Charles grabbing Frank, who still had a tight hold around Caryn's waist.

'I think I'll go and join them on the balcony for a smoke,' Paul said as he left the table.

'Probably a good idea,' Mandy agreed, rolling her eyes heavenward. 'Charles is very protective of Caryn and sometimes rather overly so.'

'Wish some guy would be protective over me,' Alice said with a sigh.

'Who's Dexter? He's rather a dishy looking guy,' Mandy asked Alice.

'He's Dexter Stevens, our environmentalist who comes to the lodges every few months and stays while looking into what's going on in our area. He then reports back to our superiors and after much discussing they decide about things like alien irradiation and burning programmes.'

'Let's have one more for the road shall we, ladies?' Ed suggested, waving a waiter over when they all agreed.

'Bring your best port, and eight glasses, please.'

'Great idea, mate,' Charles said rejoining the table followed by a subdued looking Frank with Caryn, who seemed, Kay thought, rather unsteady on her feet.

Frank glared at Kay, as if it was all her fault he was in trouble with Charles, because she had left him to dance with Ed.

'I'm going to return to my table,' Frank said. 'I'd forgotten about that damn meeting. I'll see you guys later at the bar for it.'

'I thought as much,' Ed said, glaring at him. 'I'll see you there.'

The band members finished their set and left the stage to

get refreshments. Kay stood up noticing everyone was making a move to leave. She and Alice said their goodbyes and promised to meet up with the Canadians the following afternoon for a game drive.

'Ben is going to take you both to the lodge,' Ed said. He bent down to whisper in Kay's ear. 'I'll have to take a rain check on our drink together.' He finished his drink. 'Charles wants to talk over some business ideas. I can't believe Frank will be of any use, but hey, who am I to judge?'

'No problem,' she said regretfully. 'I'm actually tired anyway. It's been a long day. Good luck with the talks.' Kay moved away from him and looked around for Alice and saw she was waiting patiently by the exit door. 'Goodnight, see you all tomorrow bright and early,' Kay said with a smile as she followed Alice out.

Chapter Six

The following morning was a Sunday and Kay's day off, so she dressed in jeans and a white shirt, relieved not to be wearing her uniform for the day. As she made her way to breakfast, she was surprised to see Alice sitting on the bench under the marula tree. Kay noticed her friend looked upset.

'What's the matter?' Kay asked.

'I hate men. Really, Kay, I'm not jealous by nature but that Caryn, and don't get me wrong I like her, but she's such a flirt,' Alice ranted. 'Did you see her smooching with Ed? Frank was all over you like a rash, and I was having a wonderful time with Colin when that Canadian woman decided to home in on him. Paul couldn't take his eyes off you by the way. He's also an artist, isn't he?' Kay knew Alice needed to get her annoyance off her chest, so sat down and let her get on with it. 'Honestly, Kay, I'm giving up on the male species. It's a good policy they have at the lodges. Relationships are frowned on between the staff, as they should be. That's why they like married couples to manage the place, with the wives usually heading the staff and the husband getting on with everything to do with the environmental side and the wildlife.'

Kay looked at Alice in amazement. 'Really? Couples?'

'Well, you did ask, and now I feel much better thanks to my rant.' Alice got up, and linking her arm through Kay's, said, 'Come on; let's have some breakfast, my friend.'

Kay's stomach rumbled on cue and both girls laughed.

After breakfast they decided to go for a swim and then brush up on their tans. Kay wore a tiny pink bikini, while Alice wore a similar bikini in deep blue.

Kay commented on how Alice's fair skin had become the colour of honey. 'You've got blonder streaks in your hair now, too,' she said. 'It looks lovely.'

Kay was surprised when Charles came over to tell them that Ed had gone to organise a tracker. They both loved the idea and promptly gathered their belongings and rushed to their rooms to get dressed ready for the safari, promising to meet back at the vehicle within the hour.

They set off to collect Mandy from the main lodge. Having radioed ahead, she was waiting at reception, so they lost no time in getting started on the drive.

'One of my favourite calls is that of the fish eagle,' Charles announced as they drove. 'Such a magnificent bird,' he told the others. 'You can't miss them sitting on tree tops over rivers waiting to catch a fish. They swoop down on their prey. Ed and I have spent hours waiting to see them in action, when I visited him before we were married. I have some superb photos of them in action that I'm really proud of.'

'OK, I get the message, a fish eagle it is,' Ed answered. 'We should find one at the river where we plan to picnic.'

'Look, girls, there's a hornbill. What's it called in Afrikaans, Ed,' Alice asked.

Before he could answer her, Kay butted in. 'They're known as boskraai in Afrikaans, and by the local natives their called kotokoto, the sound that resembles their call,' Kay explained.

'Wow, Kay, you sure know your stuff, honey,' Mandy said.

'You can say that again. She was one of the top students of her year and passed every exam with higher marks than the guys in her class. That's why she beat the lot of them and got this job with us,' Ed said with what sounded like pride.

Driving through the bush, with the wind in their hair and only the calling of the birds, and animals, brought it home to them all as to how lucky they were to be able to experience the wilds of Africa and spend time in the natural habitat of the animals.

'Ed, would you tell us more about this idyllic place you live and work in?' asked Mandy.

'I will be delighted to tell you all about my favourite topic,' he grinned. 'The others will probably be bored as they have heard it all before.' He took a deep breath. 'Sadly, so few people can afford to do this. The lodges are very expensive and out of reach of the ordinary person. Mostly overseas visitors can afford the prices. It costs a fortune to maintain the area of bush, and supply guests with their daily food and drinks, as everything must be delivered in bulk once a month, so that adds to expenses. Also, the vehicles used for viewing must be in excellent working order, as one can't afford to break down in the wilds.'

'What a horrible thought,' Mandy shivered. 'I'd die of fright if I was in a vehicle that broke down out in the bush somewhere.'

'We have to be vigilant,' he said. 'And we always are. We must train staff, be it rangers, trackers, chefs and everyday cleaning ladies and barmen. Huge laundries are needed as people usually only stay three or four days, so the changeover is enormous. Managers make good money, but their hours are long and sometimes, due to poachers, very dangerous. Having said that, I wouldn't change my life. Of course, if I ever marry and have kids, then it may have to change, as not everyone can cope with living in the bush. It's great for the single guys and girls, but we do have quite a changeover of them after a couple of years, as they often miss the city life,' Ed explained just as a huge bird flew overhead.

'Fish eagle,' Kay shouted, pointing to where the bird was landing on the top of a dead tree.

'Follow that eagle, Ed. You can chat to my dear wife later and tell her all your stories, but right now there goes my favourite bird of prey,' Charles cheered.

Ed motored towards the eagle. It was perched over the dam, just looking down at the water. Charles took out his telephoto lens which he quickly attached to his camera and started to take pictures. To their amazement they watched as the bird flew into the dam and pulled out a large fish in its talons, returning to the top of the tree.

'That was fantastic. Did you get that picture, Charles?' Mandy asked.

'Sure did, honey. Bloody brilliant that was.'

'Can you email me that photo please, Charles? Your camera is so superior to mine,' Kay asked.

'See what you miss while you sit in the office, Alice?' Kay laughed.

'No wonder you guys enjoy being out here with nature. It's not all about the poachers is it? That's the bit I usually hear you all talking about,' Alice said, as Ed restarted the engine.

Having seen the fish eagle, they continued through some dongas and thick treed areas, where a herd of elephant were grazing while their young played in the sandy soil. Everyone laughed as a bull elephant rubbed against a fallen tree. He had his leg over the trunk and was having a good scratch.

'What the hell's he doing?' Mandy asked, as the girls laughed at the elephant's antics.

'He's getting rid of the mites that infest them sometimes,' Ed explained. 'His friend is going to knock that leopard tree down in a moment, if he keeps rubbing his bum against it much longer,' he added, pointing to another even larger elephant a little further away.

After half an hour taking pictures and enjoying the group, everyone was ready to carry on the drive.

Finally, they reached the river and set out their picnic. Kay was relieved to note that Ed had brought folding chairs and a picnic table. She relished being out here enjoying the late afternoon sun as they all ate and drank. Charles had surprised them by taking it upon himself to pay for iced champagne to be included, which Kay, Alice and Mandy shared between them, while Charles drank red wine. The tracker ate with them but only drank orange juice, as it was his job to be alert always and never drink while on duty.

A family of rhinos came through the clearing in the distance, alerting Kay and Ed.

'Tshepo, you'd better keep an eye on that lot because they've a new-born and what looks like a three-year-old with them and we're down wind so only a matter of time before they smell us,' Ed warned.

As the crash of rhinos continued towards them, Kay noticed that Ed's tracker Tshepo, a Setswana native, born and bred in the bush, was becoming very fidgety, which in turn began to worry her. 'Don't you think we should pack up and get back into the vehicle, Ed?' Kay asked.

'Don't be ridiculous, they're about a mile away. They're not bothering us, are they?'

'No, but…'

'Relax and enjoy your champagne, Kay. I'm in charge today. You're off duty. Make the most of it.' Ed gave Kay a look as if to say, shut up your scaring our guests.

Turning to Tshepo, Kay asked, 'What does your name mean in Setswana?'

'It is the name my father chose for me and it means trust,' he replied.

'I like that,' shouted Charles having overheard Kay's question. 'We trust you to keep an eye on those critters while we enjoyed the sun going down,' his voice getting louder as he spoke.

Kay noticed that Tshepo was quickly and unobtrusively

packing away the picnic tables which had previously held their drinks. He then folded away the cloths. Kay was very aware that Tshepo was becoming increasingly agitated, but Ed continued explaining about the surrounding vegetation to his friends.

Kay watched the tracker turning towards the rhinos again.

'They have heard us,' Tshepo said, glaring angrily at Charles. 'We must pack up and be ready to get moving.'

'They're miles away. We're having the time of our lives, don't let those beasts chase us away, hey, Ed?' bellowed Charles, with a guttural laugh.

'Ed, look! They're beginning to run now,' Mandy said, her eyes wide with fright, as she clambered onto the vehicle and called out to her husband to join her.

'Move! Everyone on-board,' Ed yelled, hurriedly gathering up his half full wine glass and leapt into the driving seat.

Tshepo finished stowing away all the picnic things and only just managed to jump onto his seat on the front of the bonnet, when Ed put his foot down and drove off at speed, with one hand on the steering wheel and the other holding his glass of wine out of the vehicle door.

'Bloody hell, man, that was awesome, you haven't spilt a drop,' shouted Charles, as he watched Ed's glass of wine being jumped around as they drove over the bumpy ground. 'Who'd have thought those critters could run so fast, they nearly had us.' Taking a gulp of his own wine that he had managed to spill on his shirt, he reached over and took his wife's hand. Unamused, she snatched it away.

'You and your big mouth, Charles, it's your fault they heard us, with your booming voice. You know you're supposed to whisper when we're out in the bush.'

Kay and Alice looked behind them at the still charging rhinos. Ed only slowed down once they had stopped being chased. He pulled to a stop and drank down the rest of his wine in one, much to the amusement of his friends.

'That was too close for comfort, mate,' he said, pulling a face at Charles.

Kay glared at Ed, furious at having been put in danger.

'You should know better than to wait so long before moving away,' she snapped. 'You could have got us all killed.'

'Just don't you try that if you have guests, Kay,' Ed said trying to make light of the situation. 'Charles and I've been together on so many safari drives. Far more dangerous than having a few rhinos chasing us. You were never in any danger; I was in total control,' he assured her.

'Just being a typical macho and showing off to his friends,' Alice whispered to Kay.

'Imagine if the people carrier hadn't started,' Kay snapped, as Tshepo gave her a surreptitious nod of his head.

'Relax now, everything is fine. Find us a *tau tshepo*.'

'What's that?' Alice asked, never having heard the name before.

'That's Setswana for lion,' Ed explained.

'This guy speaks several native languages in case you didn't know, Kay,' Charles said turning to smile at the girls.

Kay closed her eyes and let her mind wander, as the breeze sent smells from the bush over and around her. She was relaxed and feeling uplifted as the drive progressed. Nobody spoke. She drifted off into a world of her own, listening to the sound of the birds calling to each other from the dense bush. She knew this time would pass and she would have to return to Durban and her old life teaching art. Kay had not planned on staying here for more time than it took to forget Harry. She always had a five-year plan in the past, but thanks to everything falling apart and her broken engagement, the only thing she now decided was that she would avoid men at all cost. She realised it would take a long time to trust one again, and the best way forward was not to get involved.

Who was she kidding, she thought, Edward Blake was really getting under her skin. Then there was Frank, who she was finding very attractive albeit in a mischievous way. Giving herself a mental talking to, she refocused on the wonders of the ever-changing bushveld.

Ed mentioned they would stop for sundowners under the trees hanging over a large dam, housing a family of hippo.

Kay took a deep breath as she watched Ed who had turned to speak to Charles. She studied his strong rugged face that suited the big nose, and the square determined chin. His strawberry-blonde hair streaked golden by the sun. Once again, it was curling on the collar of his shirt, as she resisted the urge to run her fingers through it.

He must have felt her looking at him. He turned and their eyes met. Why was she feeling as if she couldn't breathe, as those intense grey eyes held hers and she felt like a rabbit caught in headlights? The moment passed as Ed looked back to the road. What was that look he gave her? She noticed that Alice was raising her eyebrows questioningly. Kay spotted Ed looking at her in his mirror, smiling.

Ed turned towards the dam and parked under Kay's favourite spot by the jackalberry tree. Everyone jumped out and stretched their legs, while Tsepho organised the drinks. The sky had turned to magenta as the sun sank behind the distant mountains, but not before the visitors had taken several photos as it went down. A tree that had been burnt some time before was in the foreground of their pictures, and a lone vulture perched on one of its branches, waiting.

'I've got a great picture of that bird against the setting sun,' Mandy said in awe.

'That bird happens to be a vulture,' Charles told his wife.

Half an hour later, it was time to return to the lodge. They drove on in silence each deep in their own thoughts, except when there was an occasional excited acknowledgement of a sighting of smaller animals.

'Time to my put foot down now, guys, as it's going to get colder as we hit the valley,' Ed said to no one in particular.

'I'm ready for a beer,' replied Charles.

'How typical,' Mandy said.

The girls all laughed as Ed gathered speed as he took a steep bank. Coming down the other side they came across a herd of zebras who looked up in fright from their grazing.

The sudden arrival of the vehicle had startled them.

'Shame, we gave the poor things a fright,' Alice said.

As the lodge came into view, Ed slowed down to negotiate the sharp bend before the dam. In the dusk, the elephants and more zebra were at the waterhole for their usual evening visit. The shy waterbuck and her calf ran into the bush as the lights of the vehicle shone on the water where they'd been drinking.

Ed parked under the thatched open garage, and everyone collected their belongings and jumped off the vehicle.

Charles gave Ed a hard slap on his back. 'Well, my mate, that was just like old times. Pity the girls nearly shat themselves with fright when the rhino charged,' he said quietly.

'Thanks so much for giving us a wonderful fun day. I can't wait to go and show Caryn and the others all the great pictures I took,' Mandy said, before she and Charles said their goodbyes.

Alice excused herself saying she needed to call home from the office landline. It was her once a week concession from Ed. Kay collected her belongings and started to leave the lodge and make her way towards her room.

'I'll walk you back to your room,' Ed said. 'I don't like you girls wandering about camp on your own,' he added, joining Kay, hands in his pockets, his long loping strides, meaning that she had to almost run to keep up with him. He stopped without warning, grabbing her arm in a vice-like grip. Kay winced, wondering what had happened.

'Look, we've got company,' he said releasing his gun from its holster which hung, as always on his belt. He pulled

Kay into the doorway of one of the chalets they were passing. 'I've a master key. Hold my gun while I unlock the door.' Ed thrust the gun at her as he turned to the door.

'What have you seen, Ed?' she whispered in a nervous voice.

'Look over there, behind that thorn tree, in that hollow, there's a male lion. How the hell did he get into camp?' Ed pulled her into the room and closed the door behind them. 'Check the window while I call security,' he said taking his phone from his pocket.

She did as she was told.

'Right, Ben's on his way with transport,' he announced. 'But he might be some time. We can't risk walking, as I only have my handgun and I've no intention of killing one of our kings of the bushveld.' He moved closer to Kay and looked out of the window over her shoulder.

Kay's heart beat a little faster at his closeness, as he put his one hand on her shoulder and pointed with the other.

'Can you see them? They seem to be settling in for a sleep, so that means you are stuck with me until our rescuer arrives, he said, moving away and sitting on the side of the bed. 'Come and sit, Kay, it could be a while before he gets here as they are all out at the other lodge.'

Kay sat on the armchair directly across from Ed, so that they could face each other. 'Would you tell me about some of your experiences?' she asked, feeling awkward about being alone in a bedroom with her boss who clearly didn't want a woman ranger on his team.

'Sure, I'd love to regale you with stories. It's just a case of where to start really. What would you like me to tell you about?' he asked a huge smile on his face as Kay had asked about his favourite topic.

'What is the most scared you've ever been since working in the bush?' she asked.

'That's an easy one, I've told it many times. Probably gets a bit exaggerated over the years, too. It happened three years after I joined the team.' Ed crossed a long leg over his knee and made himself comfortable as he continued. 'Being on the environmental side of things when I got the job here, I stayed in my own house some distance away from the main camp. My job was to burn the old grass to make way for new shoots for all the small animals. We have done a huge amount of work in that department over the years. Sorry I digress.' He rested back on one of his elbows. 'I could keep my two dogs with me as I worked alone with just a couple of the Shangaan trackers.'

'You mean you were allowed to keep dogs?' Kay asked in surprise.

'Sure was in those days, but let me finish and then you will appreciate why they changed the rules.'

'I'm sorry, Ed, I just can't believe they let you have dogs on the property.'

'Well the thing is, I took the dogs out that evening; well it was late afternoon when I set off. I drove to that area about a mile from here to check on some work the gang had been doing in clearing the stream. I left the bakkie and walked with the dogs into the bush as it was rather difficult to drive over that area. Suddenly I came across a pride of lions with their kill. They were all full from eating and lazing in the veld. I quickly picked up one of the dogs, a mastiff, but the other one ran into the bush. The male lion stood up and roared at me.'

'No!'

He smiled. 'There I stood, with one dog in my arms unable to use my rifle, even if I had wanted to. Moving very slowly I crawled under the huge thorn bush to where the other dog had run. It was one hell of a job to get to him. He was young and terrified, so it took all my strength to hold onto the one I had and pull the other out. It took about five minutes before I managed it. Then I stood up very slowly as the lions were now watching me, as I watched them, wondering, what now?'

Enthralled, Kay asked, 'What did you do?'

'We eyeballed each other for what seemed hours. Then as nothing happened, I started to slowly walk backwards until it felt a safe enough distance away to turn and walk. I didn't dare look back and hoped that I wasn't about to be attacked from behind. The dogs were trembling, probably because they could feel my pulse rate going over the top. Both my young dog and I were covered in scratches and bleeding badly. A small price to pay for having survived what could have been a disastrous experience. And that was my most dramatic and scary experience.'

She shook her head in amazement. 'You were lucky they didn't attack you or the dogs. I think I'd have passed out with fear. You won't catch me wandering around the bush on foot, that's for sure.'

'Just be aware if you do. I was lucky that day, as the pride had just finished off a carcass and their bellies were full. It could have been a very different scenario if that had not been the case.' He pushed the hair out of his eye as he spoke. His long fingers making Kay think he could have been an artist. Far too elegant for someone who worked in the bush, she mused.

'Hello?' Ed said, making Kay realise that she had been lost in thought and missed what he must have been telling her.

'You haven't heard a word I just said, have you?' Ed said, giving Kay a puzzled look.

The sound of a vehicle made Ed jump up and look out of the window. 'It's Ben, come on, let's get out of here before we have a memorable situation with these lions. You go first,' he added with a laugh, which in turn made Kay chuckle. She had never seen this side of him before, and she liked him enormously when he was relaxed and not being chauvinistic.

Ben stood on the people carrier with his rifle aimed at the lions, while Ed ushered Kay into her seat and jumped in after her.

'How?' the tracker said with a wild look in his eyes as he spotted the lions.

'Get the rest of the gang and get those buggers out of here before more guests arrive. Check the fences. Where the hell did they get in? I had all the boundaries checked only last week. I reckon an elephant did the work and they took advantage.'

Kay was aware of Ed's change of mood from the man she had just spent the past half hour listening to.

He seemed to sense she was thinking about him and turned around looking at her with an amused expression. 'You recovered?' he asked. 'It's back to the office for me and you'd better join me until we move those lions out and it's safe for you to return to your quarters.'

'Yes, fine thanks. I'd very much like to wait until it's safe to walk back on my own again.'

'No, you're not doing anything of the sort. I'll see you safely to your room myself, just as soon as they get rid of these lions.'

Why did her heart do a summersault with hearing those words? Something had changed with the dynamics of their relationship since spending forced time in that room with Ed. She followed him to the office and sat looking out at the dam where a mother and young waterbuck were making their way towards it in the evening light.

'Instead of us trying to focus on work, why don't we go and get a drink. It'll take some time to move those lions, so let's make the most of it shall we?' Ed said over his shoulder as he stood up and walked out of the office.

Kay picked up her bag and followed him. She couldn't believe the change in Ed, and just hoped it would last.

The bar, as always, was laid out with cocktail sausages, olives and other appetisers. There were African pottery dishes filled with amazingly appetising chef specialities, huge silver-plated bowls, filled to the brim with ice, as white and rosé wines sat looking very impressive. Decorative handles on either side of the bowls added a final touch.

Kay felt good to be acting as one of the guests, even if for only a short while. The barman gave her a smile as she seated herself on one of the oak bar stools. Ed stood very close to her and as he put his hand on her shoulder, a shiver ran all the way down her spine. She shivered.

'Are you cold?' he asked looking into her unusual amber eyes. 'Maybe our friend here could make you a hot toddy instead of something cold?'

'Gosh no thanks, I'm not cold, just got a shiver. I'd love a white wine please.' Kay felt the heat rising in her cheeks as he continued to look deep into her eyes.

Just as Ed ordered their drinks and was about to say something to Kay, they were interrupted by a loud commotion coming from the watchman standing guard at the entrance to the lodge. He was shouting to someone. Then they heard a voice they recognised immediately as Frank's, followed by loud laughter as footsteps approached the bar.

'Hi, what's all this I hear about lions in camp? It's all over the radios and all the other lodges in the area are talking about it. Bloody serious stuff, Ed. Thank God, we don't have any guests scheduled until tomorrow afternoon. I'm gasping for a beer. The coldest bottle you've got, please,' he said waving towards the barman. 'No glass, I'll drink it out of the bottle,' he added as his eyes locked onto Kay.

'This must be my lucky day, finding you here, Kay. Not like you to be propping up the pub at this time of the day. How did you get her here, Ed?' he sounded irritated as he spoke.

'It's a long story, but suffice to say, it's the lions' fault that Kay can't get to her room. She might as well have time to relax, and now that you've arrived, no doubt a party,' Ed said sarcastically.

Kay didn't mind having these two very different men vying for her attention. A bubble of contentment spread through her as she sipped her wine and listened to them discussing the pros and cons of conservation and its problems.

'By the way, Frank, any update on Tom?' Ed asked. 'I gather he's out of hospital but that's all I know.'

'He's feeling tons better and will be back at the lodge Monday next,' Frank replied.

Meanwhile Frank was making eyes at Kay and giving her a sly wink whenever Ed's attention was elsewhere.

She realised what an incorrigible flirt he was, but at the same time couldn't help responding to his infectious humour. He was the sort of man that one could have fun with, but could not take too seriously, as he was always seen with a different woman. Any new attractive visitor to the lodge would fall right under his spell, which Kay was only too aware of. Luckily for all the staff, they were encouraged to keep the guests happy, especially if they were invited to share dinner of the alfresco evening with any of them. Frank grinned at her mischievously. 'How about I see you back to your room once the coast is clear?'

'Well, Ed has already very kindly offered,' she said giving him a stern look.

'Right, then why don't we all have a bite together, and then

I shall head back and find a pretty girl to console myself with. But I warn you, Kay, I plan to take you to Kruger when we're both off duty together. There's an elephant museum that I think you would find most interesting. It's a long drive so we may have to spend a night at the campsite near there.' Frank looked very pleased with himself as Ed scowled at him.

'Kay's not due any leave for months yet, are you, Kay?' Ed asked.

'I'm not sure, but no I don't think so. I'll have to let you know, Frank,' she said.

They had dinner in the dining room, served with the best of everything. The chef delighted them with his experimental new recipes for game pie, followed by a French torte, which Kay wanted the recipe of. She had never felt happier than at that moment. She was aware she had changed profoundly since joining these dedicated people in this amazing setting. Her old life seemed worlds away. As Frank and Ed talked as if she had become invisible, her thoughts turned to Harry. Was he doing well with his gallery? Did he ever give her a thought these days? Try as she might, her mind would return to her ex and their life together and all the doomed plans she had made.

Frank interrupted her thoughts. 'Sorry, we've been ignoring you. Very rude of us and I'll make it up to you I promise,' he said with a smirk.

Ed turned away to greet the chef who was arriving at their table.

'Well I hadn't realised how ravenous I was,' Kay said. 'Thanks for that, Chef.'

Frank added his appreciative comments as the chef came to ask what they had thought of his menu.

Having all agreed it was simply the best, he departed with a happy smile on his face. They all stood up as Frank was leaving, and before Kay knew what was happening, he gave her a quick kiss on the lips, taking her by surprise. With a wave he was gone, but not before she had seen the look of annoyance Ed gave his departing back.

Just then Ed's phone rang. 'Good, thanks,' he said and switched it off. 'Right, now I can get you back to your room. Lions have moved out and the electric fence has been repaired and is working again. The elephant that broke it must have shocked himself, so hopefully he won't be back.'

Ed's face relaxed as he looked at her, which made her feel better as she followed him out of the lodge towards her room. Looking to where the animals had left the flattened grass, Kay was very grateful that she hadn't been on her own earlier. She may not have spotted the lions as they lay half hidden in the long grass. Reaching her door, Ed turned suddenly, and she bumped into him. He grabbed her arm to steady her.

'Sorry, Kay, are you alright?'

'Um apart from being embarrassed, I guess I am,' she giggled, wondering why he was still holding onto her. Then to her utter amazement Ed pulled her into his arms and kissed her with such force her lips parted, and he took that as permission to explore her mouth with his tongue. Her head spinning, she was lost in the moment as her arms seemed to have a mind of their own and moved up around his neck. She pulled him closer as their tongues met and continued to explore each other. As suddenly as it had happened, so it ended. Ed pulled away.

'What the hell am I doing? I've just broken all the rules in the book. No getting involved with staff, that is the cardinal rule here. Kay, I don't know what to say, or what came over me. I can't blame it on the wine, now can I? This means it's you who's gone to my head.' He turned to leave, before adding, 'It won't happen again I promise.'

Kay stared at Ed's back as his long strides took him back towards the lodge. She was trembling with emotion as she let herself into her room, closing and locking the door behind her. In a daze, she collapsed into the huge armchair. Waiting for her heartbeat to regulate, she marvelled at the kiss they had shared. Never had she felt such passion from a kiss. It was fantastic she thought as she hugged herself and smiled.

She ran a hot perfumed bath and lay in it going over the evening in her head, feeling the tightening in her stomach as she thought of Ed's kisses and the way he had looked into her eyes, with such passion. If Ed had taken things further, she wasn't sure she'd have been strong enough to stop him, or even wanted to. It was a thought that astonished her.

Since leaving Harry and Durban, Kay vowed no man would steal her heart again. Sex was another matter she analysed. It would be without strings and not because she fell in love. No, she could not let that happen again. She was determined those feelings would not be allowed to surface. That life she shared with Harry had been over for a long time, left behind in Durban.

Chapter Seven

Early the following morning, Edward Blake ran his long fingers through his hair, as he looked out of his office window at the land he was the custodian of. The frustration he was feeling was unusual for him, being a man of action and not one to dwell on thing he couldn't control. Now he was feeling very frustrated. What was he missing? How could the poachers know how to infiltrate his concession of the Sabie Sands area? They were either incredibly intuitive or someone from the inside was feeding them information. His gut told him it was the latter. He vowed to speak to Frank about this situation when he arrived for their meeting.

Instead of catching up with his phone calls, Ed's thoughts turned to Kay. He couldn't believe the effect she was having on him. After the death of his adored wife Claire all those years ago, he vowed never to let his heart get involved with another woman. He enjoyed sex, and it was always available to him, either in the form an attractive unattached guest or when he went on leave. Women fell at his feet. He used to think it was because he was someone of importance and the glamour of being a ranger, but of late he had been told they fancied his good looks and toned body. He was sure the uniform helped somewhat. Thanks to an experienced wife who had taught him how to satisfy a woman, his close friends called him a stud, much to his amusement.

Ed couldn't stop thinking about how Kay had such a sensual walk, with the swing of her hips as she moved. Her voice when she spoke, sent him down memory lane once more, as again she reminded him of Claire. Was it why he couldn't stop thinking about her? he wondered. Her laugh which ended in a little girly giggle fascinated him as he remembered hearing it when she and Alice had been in his office when he'd arrived one morning. The warm feeling in the pit of his stomach when he thought of Kay frightened him. He would make a determined effort to get her out of his mind. He realised he couldn't afford to cause a problem by getting involved with one of his staff.

'Ed mate, what's the problem? You made it sound serious when you called me earlier,' Frank said as he rushed into Ed's office.

'Hang on while I take this call,' Ed answered, as he picked up his ringing phone. 'Right, let's get on with the problem at hand. I'm seriously worried as to where these poachers are getting their information from, Frank. I've spoken to the other lodges in the area, and they too seem to think this is an organised gang and not just some random chaps taking a chance. The locals have only ever put snares down for small game, which they use for their family meat rations. Now this rhino poaching is much bigger and strikes of international backing, and huge money involved. It's a bloody dangerous game they're playing and I'm afraid it's a bit out of our league. What are your thoughts on the subject and who do we turn to? We can't allow these bastards to desecrate these precious beasts.' Ed thought briefly about what to do next.

'Let's leave it to the park board, guys,' Frank replied. 'It's not something we can sort out even with the help of the other lodges in the Sabie reserve. I'll have a word with the locals and ask if they have heard of anyone giving inside information to the poachers.'

'Good idea, I'll leave it to you then to find out what you can. Let me know what you find out, and then I can get back to the park board chap who just called me.' Ed was relieved to have a plan.

'I'll check in with you later today. I have to go into Nelspruit for some spares. I'll have a word with the guys after that,' Frank told Ed.

As Frank was leaving the office, he literally bumped into Kay as she entered.

'Sorry, but thanks for the hug,' Frank laughed and pulled Kay into his arms. 'That has just made my day, having you in my arms, sweet lady.' Releasing her as he left the office, he was unaware of his friend and boss's look of thunder as he saw Kay with Frank.

Ed was feeling very uncomfortable as he watched the interaction between them. Having just convinced himself he would have to keep her at arm's length, here she was again looking like a million dollars, he thought. He tried to pull his eyes away from her face. Did she have feelings for Frank?

Ed had no time to ponder on this as Kay started to speak.

'Hi Ed, I was just wondering,' she said. 'Has Alice arrived yet? I said I'd help her with the orders this morning as I have some free time.'

'Morning, Kay, no she's not here but I did see her heading towards the kitchens when I arrived. And about last night. I hope I didn't embarrass you, or make you feel uncomfortable? It won't happen again I promise,' Ed added as he watched her face change from the smile she had first given him to one of annoyance.

He thought she must have regretted it had happened by the look on her face, as he turned and picked up his phone off the desk. Turning back to her, he was in time to see her turn and hurriedly leave his office. Going to the door, he watched her walk to the carports where her people carrier was parked. He then heard her revving the engine as she left the lodge going in the direction of the dam area, where her tracker Ben was working. Ed watched until she had picked up Ben and carried on into the veldt when he lost sight of them.

'Now what's got into her?' he said in a puzzled voice to himself. 'Women, I'll never understand them,' he said. 'Never did and never will.'

'You taking to yourself?' Alice asked as she barged into the office.

Ed glared at her as he marched out and slammed the door behind him.

'Now what have I said,' Alice asked. 'Hell, he's got me talking to myself as well. Must be catching,' she added, grimacing.

On his way to the main lodge, and driving very slowly, Ed's thoughts went back to his conversation with Frank. They had been together for many years and he knew Frank could find out what was going on with the natives. Even so, he would do a little digging himself, just to get another perspective on the situation. Things were getting out of hand and if this carried on they would lose many more rhinos and it was obvious from what he had seen of late, that there were a few calves to be born soon. It wouldn't do for these females to be butchered by poachers, who had no qualms about killing a pregnant female for her horn.

It made his blood boil at the thought of the agonies these poor beasts went through and the loss of their young, being orphaned or dying in their mother's womb. He was deep in thought when he heard Kay's voice coming over the radio. He turned his radio full on to hear her better. She was obviously letting the other rangers know something.

'We're just over by the far ridge on the north side,' she said. 'A pack of wild dogs are feeding on the remains of an impala. Good opportunity if you have guests. I reckon they will be here for at least another half hour,' she added.

'Thanks, Kay, we're on our way. Just what my guests ordered and have been trying to find them this past hour. Let us know if you spot the leopard, as that's next on the list,' Matt, a ranger from one of the other camps replied.

Ed listened, with a feeling of pride at one of his rangers finding the wild dogs that another very experienced ranger and tracker had missed. He was still feeling frazzled by Kay's mood change so suddenly when she had been in his office earlier. The more he thought about it the more puzzled he became. Never had he felt the rush of jealousy before as when seeing her in Frank's arms. Maybe Charles had been right when he said he had feelings for Kay. Well he had better hide them, or he'd be the laughing stock of the lodge, he reckoned. Just as his thoughts turned to the meeting he was going to, his radio crackled again and broke into his thoughts.

'Hi gorgeous, well done on finding the wild dogs. I'll be doing a run later this afternoon with only a couple of guests, so if you'd like to join me, I'd like that. See you back at the lodge and you can let me know then. I'll be turning off now as I've business to sort out. Cheers. Over and out.'

Ed realised that Frank was making a play for Kay. He would have to nip that in the bud before Frank got carried away, as he did so often. He had lost count of the number of times Ed had bailed his friend out of embarrassing situations when he had a few drinks under his belt. Frank never let up when he spotted a pretty girl he fancied. Ed had to admit it, he wanted to keep Frank away from getting close to Kay. What the devil did Frank need to do business wise? Ed pondered. He should never turn his radio off when out in the bush either, so that's another thing he would have to talk to him about.

Just as he parked his vehicle, Ed saw Sally Pope walking towards him. He had to admit that she was pretty, but not in the way Kay was, he mused.

'Hi Ed, I saw you driving in and thought it would be a good time to catch you before you got inside,' Sally said.

'Mmm, you're wearing aftershave? Who are you trying to impress? Smells lovely. Are you trying to impress me?' Sally asked, playfully punching him on his arm.

'Stop messing about, Sal, and tell me what's so urgent that you've collared me here?' Ed said, feeling flattered by her comments.

'I just felt you ought to know that we've had the top brass from the Parks Board staying here this past week. Incognito I hasten to add. It's just that one of the handsome guys made a pass at me and we had a drink together, so we got talking. The more he drank the more he talked. Apparently, they are keeping this lodge and yours under surveillance. He obviously thought that I have few brain cells as I'm the beautician here, so thought it would go in one ear and out the other. I did try to give him that impression mind, to get more info out of him.'

Ed caught her hand and pulled Sally towards a bench that was hidden from view, behind huge boulder covered with a display of shrubs. She sat beside him as he turned his troubled grey eyes towards her.

'Bloody hell, Sal, don't go shooting your mouth off where we could be overheard. Who is this chap you were talking to and is he legit?' Ed asked in a whisper.

'Yes, he's the real deal, Ed, and there are two more of them. Keep to themselves and in civvies so as not to stand out. Look, I don't know if I should make this sound more important than it is, but just thought you ought to know. What are they looking for do you think?' she asked.

'Keep this to yourself, Sally. I suspect it could be to do with the poachers.'

'Why would you think that?'

'Because the Parks Board thinks it's an international ring working the Sabie area, and that one or more locals are on their payroll. Heavy stuff, and very dangerous to get involved with. These chaps will stop at nothing to get the rhino horns. Big money, as in millions,' Ed explained, as he watched a worried expression cross Sally's face, quickly changing back to her usual smile.

Deep in thought, Ed watched two hornbills who sat above them on a large leaf rock fig, their squawking was beginning to irritate him.

'Ed, I have to get back as I have a client in ten minutes. You okay?' Sally asked.

'Those birds think they own this place,' he groaned. 'Bloody racket. Can't hear myself think. Come on, I'll walk you back. I've got a meeting in half an hour about burning the veldt and want to grab a coffee before it starts,' Ed said, already moving away from the noisy birds.

'I'll keep my ears open for any more info, Ed, even if it means flirting with that gorgeous Parks Board guy,' Sally laughed.

'If that's okay with you. Seriously though, Sally, be careful. We don't want them to think he's passing on any information. He could lose his job if they find out he's been talking, especially as it would be a warning to anyone involved in the ring of poachers. We certainly don't want anyone to know the place is being watched by the Parks Board. Let them find out who's at the back of all this business. Cheers for now, have a good day,' Ed added, as they reached the entrance to the lodge and separated.

Sally headed for the spa.

Ed was deep in thought as he sat alone on the balcony that overlooked the waterhole, while drinking his coffee. He had to think clearly. Could he trust Frank to keep his mouth shut if he shared Sally's news with him? What was it that Sally had mentioned that was like a thorn in his side?

After much thought he decided to keep their conversation to himself for a while until he had time to think clearly. When his friend was fired up with whisky, he was inclined to mouth off or show off. He couldn't risk Frank letting some valuable information slip out to the wrong ears. He would never forgive himself if it was due to his neglect that the poachers got a warning of the plans to catch them. He would spend more time at the main lodge to check out these undercover guys.

If Sally could work out what they were doing, it was high time he found out more. How dare they infiltrate his domain without first talking to him about what they were planning? His mood changed as he became angry. Putting down his coffee cup, he went to his meeting. He would get to the bottom of what was going on once the meeting was over.

Chapter Eight

Kay didn't set eyes on Ed that morning when she arrived at the lodge at six-thirty. She joined Alice for breakfast and was told that Ed was tied up with more meetings and after that would be going to see an old chief who he knew as a young boy.

'Don't let on you know all the boss's business, Kay, or I'll be in trouble,' Alice said quietly. 'He insists that anything concerning his movements is to be kept very quiet. I gather even Frank isn't aware of what Ed's up to.' She took a sip of her coffee and gave Kay a knowing wink.

'What do you mean? What Ed's up to?' Kay asked, perplexed. 'Sounds very cloak and dagger stuff if he isn't telling Frank what he's up to. Is it anything to do with the meetings he's been having at the main lodge, do you think?'

'Not really sure, Kay. He's even been out in the bush very early this morning long before anyone else was up,' Alice said leaning in closer to Kay. 'The chief he's gone to see is quite a long way out of the park, so he'll be back late. He said I'm to tell anyone that asks for him, that he had a meeting in the Kruger Park. All very strange for Ed to be behaving so secretly though.'

The girls finished their breakfast in thoughtful silence and were about to leave the table when Frank greeted them.

'Morning, girls, looks like good viewing today, the weather is perfect, not too hot. I'll join you for a quick coffee, if I may. Then I'd better get off to the main lodge where I'm to pick up a group of Japanese tourists. That's usually Ed's call, so I was a bit surprised to receive a message from him that I should go in his place.' He waved the waiter over. 'Where is he, Alice? Not like him to skip out on a busy day.' He ordered his coffee and Kay could see Alice was relieved to have a few seconds to think of an answer.

'All I know is that Ed had a meeting at the Kruger offices, so left very early before light. At least that is what he told me when he called me last night,' Alice answered.

'Did he say what it was all about?' Frank asked.

'No.' She glanced at the clock on the wall and stood up. 'I'd better go. I need to open up the office and see if I've got any mail to answer. Wouldn't do for the boss to get back and find me slacking. You coming, Kay?'

'Yes,' Kay said relieved for an excuse to leave. 'I need to see the fixture list of today's guests.'

Kay followed Alice, but not before she noticed Frank's displeasure that they were leaving him. He's not one to manage hiding how he felt, she thought. One minute he would put on his boyish charm and another, he seemed almost threatening if he didn't get his own way. She had no time to bother about Frank and his moods, she mused hurrying after Alice.

'He's a moody sod,' Alice said over her shoulder as she

stopped to retrieve the office keys from her pocket. See the way his charm disappeared when I suggested you leave? He's got the hots for you, my girl.' Alice narrowed her eyes and gave Kay a pointed stare. 'I'd be very careful if I were you. The way he looks at you when you're not aware, is near scary.'

'Don't be silly, I can handle Frank,' Kay reassured her. Deep down though, she was less confident than she wanted her friend to think.

Alice unlocked the office door and went inside. Picking up the list of Kay's guests and the note showing who would be her tracker that day, she handed it to her. Kay was relieved to see it was Ben. She always felt more relaxed around Ben. He had never shown any opposition to working with a woman. It made a welcome change.

The group were woken at six o'clock by the night watchman. Kay hoped with a bit of luck that they would be ready to leave in the next half an hour after enjoying a snack of coffee and biscuits.

Ben organised the kitchen staff to pack picnic baskets with all the group needed for their morning break. Bottles of water, still or sparkling, would be ready to offer the guests as they left for their drive. Kay looked forward to meeting Ben at the vehicle once she had gathered her group of guests together. She returned to the lodge lounge to find out how many of them had got up for the early drive.

She could hear laughter as she reached the lounge and was relieved to see no sign of Frank.

'Good morning, Kay,' shouted a large, jolly chap, who

introduced himself as Richard. He walked up to her with a wide smile. 'My wife will be with us in a minute, and I've been instructed to get her a strong coffee,' he said making his way to the buffet counter.

'Nice to meet you,' Kay said, shaking his hand. 'Great morning for viewing. With a bit of luck, we'll find a cheetah for you.'

Richard's wife, Cherry, arrived with Brian and Joan, their friends from Cape Town. Shortly after them, a tall handsome Irishman called Alan and his tiny French wife Monica hurried in. They were in South Africa to look for artistic talent and give bursaries to an art gallery in France. Kay discovered that they currently stayed in rooms above an art studio in Durban. Then a short while later, the final couple arrived.

'Hi, sorry we're late,' the woman said. 'It was his fault,' she gave Kay a wink to show that she was teasing her husband. 'I'm Sheena and he's Colin. Is it okay if we quickly grab a coffee?' she asked hurrying to stand at the end of the short queue.

Kay smiled. 'We have a few minutes left for you to drink your coffees,' she said, impressed to see that everyone in her group had made the supreme effort of getting up early on their first morning to go on the drive. She instinctively liked this group; they were obviously intent on having a good time.

Colin was the first to make his move. Without waiting for his wife or friends he picked up his gear and made off to the people carrier. When Kay followed him outside to check he was all right, she discovered he was determined to sit in the front next to her, so that he could hear what was being said over the radio. Kay and Ben often remarked how funny it was to watch adults rushing to get the seats they wanted. She had learnt that the nervous guests preferred to sit in the middle of other guests, while some liked to be on the sides, to get a better view. Keen photographers usually sat way at the back on the higher seating, to take the best panoramic pictures.

The others arrived and once everyone was on board and comfortable, Kay put the radio on and the headphones in her ear. Aware that there would be lots of questions asked by the guests, she now only put one ear piece in.

Kay intended to impress these important guests. She drove towards where the young male lions were last seen by one of the staff members on his way to work. Everyone was thrilled to find them not far from camp. The lions were playing with each other, biting and growling, just like oversized kittens. Everyone had cameras at the ready and managed to take some great pictures. The group stayed watching and taking videos for the best part of an hour.

'Everyone ready to move on?' she asked, smiling. Of course they were, she smiled recalling her first few times on drives, loving every second although always exhausted from concentrating on trying to spot the animals. 'I know it's a bit chilly now, but it'll soon warm up when the sun rises.'

By midday, the sun was beating down on the dusty dirt road. The group took off their jackets and rolled up their sleeves.

'When are we stopping for coffee? I'm desperate for a pee,' Brian asked.

'For goodness' sake can't you wait,' his wife, Joan, hissed. 'You went just before we got into the vehicle.'

'That was over an hour ago, and I had all that coffee before we left. Surely someone else needs to go?' Brian said, looking at his friends hopefully.

'Sure do, my friend, just as soon as we stop I'll be with you,' Alan answered, in his lilting Irish voice, which reminded Kay of her late grandfather.

Her radio crackled into life and the guests stopped talking, as news came through from another ranger.

'He's spotted a cheetah with her three cubs, just over the ridge from we are,' Kay said, in case the guests hadn't realised it. We'd better stop at the dam on the way, Brian,' she added. 'But you'll have to stand behind the vehicle as we're too vulnerable to move away from it around here. No knowing who or what's around.'

'Don't worry, I can hold it,' he said grimacing. 'Don't want to miss seeing the cheetah. This lot would never forgive me.'

'Good decision, Brian,' Colin said.

Kay was excited to be sharing this viewing with guests that appreciated life in the bush and didn't mind if they didn't get to see the big five. Nearing the sighting, she slowed down as she manoeuvred her way across the veld where another crowd of guests sat in silence, their cameras pointed at the animals.

'Look at those little darlings,' Monica whispered.

'This is such a real treat,' her husband Alan said quietly, training his binoculars onto the family of cheetahs.

The rest of them gazed in awe as the young cheetahs played around, falling over each other. Their mother kept an eye on both vehicles and Kay noticed she didn't appear to relax for a second. Seeing another ranger arrive with his vehicle full of guests, Kay slowly drove away.

'Wow that was stunning, simply stunning,' Sheena muttered to herself.

'I think we can take a pit stop now everyone,' Kay said steering the vehicle to a safe clearing overlooking the waterhole.

A couple of hippo could be seen in the middle of the dam, as they blew water into the air. Ben jumped from his seat on the front, and started to get a folding table out, onto which he put cups biscuits and muffins.

He asked each person what they would like. 'Tea, coffee or hot chocolate?'

Kay helped pour the drinks while Cherry passed around the nibbles. The others joined in to help, while the men rushed off to hide behind some dense bushes so that they were just out of sight while they took a bathroom break.

'Just look at that view, guys,' Colin said, returning to the others.

'Awesome,' Richard said, coming back to join them.

Kay asked them all to pose for a photo. She made a habit of doing this and when she had time downloaded them onto her laptop and added their names to the pictures. This way she would always be able to refer to the pictures, should any of the people return to the camp. It was a tip Frank had given her soon after her arrival.

After the photo, they finished their drinks, helped Ben and Kay pack up the vehicle and drove off. On the way to the camp, Ben delighted the guests by pointing out some elephants and a pack of wild dogs, relaxing with pups near a dried-up riverbed.

'My goodness, however did you see the puppies, Ben? I would never have noticed them sleeping in the sand.' Cherry asked, her eyes wide. 'Seeing those wild dogs was such a thrill. That was a real bit of luck, wasn't it, Kay?'

'Yes, so many people never get sighting of wild dogs, especially when they have pups,' Kay answered as she turned the steering wheel to take them back to the camp. 'Time to get you guys back for some breakfast I think.'

Arriving back at camp, Kay was hoping to find Alice. Unfortunately, she could only see Frank who was talking with one of the rangers from the main lodge.

Joan amazed everyone by suddenly announcing, 'The most exciting thing I saw all day was that dung beetle on the way home.'

'Really?' Brian gasped. 'What about the lions and the cheetah with her cubs?' Brian boomed at her in a rather annoyed voice.

Everyone looked at each other and some shook their heads. Kay came to Joan's rescue by explaining that everyone could have their own idea of what made it the best of a day for them. Before anyone could make more remarks, she added, 'You must be hungry, so why not help yourselves at the buffet counter to cereals, fruit and yoghurts. After that, the staff will take orders for the main course.'

She knew the cooked breakfast at the lodge would probably surpass all their expectations.

'Just another word, folks,' she said. 'I'm going to leave you all now, so please enjoy the rest of the morning and lunch will be served at twelve-thirty. After that you can relax and have a nap or enjoy our pool area. Afternoon tea is served at three o'clock, and we meet for the night drive at four sharp. We'll be going a long way from camp, so please bring something warm as it will cool down by the time we return to camp around seven.'

She was used to this speech now. She noticed them wanting to get to their breakfast, so quickly added, 'Tonight's arrangements for dinner will be on the board when we return. Have a lovely day and I'll see you all this afternoon.'

A chorus of, 'Thank you, Kay,' rang out as Kay waved, and left them to go and find Alice for a catch-up chat.

Everyone returned after their afternoon rest or from lazing by the pool. They joined Kay and Ben for the afternoon drive, and she was delighted to hear that everyone had enjoyed a perfect day so far. It was fun having everyone on board again, although the afternoon turned out to be very uneventful.

This time they only saw smaller animals, a few vultures and the fish eagle. Kay made a hurried stop at the dam for drinks as it started to rain, which cut short their stay and by the time they arrived back at the lodge everyone was cold and wet and far less cheery than they had been that morning.

Colin added to the annoyance by taking photos of the women looking bedraggled in their rain gear. Kay found it amusing when they turned on him, shouting their disapproval, which only made him laugh more and carry on taking photos.

Later that evening as all the guest were relaxing around the veranda with drinks or coffees, Ed and Frank arrived from the main lodge with two stunning women who Kay thought could easily pass for models.

Her heart pounded, and she realised she must be jealous. Both men looked very handsome in their smart chinos and crisp shirts. Everyone stopped talking and stared at the two handsome couples. Ed disentangled himself from the woman whose arm was linked through his as soon as he spotted Alice and Kay. He walked over to speak to them.

'Hi, ladies, this is Andrea and her friend Hannah,' he said. 'They are jewellery designers from Cape Town and will be staying for a few days at our main lodge. We thought it would be a good idea to bring them over for a quick night cap with everyone. It's their first visit and they're keen to see everything and meet everyone.' Kay and Alice exchanged greetings with the two other women. 'They're friends of our boss who, you probably know, also lives in Cape Town and they supply the lodge with all those amazing trinkets and jewels that you see in the display cabinets near the reception area.' Ed gave Alice and Kay a quick smile.

'Ladies, what's your poison?' Frank asked, walking over to the bar.

'Same again for us, please,' Alice said raising her eyebrows at Kay to check that was what she wanted. Kay nodded.

The next hour passed in a daze for Kay. She enjoyed getting to know the two women and finding out where they got their inspiration from for their unusual designs. Eventually, noticing that Ed had not said very much, she glanced over in his direction, just as he looked up and caught her eye. Was it her imagination or was that a wink she saw as he raked his right hand through his hair?

Finding it difficult to concentrate, she looked at the clock in the corner of the room and was amazed to see it was already eleven-fifteen. She had an early drive in the morning, and as much as she was enjoying herself, she was tired. She was getting used to the early mornings and long days, but still found it hard to stay up late drinking when she had an early start the following morning.

'We heard two of your rangers discussing poachers earlier today,' Alan said, as Richard and Colin leant forward to hear what Ed had to say on the matter.

'It is a big problem,' Ed admitted. 'We have to constantly be on the lookout for them, but it's difficult to protect all the animals over such a huge expanse of land.'

'It must be,' Richard agreed. 'They were saying how you are determined to publicise the plight of the rhinos, especially, to as many people as possible.'

Kay wanted to hear more, liking that the man she worked for was such an enthusiastic conservationist. Unfortunately, Sheena and Monica waved her over to go and speak to them where they were sitting by the fire drinking their cocktails.

She quickly went over and wished them a goodnight.

Then going back to the group of men, Kay waited for a lull in Ed's conversation and stifling a yawn, said, 'Sorry, I'm going to have to go to bed now.' She waved to the others by the bar and smiled.

'Hold on, I need to discuss something with you,' Ed said, catching up with her as she reached the exit where they were out of sight of the lounge bar. He caught her by the arm and turned her towards him.

'Everything's alright, isn't it?'

'Yes,' she replied, confused. 'Why?' She tried to think how she might have given him the wrong impression about how she was feeling. 'I'm just tired, that's all.' She hesitated. 'I think it's great that you're such an avid conservationist,' she said.

He looked touched by her comment. 'I don't understand how anyone could choose to kill any of these magnificent creatures, and I'll do my utmost to see that they're protected.'

Kay opened her mouth to assure him that she was happy to support him in his quest, when Andrea arrived and slipped her arm through his in what Kay thought to be rather a possessive way. 'Edward, there you are,' she gushed. 'I've been looking for you everywhere. Hannah wants to leave, and Frank said he was happy to do so, but needed to wait until he saw you.'

Ed gave Kay a frown that only she would have noticed, before disentangling himself from Andrea.

'I'll catch up with you tomorrow,' he said. 'Goodnight, Kay.' He turned and left with Andrea, who glanced at Kay over her shoulder and shot her a triumphant smile.

Kay was furious that she and Ed had been interrupted deliberately by the woman. What else would Ed have said, given time she mused as she walked to her room, guided by the porter's torch light? She heard loud laughter coming from the open vehicle as it departed for the main lodge. A feeling of dejection overcame her, as she made her way to the bathroom.

Kay cleaned her teeth and felt homesick for the first time since her arrival. She missed her grandmother and her little cottage. Tomorrow she would put a call through from the office. She wished her grandmother had agreed to learn how to use a mobile phone before Kay had left Durban, but she understood that it was not something she would probably ever use unless it was taking a call from Kay. She couldn't even email her, she thought, recalling how internet access was often inaccessible where their lodge was situated, although the main lodge was geared up for everything technologically, which was why most of the international visitors stayed here so they could be in touch with their businesses even when travelling. She might be miserable right now, she thought, but she had not regretted having joined this group of dedicated people, not for one second.

After a very restless night, Kay left her room at five-thirty. It would soon be dawn and she concentrated on making sure there were no predators lurking in the tall grasses on her way to the lodge from her room. The kitchen staff were not at work yet, so she sat on the veranda of the lodge and picking up her binoculars, studied the dam. Before long she spotted giraffe and zebras making their way across the veldt, followed by a family of wild boar. In the distance a lone elephant was working hard to pull down a tree to reach the top leaves.

The silence of the early dawn, interrupted only by wildlife, enveloped her senses and Kay felt the calm seeping through into her very soul. Taking in deep breaths and exhaling slowly, she felt more relaxed than she had for a long time. Maybe this was the way to start every day, before another person was around, she thought. The smell of the animals wafted across to her as she shielded her eyes from the early rising sun.

The noisy chattering of staff arriving shattered her peace.

'Hi Kay, you're up early,' Alan said. 'Couldn't you sleep last night? I had too much to drink so I knew it was no good trying to go back to sleep. My dear wife is still fast asleep. I've asked the porter to go give her a call in half an hour. Hope you don't mind if I join you?'

'Not at all,' she said. 'Come and look at our early morning visitors at the dam.' Spotting he had brought his expensive camera, she added, 'Great you've got your camera with that amazing telephoto lens. You must try and capture the haze rising out of the dam. I'll get our coffee while you enjoy the view.' Kay left him and went to the kitchen to see how the staff were getting on and if they had begun making the coffee yet.

By six-thirty everyone was assembled and ready to leave. The excitement of the group was palpable as they made their way to the people carrier where Frank and his tracker, Zumbe, was waiting. Kay realised it must be Ben's day off.

She would have preferred working with another tracker as she couldn't help feeling that this man didn't approve of a woman being a ranger. The knowledge made her apprehensive and determined not to make any mistakes. Zumbe helped those who needed a hand onto the vehicle but didn't greet them as Ben would have done. He had a sullen look about him Kay noticed, more so than usual. Was it was something Frank had said?

As they departed, Kay drove towards the river. The call of a fish eagle rang out as it rose into the sky. Another seemed to answer from a different direction. Before they reached the river, Zumbe put up his hand to stop.

'What have you seen?' Richard asked.

He was pointing a little ahead towards the ground. He indicated for Kay to move slowly forward which she did, until she saw what all the excitement was about.

'It's a dung beetle,' Kay explained. 'Look at the enormous dung ball it's rolling with its back legs as it pushes it up the path.'

The guests leaned out to get a better look, entranced the clever little beetle. More photos and videos were taken and when they were finished, Kay drove slowly onwards.

'I can't help being amused by Joan being so excited about the dung beetle,' Richard laughed, the others immediately joining in.

'I bet you're happy now you've seen your favourite animal this morning,' Brian said teasing his wife.

Then the questions started coming. Kay always carried her little book of all the names and habits of the animals and insects. She often referred to it when she needed more information than she could remember. Alan seemed to be the ringleader when it came to the group's queries. He was interested in everything that happened, and Kay was glad to see him making the most of his trip.

They passed a herd of impala and zebra and Kay explained to the group, aware that Frank was listening to every word, that the animals always seemed to enjoy each other's company. It was getting warmer and the group began removing their thicker jackets as the sun warmed them as it rose.

'Tell us some of the reason why the zebra have so many stripes, Kay?' Alan asked.

'Well, the stripes of each zebra are different like our fingerprints. Then, when a predator attacks one of the heard, they all take off at a gallop and the predator is dazzled by all their stripes.'

'Wow! That's amazing,' Sheena shouted in excitement.

'Shush, woman, you'll frighten all the animals away with that booming voice,' Collin admonished his wife.

Kay noticed Sheena giving her husband a surreptitious glare which made him sit quietly for the next half an hour and had to hide her amusement.

Crossing a dry riverbed, they noticed a few vultures perched on top of a dead leadwood tree. It was still early and but unusual for them to still be perched where they roosted the night before, Kay explained to her guests.

'They usually look for a good rising thermal to climb and begin their days searching for decaying flesh as soon as it's light,' she said, as Zumbe stepped down from the vehicle.

More vultures flew overhead. Becoming concerned that something was wrong at the base of the aerial restaurant, Kay checked to see what Frank was doing, and seeing he was on the radio to someone, decided to go and see what was going on.

Richard was the first to smell the rotting meat of the dead animal as they approached some huge rocks just over the ridge. He put his hand over his nose.

'What the hell is that disgusting smell? Good thing I've not eaten breakfast yet,' he whispered.

'Eugh, what a pong,' Sheena said as the others grimaced and covered their noses.

Kay drove slowly around a bend towards where the vultures were circling. They came across a pride of seven young male lions feeding off the carcass of a buffalo bull. One of the larger of the lions looked at the approaching vehicle and started to growl at it, only to return to his feeding once they had come to a halt some distance away.

'Can't we get closer? I want to get a close-up of these chaps to show my kids,' Brian asked.

'We'll let them settle first, Brian,' Kay said. 'That big lion seems rather annoyed with our presence already, and we don't want him to feel threatened. I don't know this pride, so they may just be passing through our camp.' She glanced at Zumbe. 'I suggest you get into the vehicle until we move away,' she added aware she might have to drive away if the lions turned on them. Without a word, he got into the front seat next to Colin.

Kay drove slowly closer, when she felt it was safe to do so. The lions seemed comfortable with their presence and carried on eating, giving only the occasional look their way. The group watched silently as the lions chased each other off the kill, and the vultures swooped down, landing close by. Kay heard the quiet whirr of cameras as the people she was with took their photos.

Frank radioed the situation to the lodge and another three vehicles arrived. It was Kay's cue to leave, so that they did not encroach on the game. Once on the move and some distance from the lions, Kay stopped to let Zumbe back onto the tracker's seat on the front. Unsure whether she had mentioned the process to the guests on their first drive, she explained that whenever a ranger approached one of the predators, the tracker would get into the people carrier until it was safe to return to his seat.

Before leaving the lions behind, Zumbe jumped into his viewing seat, as she motored on towards the river where the hippo and crocodiles would be. There in the clearing they stopped for the morning break.

'Right, guys, anyone for a pee?' Brian asked being the first to get down and walk towards a nearby bush, closely followed by Alan and Colin.

'I also need a wee, but I'm not squatting behind that tiny bush,' Cherry whispered to Monica.

Zumbe must have overheard her and pulled a blanket from the back of the vehicle and walked towards a thorn tree some distance away, without saying a word. He hung the blanket on the thorns and draped it across to make a shelter of sorts. Returning to the waiting fidgeting girls, he said, 'For you,' as he pointed towards the temporary curtain.

'Zumbe, thanks so much. That's amazingly clever of you,' gushed a much-relieved Cherry, as she and the other girls make their way towards the now concealed ablution area.

Meanwhile Kay was pouring coffee and tea orders to be ready for their return. She laid out the biscuits and homemade muffins onto the bonnet of the vehicle, for everyone to help themselves. Kay listened to the peals of laughter coming from behind the blanket, as the girls hid from view and could imagine the chaotic scene. She had been in the same situation many times.

Once everyone had eaten and drunk enough, it was time to carry on.

'Please, Kay, I'd like to see a leopard if possible?' Sheena said.

'I'd like Zumbe to find a cheetah for me,' Colin added, just as he gasped at a bird, Kay noticed was an exquisite purple lilac roller as it swooped right over his head and landed in the nearby tree.

'Look at that bird,' shouted Monica as she aimed her camera.

Everyone laughed. Kay stopped and turned to her guests, explaining a little about the bird population and what she had seen since her arrival at camp. 'Right, let's go and try to find the cheetah and maybe a leopard,' she said.

They were passing a bend in the river, when Zumbe pointed to where a fish eagle was sitting on a dead branch looking down into the water. Kay stopped and told them to get the cameras ready. They waited for about five minutes when the huge bird took off in a steep dive right into the water, surfacing with a large fish in its talons before flying back up to his perch. It landed still clasping the fish, which it then proceeded to eat. She smiled as she heard the group's gasps as they watched the bird's mate join it and share in the delights.

'Did you know that the fish eagle mates for life?' Kay asked her group, aware Frank was paying attention to what she was saying. She tried not to make any mistakes in what she was telling them. The last thing she needed was Frank telling Ed he did not think she was good enough for the job.

'Really? What else can you tell us about them? Slowly mind,' Alan said. 'I want to write it all down to tell my friends back in Ireland.'

'Okay, to start with let's talk about their colour,' she began. 'The body is brown, and the wings black, eyes are a dark brown and its head and tail white. They have a yellow face, which I think is most attractive. As you saw when the fish was caught, the eagle has long talons.' She pointed up to the birds. 'Can you see their beak has a black tip which is very hooked and that's ideal for carnivorous lifestyle. The female weighs more than the male at about eight pounds. The male's wingspan is about six feet, while the female's is two feet more.'

'Where do they lay their eggs?' Cherry asked, intrigued.

Kay was enjoying herself. She loved anything about nature, and this was her favourite part of the job. 'In the nest built on top of large tall trees. The nests are made of sticks and bits of bark and any moss they find. They usually lay up to three eggs and manage to rear them with ease. The eggs are white with reddish speckles.'

'How long do the eggs take to hatch?' Joan asked.

'Incubation can last up to forty-five days before chicks hatch, and the interesting thing is, it's the male who incubates while the female goes off hunting for them both,' Kay added.

'Last question I promise,' Monica laughed. 'How long before the chicks can fly away from the nest?'

'The chicks fledge at approximately seventy-four days, so that's about three months,' Kay answered.

She could feel the admiration from them all as they chatted amongst themselves and didn't hide the fact that they thought it was their good luck to get such a knowledgeable ranger and a woman at that, Kay heard one of the men remark. Kay felt her hackles rise at his comments. Why would female rangers be any less expert at their job? she wondered. Physically they might sometimes be less strong, but what she lacked in strength, she knew she more than made up for in knowledge. It was just one of the many irritations that she had to put up with where men were concerned.

'I think that's enough excitement for one morning,' she said trying not to let his comment annoy her and spoil what had otherwise been a fun time. 'Let's hit the road and find that elusive cheetah.'

She drove on until they found a herd of elephant, some

wildebeest and rhino. Kay stopped further on to let the guests spend time watching a huge male kudo bull but was disappointed not to be able to locate a cheetah.

'That's the brilliant part of being out in the bush,' she said. 'Nothing is certain, and you can't always manage to see the animal you're hoping to come across.' She drank some water from the bottle she always carried with her. 'Time to get you guys some culinary delights, which I'm sure the chef has waiting back at camp,' Kay said as she started the engine and slowly turned towards camp. She heard a chorus of agreement from behind her, which made her smile. A feeling of deep content came over her as she drove on in silence the sun hot on her back and the breeze on her face, her earlier irritation vanishing.

'We'll try and find your leopard or cheetah on our next drive, guys. Hopefully we'll find one or the other.' She glanced at Frank, sitting quietly in the back and he nodded.

Back at camp, the guests rushed to their rooms to wash and prepare for lunch, which was to be served on long tables under the marula tree overlooking the dam. Staff waited, ready to take orders for a choice of drinks. Salads, cold meats and other delicious looking savouries, including homemade breads and muffins were on display, covered to keep away insects.

'Even the croissants are as near perfect as the French could make them,' Monica remarked, tearing the end of one and popping it into her mouth.

'I'll meet you all back here in two hours and then we can go out on our afternoon drive,' Kay said, looking forward to returning to the staff quarters and enjoying a well-earned lunch herself.

Approaching the staff dining room, she could hear deep laughter, and immediately recognised Frank and Ed's voices.

'Hello there,' boomed Frank as she entered the room.

'Hi guys, what's on the menu for us today? Are we having the same as the guests?' Kay asked, as she looked from Frank to Tsepho, and another young trainee ranger. She could sense Ed's eyes boring into her back as she moved past the men and made her way to the staff buffet near the kitchen. Why did she feel so awkward when he was in the room? She knew that it was down to her growing feelings for the man she had come to admire.

'How was your viewing this morning?' Ed asked, standing up and joining her next to the lavish spread on the buffet table.

'It was great, thank you,' she said. 'I did radio the other rangers when we came across a pride of young lions that had killed a huge buffalo. My guests were in their element and took masses of photos,' Kay added, as she turned to face Ed.

'Congratulations are in order, Frank tells me. I've heard first hand that you're making a great impression on everyone here since you joined us.'

'Does that include you?' Kay asked, looking him straight in the eye, feeling a strange sensation in the pit of her stomach.

'What do you think?' he asked lowering his voice and staring deep into her eyes.

He had such a serious look on his face as he asked the

question, that Kay felt it had to be answered, but before she could do so Frank called across the room to them.

'What the hell is keeping you two? Anyone would think you're making the food, instead of filling your plate, Kay. Ed, yours is sitting here getting cold.'

'Come on, we can finish this conversation another time,' Ed said, leading Kay back to the table, where the others were halfway through their lunch.

'I was asking Kay how her morning went with the guests,' Ed snapped at Frank as he sat down opposite him and next to Kay. 'You know I like to keep up with what my staff are doing, especially as there were so many negative comments when most of the men discovered that a female ranger was starting here.'

Frank scowled at him. 'I seem to recall that I wasn't the only one with something to say about it.'

'Eat your lunch, Frank,' Ed said, without looking at him.

Kay didn't say a word. She wanted to eat and leave as soon as possible, not wishing to become involved any more than she already was with their conflict.

After lunch, they all went their own way, leaving Kay to go to her room for a doze. It was going to be a long, hot afternoon and after a bad night's sleep, she was aware she could not afford to relax while all the rangers seemed to be watching her every move, and reporting back to Ed. They can watch, she told herself, as she drifted off into a dreamless sleep, waking in what seemed like moments when her alarm went off at three in the afternoon. She showered and dressed and went to meet her group.

The afternoon drive was successful. Kay was relieved when Zumbi spotted a cheetah on the way back from the evening sundowners by the river. It was soon dusk, and the sighting was not that good, but everyone seemed delighted when a lone leopard walked through the veldt. It sauntered right up to the vehicle Kay had stopped only moments before to allow the guests to take pictures.

'Everybody finished taking photos?' she asked, moving off when they agreed that they had.

Kay promised to find another cheetah, if possible, the next day. She explained that the leopard would probably still be in the vicinity of the lodge's concession, so should not be too difficult to locate. She cut the drive short as it was their evening in the boma and everyone wanted to return to their rooms to be ready for the cocktails they knew would be served from six-thirty.

Kay was also excited about the evening, as all the rangers and trackers who worked with Ed were allowed to join in. She suspected that Ed's reasoning behind their invitation was to ensure that after a few drinks none of the guests wandered out of the boma to the lavatories, or back to the lodge without porters accompanying them with torches.

Ed always made a rule that at least two or more rangers and trackers would be present at the alfresco evenings. He also tried to attend, unless he was required to entertain important guests at the main lodge.

Kay was the first to arrive and check that everything was in order for the evening's entertainment. It was the highlight of the guests' visit. Presentation was paramount, so she first checked the food section which was set out on long tables. The chef had made tasty morsels of prawns, langoustine and mussels, placing them on forks that were positioned in a row ready for the visitors to sample. Then there were the steel dishes on a row on hot trays consisting of beef, sausages, game, potatoes, phuthu, an African dish made of maize. An onion and tomato sauce had been added to the phuthu to moisten the dryness of the dish. It was something different and a talking point with the guests. Kay liked it and had only tried it for the first time when she had started working at the camp.

She sensed it was going to be a fun evening. She always enjoyed outdoor parties and the added sense of security by holding the party in a fenced off space. Her guests were a jolly lot, she thought smiling. They would enjoy this evening eating under the stars. Kay stepped into the boma and gazed around at the many lanterns and fairy lights hanging from trees lighting the area. The large fire in the middle of the area was in full blaze with the tables and chairs arranged neatly around it. Kay gazed at the enchanting scene in front of her. One of the staff smiled and Kay tried to imagine how long it must have taken to create this vision.

The full moon added a magical aura to the setting, Kay thought, just as a lion roared somewhere in the distance. She spotted a few porters ready to accompany guests and staff between the boma and the lodge and was glad that Ed never scrimped on security.

Frank arrived with Tom, who seemed to have shrunk since his time in the hospital. 'Good to see you, Tom,' Kay said, wondering if Frank was right about Tom losing his nerve and not wishing to assist with the tracking of poachers any more. She could not blame him and doubted she would want to go out again after being shot and nearly dying.

'Hi there, what's your poison?' Frank asked Kay and Tom, just as Alice arrived.

'I'll have a lager,' Tom replied.

'White wine for me please,' Kay said to the barman.

'Same for me please,' Alice said.

The four of them sat around the log fire waiting for the guest.

'This is the best time of the day,' Tom said raising his glass. 'Cheers.'

The sound of excited chatter reached them as the guests arrived and spotted the three chefs standing proudly behind their elegant display of food on the long tables. The staff in their pristine black and white uniforms waited to attend to their every whim.

'Gee whiz, just get a look at this, guys. Have you ever seen anything like it in your life?' Sheena said, looking around in awe. 'It's like fairyland. Just look at that full moon, Kay. Did you also order that to complete the perfect picture?'

Kay smiled, enjoying the banter and comradery that was going on between everyone, as the staff poured drinks and began joining in.

'Hi everyone, we made it,' Sally Pope shouted above the noise, entering the boma, closely followed by Ed, with one of the guests from the main lodge, clinging to his arm, yet again. Kay couldn't imagie how he managed to cope with these silly women when they acted in such a way.

'Let's get the party started now the boss has arrived with his entourage,' Frank said in a sarcastic tone, which did not go unnoticed by Ed, Kay noticed. She watched him glare at Frank.

'There's no need for that talk. You're all here to enjoy the evening and let your hair down,' Tom said to Frank, before nodding a greeting to Ed.

'Only joking, mate,' Frank thumped Tom on his back. 'Sorry, hope the shoulder's not still sore?' Frank added as Tom winced.

'Still a bit tender thanks,' Tom replied, moving closer to Kay, when Frank walked off to the bar.

'That sod never knows when to leave well alone,' he said through gritted teeth. 'He's got an annoying habit of having a go at Ed whenever the opportunity presents itself. I reckon he's after his job. Plain jealousy, that's what it is.'

'What are you two plotting?' Alice asked with a laugh.

Before Kay could answer, she and Alice were surrounded by her group of guests. Tom greeted them politely then went over to chat to Ed and the people he was with.

Colin and Richard praised Kay to Alice. 'She's a wonderful ranger,' Richard said, as Colin then went on to regale Alice with all that had happened that day.

Thrilled by their enthusiasm, Kay realised it was heightened by the alcohol they had consumed, as the stories had become crazily exaggerated, making Kay laugh more than she remembered doing for a very long time. Tears ran down her cheeks from laughing so much. She rummaged around for a tissue in her jeans pocket, when a hand from behind passed a clean cotton hankie over her shoulder. Looking around in surprise, she gazed into a pair of warm grey eyes.

'Why, Ed, thanks so much,' Kay said.

'You're welcome,' he said, smiling. 'I couldn't help overhearing some of the remarks about you're drives today. Well done. You sure made a hit with this lot,' Ed said eyeing her guests.

Kay's stomach contracted into a knot of pleasure.

'This kid needs a raise in salary, Ed,' Brian roared above the noise, winking cheekily at Kay. Everyone laughed, raising their glasses to her.

Kay had never felt so happy and appreciated. Her delight was compounded by Ed hearing all their wonderful praise.

She was sure Ed would be pleased that the evening was a huge success. She scanned the room watching everyone sitting around chatting and enjoying the huge fire in the middle of the circle in the boma.

Her thoughts were interrupted when a group of dancers in brightly coloured clothes ran into the middle of the circle chanting in their native song. The guests clapped in excitement. The dancers took guests by the hand and pulled each of them up to follow in crocodile file singing and dancing around the fire. After a bit of persuasion even Ed joined in. He stepped in behind Kay placing his big hands around her tiny waist, much to her embarrassment but delight. Kay noticed Sally chatting to Ed's guest as he danced.

Sally, Kay noticed, was very chatty to one of the senior lodge guards which surprised her. Sally wasn't one to fraternise with the staff. Maybe the drinks had made her friendlier, Kay pondered.

The staff began taking all the pots and pans back to the kitchen and when the dancing finished everyone was amazed to see the boma cleared of food and crockery. Only the bar remained.

Frank made a point of putting his arm around Kay, offering to see her safely to her room. Saying goodnight to all the visitors, Kay realised there was no getting out of it. She was tired and needed to leave and Frank seemed to be the only one also ready to go. Sally was still chatting to the guard as Kay turned to leave.

'Is something the matter?' Ed asked her as she passed them on the way to the exit.

'No, just my battery seems to have rundown,' she replied as the blush rose into her cheeks. She hoped he wouldn't notice in the candlelight. 'Goodnight, enjoy the rest of the evening,' she said following Frank to the exit. She glanced back at Ed noticing he was watching them with a strange expression on his face, unsure what he could be thinking.

Arriving at the staff quarters, Kay thanked Frank for walking with her, having only accepted knowing he was expected back to the boma to drive to the other lodge with Ed, to welcome a delegation of Chinese visitors on the drive early the following morning.

The guard led the way to the staff rooms. He waited to see Frank back to the boma.

'It's okay, I have my firearm with me,' Frank told the porter. 'I can see myself back. You see to the other guests in case they need you to light their way.'

The guard turned and left them, but not before Kay saw a look of concern cross his face. She wished him goodnight, as she turned and unlocked her door, moving away from Frank.

'Now don't think you're getting away with it that easily,' Frank slurred, as he pulled Kay into a bear hug and forced her lips apart with a violent kiss.

'Frank, please, you're hurting me,' she cried, her voice muffled by his mouth as she tried to push in away.

'I see how you look at the boss with those big hungry eyes. Why don't you look at me like that? Here's a taste of what I could give you, if only you'd give me a chance.' With that, he grabbed one of her breasts and kissed her as he held her in a vice like grip. She couldn't do anything about it he was so strong, even as she kicked him, it had no effect. Then from out of nowhere a torch light shone on them.

'Mr Frank, boss says he's ready to leave. Is everything alright?' Zumbe said.

'Bloody Ed,' Frank said, letting go of her.

Furious and a bit shaken, Kay tottered sideways against the pillar of the cottage. Frank marched off in the direction of the cars, closely followed by Zumbe, but not before Kay's rescuer gave her a worried look.

Kay hurriedly stepped into her room, locking the door. She felt violated and was reeling from the shock of Frank's behaviour. She thought about his flirtatious ways, but never imagined that his bantering could turn into something so unsavoury. Kay determined not to be left alone with him in future. Still trembling, she stripped off her clothes and showered, letting the hot water beat down on her skin to remove the bruising in her arms where he had held her tightly. Her lips were slightly swollen. What worried her the most, was, what would have happened if Ed hadn't sent Zumbe to call Frank?

Chapter Nine

Kay got into bed wondering if she had been wrong thinking she could live here with these men. It had always been a man's world and maybe she should focus more on the reality of her situation, rather than what she wanted to achieve. Suddenly the tears began sliding down her face wetting her pillow. She missed her grandmother but knew that to tell her would only mean that she would insist Kay return home to Durban. It would be easier to cope with having lost her boyfriend than having to deal with the likes of Frank and Ed, she decided. Her thoughts of quitting the job and going home filled her head as she drifted off to sleep.

The following morning, Kay's resolve had strengthened. She arrived at the lounge where Ed was already having coffee, happy not to find Frank there instead of him. Recalling Ed's meeting with the important guests he had been supposed to meet that morning, she could not understand why he hadn't left.

'Good morning, Kay,' Ed said motioning for her to take a seat next to him. 'I hope you don't mind me asking, but is there anything going on with you and Frank?'

'What do you mean?' she asked, annoyed by the question.

'I was surprised to hear Zumbe telling the barman, he was worried when he saw you and Frank kissing on your doorstep last night.'

'That's absolute rubbish. You should make sure of your facts before making vile accusations. If you must know, Frank was very drunk and forced himself on me. It was only thanks to you sending Zumbe to call him that he let me go,' Kay snapped.

He opened his mouth to speak when some of her group arrived in the lounge and called out to her. It was their last morning at camp, so she gathered herself and forced a smile.

'We're all ready,' Alan said in his lovely Irish accent.

She was aware of Ed walking away but ignored him. 'You look tired this morning. You work hard and need a day off to relax a bit. How about you take us out on a shorter drive this morning, after your late night looking after us all?' Alan suggested.

Ed turned back to the group. 'Actually, I have a better idea,' Ed said. 'I'll drive. Kay can come with us and relax. That way I can also give her a few tips as we go. How about it?' Ed said, giving Kay a warm encouraging smile.

He seemed to be apologising to her, but Kay was still stung by his assumption that she had kissed Frank by choice. 'I thought you had a group of guests from the main lodge to drive today,' she retorted, irritated.

'No, they cancelled. Everyone's hungover this morning, so I'm not needed.'

'Okay, fine,' she relented. 'At least it's your responsibility to find Sheena her cheetah.'

He smiled. 'Good. And if we have time I'll take you all to see the cheetah orphanage where they are raising abandoned young, whose mothers have been killed. There's a set of three cubs whose mother was bitten by a snake. The poor little chaps were found trying to feed off her as she died. The tracker tried to save her, but he discovered her too late. They also have a male cheetah who's recovering from an injury. He won't be able to hunt again so they'll use him for breeding when one of the female orphans is old enough.'

'That sounds great, Ed,' boomed Colin. 'Thank you.' He turned his attention to Kay. 'Have you seen the orphan sanctuary, Kay?'

'No, I haven't,' she said honestly. 'It is something I planned to do on my day off, so I'm delighted that Ed's taking us there. Right, if you all have your coffee and biscuits, we can make an early start. If that is okay with you, Ed?'

Kay felt her spirits lift as they drove out of the camp and the guests' enthusiastic chatter filled the air. They soon discovered a herd of buffalo making their way down to the dam. In the distance a lone bull elephant was ambling towards the camp, probably to the waterhole. It was a balmy morning with a light breeze. Everyone quietened as they took in the scenery, each lost in their own thoughts.

Sitting beside Ed, Kay started to relax. He was a different man when he was driving through the bush. She couldn't stop thinking how much happier he seemed, less abrasive towards her. As she stared at his profile, he suddenly turned his head and looked at her. She couldn't see his eyes through his dark glasses, but the smile he gave her make her heart race.

It took over an hour to reach the cheetah sanctuary. The guests amused her and Ed, chatting and laughing as they tried to outdo each other spotting wildlife. They were lucky enough to pass zebra, kudu, impala, giraffe and elephants on the drive, which Kay knew was a huge bonus. Richard pointed out the most birds and when they congratulated him, he admitted that it was a hobby of his, so was something he was used to doing.

The sun beat down on them and Kay almost felt as if she was one of the guests on holiday. It was pleasant not having to concentrate at all times or be the one in charge of the guests. She noticed Ed's tanned muscled arms as he changed gears and the sight sent shivers of delight down her back. She couldn't help imagining how it might feel to be held by them. Lost in her own world, it was only hearing her name being called that she became aware of Cherry asking her a question.

'Sorry, Cherry, I missed that?' she said.

'You looked so far away and had such a happy smile on your face as you looked at Ed, just then,' the woman said. 'I was wondering if you enjoyed being driven like the rest of us?'

'I doubt very much that I'd be the cause of Kay's happy look,' Ed laughed.

Kay felt herself blush and quickly changed the subject,

grateful to notice a large kudu male with the most remarkable horns she had ever seen. 'Look over there,' she said, clearing her throat as she pointed at the magnificent animal. 'Quickly, take some pictures before he disappears into the bush.'

'Be quick, guys. This chap is very shy, and we seldom get such a good viewing. Well done to Kay for spotting him,' Ed added as he brought the vehicle to a sudden halt.

When everyone had taken enough photos, the kudu turned and moved into the bush where he was immediately camouflaged by the foliage.

'Well did you ever,' Monica asked in awe. 'He looked so proud standing there letting us take his picture, just like a professional. That was utterly amazing.'

They motored on to the sanctuary just a few miles away. It was better than any of the guests, including Kay, thought it would be. The male cheetah was in an enclosure of his own and growled at the visitors, his teeth bared as he glared at the faces peering at him through the wire fence. The attendants allowed them into the area two at a time, where the young cubs were playing, so that they could pat them and have photos taken with them.

Everyone agreed it was the highlight of their visit so far. They were exuberant in their thanks to Ed for suggesting it and breaking away from protocol to leave the camp and drive all the way to the sanctuary.

Only he could have organised such an unplanned treat, Kay realised.

On the return journey, everyone was in their element as

they traversed the river which led back to camp, seeing several of the hippo with their young, and a large herd of elephant with calfs and teenagers who tried to hide behind their mothers.

Ed brought the people carrier to a sudden halt when he spotted a large buffalo bull about to cross the path they were on. Kay heard the gasps as the guests spotted the herd following on behind him as they moved towards the river before crossing to the other side.

'There must be at least fifty of them,' Richard said quietly.

'Wow, was that a sight for sore eyes,' Brian said. 'Never seen so many of those critters at once. If we hadn't gone to the sanctuary, Ed, we'd have missed them.'

'As it's our last drive this afternoon, could you and Kay take us out? We have had such a wonderful time and you've both been such stars, it would be great to have the opportunity of spending the rest of the day with you both,' Alan asked, to a resounding plea from the rest of the guests.

'I thought you guys were leaving after lunch today?' Kay said, confused.

'Our wives persuaded us to leave early tomorrow morning instead,' Colin said. 'We've arranged to have breakfast in Hazy View. So, that means we get to have this afternoon and evening staying over. I checked it out with Alice just to make sure we could keep our rooms for tonight, and she told me that it's a day off tomorrow with no new guests arriving. Said she would let you know, Ed,' he added with a questioning look on his face.

Kay looked at Ed and saw his surprise turn to delight.

'I don't see why not,' he said. 'If Kay is happy for me to join her guests, especially as it would get me out of entertaining a VIP at our main lodge,' he added lowering his voice. 'I can ask Frank to do the honours for me. So yes, I'd be happy to be a part of your last drive. Maybe we can find that elusive leopard?' Ed laughed.

They returned to camp just in time to have a quick wash and drinks before lunch. That over, everyone went for a sleep and arranged to meet at three that afternoon for tea.

Just as Kay was leaving, Ed called her over. 'I really do apologise for what I said this morning. I was out of order about last night.'

'That's okay,' she said, relieved that he was so contrite and did believe she had nothing to do with Frank kissing her.

He stared down at his feet thoughtfully before looking at her and saying, 'I was jealous if you must know. It's not a feeling I've experienced much before. Well, not until Zumbe told me he had witnessed you kissing.'

Kay wanted to trust him and felt that she could. 'I was really scared when Frank attacked me like that,' she said. 'He was roaring drunk and is physically much stronger than me. I was incredibly relieved that you sent Zumbe to call him, I really hate to think what would have happened, if…' She saw Ed's face redden. He looked furious and she was unsure whether to continue with what she was saying.

'Frank never did arrive for the lift, so we went without him,' he said quietly, his eyes narrowed. 'I'm sorry to say this now, but I thought you and he had spent the night together.'

'Is that what you really think of me?' she asked, furious once again.

'No, of course not,' he shook his head. 'I was being a jealous idiot. I think he must have spent the night in one of the vacant staff rooms. He's done that before now. Seems to me I should keep an eye on him. If he ever tries another trick like that on you again, tell me immediately. Do you understand?'

'Anything the matter, Ed?' Sheena asked when she reached the vehicle to collect her sun tan lotion from the pocket of her seat.

'No, everything's just fine,' Ed told her, moving slightly away from Kay and smiling.

'Good, Monica and I are off for a swim. You coming, Kay?' she asked, staring at Kay inquisitively.

Kay realised Sheena was concerned for her. Kay smiled at her trying to reassure her. 'Not this time, I'm heading for a sleep after our party last night. Thanks for the invitation though,' Kay said.

Ed sighed. 'And I have some work to do and people to speak to,' he added pointedly. 'See you all later.' Giving Kay's shoulder a gentle squeeze, he left and headed for his office.

They set off into the bush after tea at three-thirty that afternoon. The entire group were excited and prepared for another adventure. Kay liked that none of them ever knew what to expect and that there was never a dull moment out on the drives. She discovered that Ed had organised his own tracker, Tsepho, to join them and give Ben the afternoon off.

It was common knowledge amongst the staff and guests that there was no one to touch Ed and Tsepho when it came to finding elusive beasts and Kay was as delighted as the rest of the group.

Half an hour into the drive Tsepho asked Ed to stop and jumped out of his tracker's seat, immediately studying the ground. He pointed out a set of leopard tracks, and indicated the direction the animal had taken before jumping back onto his seat. Ed drove on, slowly coming across footprints in the sandy soil. The tracker raised his hand in a command to stop and pointed upwards. Almost directly above them in an acacia tortillas tree sat a female leopard. There was an echo of gasps from the guests and Kay. Ed whispered that she had a cub with her and they all noticed the mother and cub were feeding on a small duiker she had managed to carry up the tree and secure it in the fork of the branches.

'Aren't they just darling?' Monica whispered.

'She's the most relaxed leopard in the area,' Ed explained quietly.

'Let's stay with her for a while, please, Ed?' Colin pleaded, his voice barely above a whisper. 'This is too amazing. Well done, man, what a coup.'

They watched for the next half hour, taking videos and photos with telephoto lenses. Just as they were about to leave three jackals appeared from the bush, followed by four huge vultures who sat on the high branches of a nearby tree hoping to get some titbits before the remains fell to the jackals, who sat under the tree staring up at the leopards.

'How did they know she was up there?' Brian asked.

'It's the smell of blood from the meat,' Kay told him, wanting to prove to her boss that she knew.

'But it's up in the tree, surely they can't get to it can they?' Sheena questioned.

'They're just hoping she drops her kill, so they're prepared to sit and wait. It happens sometimes when the cats feed, they dislodge their kill and it falls, and that's why the wild dogs, hyenas and jackals sit patiently waiting. If it doesn't drop, then it'll be the vultures' turn to get lucky,' Kay explained.

'You're all in for a big surprise tonight, folks,' Ed shouted as soon as they had driven far enough away from the leopards. 'Instead of returning to camp, I'll be driving to a new venue, so no stopping for sundowners I'm afraid. We have an appointment to keep and we're still miles away. So, if you don't mind, I'm going to put my foot down and only stop if the sighting is exceptional.'

'Aww, I really enjoy our sundowners,' Joan moaned. 'I don't think you can see a sunset anywhere else like the brilliance of the red and golden one out in the bush.'

'Shush, woman, it must be something good, or Ed wouldn't miss his sundowner for anything.' Brian scowled at his wife.

Almost an hour later, the sky was black, with the only light coming from the moon and the vehicle's headlights. Kay noticed that they had arrived at an airfield. Her excitement grew when Ed slowed down and drove into a clearing. The anticipation of the group was electric. Kay could tell Ed was treating them to something special when they neared gigantic trees filled with hanging lanterns sparkling in the lowering light. Long tables had been set up, each laden with pots of food and behind them chefs and waitresses waiting. They spotted the guests and began clapping. Kay could not believe her eyes.

Ed parked the people carrier and everyone jumped off.

'This looks just like fairyland,' Cherry gasped.

'What a way to spend our last night in the bush,' Alan said slapping Ed on his back. 'Just imagine the preparation it must have taken to organise this amazing venue. Ed man, this is the best!'

'I need the ladies desperately,' Sheena said.

'If you follow those lights in the paper bags,' one of the waitresses said, 'you'll see the vanity pod, with towels and creams all ready for you ladies.'

Colin asked his wife if she wanted him to accompany her there, as it was so dark in the little cluster of trees and bushes.

'Please come with us, in case a wild animal is lurking,' Sheena laughed nervously.

'I wouldn't worry too much, not with the guards, our tracker, Kay and Ed. As rangers, they all carry guns, don't forget, so you can rest assured they'll be on the lookout for any predators. Hurry up then, ladies, I need a beer.'

Sensing Colin liked the idea of being bodyguard for a short while, Kay let him lead the women along the candle-lit path. The women followed in single file, chatting in hushed voices as they went. Arriving at, and going into the little pod, they were impressed to see candles and flowers, plus hand wash and creams ready and waiting.

'What luxury, just like in the lodges,' Monica whispered as they took it in turns to use the facilities.

Kay watched from a distance as Colin waited outside, the frown he had on his face disappearing when the security guard arrived to stand and chat with him.

When everyone was seated, and had their preferred wine or beer, Alan announced that he wanted to give a toast.

'To all the staff and management for the best care and attention they could have given us, and especially to Kay, Ben and Tsepho, and tonight, Ed.'

Everyone clapped.

'Thanks very much,' Ed said. 'Now go and help yourselves to the buffet and drinks.'

Kay watched Ed laughing and chatting to his guests, catching her eye on occasion and giving her secretive smiles. She could see he was more relaxed with her than he had been Was it because she had opened up to him about Frank?

Unable to forget her role as ranger, Kay kept her eyes open for any predators, despite Ed arranging for the staff to stand at the perimeters with guns at the ready. Ed came over to see her and sat down in a recently vacated seat next to her. As he leant over towards her, she felt him put his arm around the back of her chair, casually letting his hand touch her on the shoulder. She shivered at his touch.

'Are you cold?' Ed whispered in her ear. She could

feel his hot breath on her skin, and her stomach clench with excitement. She nestled closer to him, feeling relaxed after a couple of glasses of wine, enjoying the feeling as his fingers traced a line across her arm and ended up holding her hand under the table briefly. It was over in a moment as then Ed pulled back and turned away from her. Had she imagined the whole incident she wondered as he turned his back to her and chatted to the guests.

Sheena called her name from across the table. 'This is the most magical evening and one none of us will ever forget,' she said raising her glass to Kay. 'You are so lucky to be living in this idyllic piece of paradise, Kay. Not to mention having the gorgeous Ed in attendance.' She lowered her voice. 'You should snap him up before one of those girls I've seen hanging all over him does. Food for thought, but I think you'd make a fabulous couple.' She raised an eyebrow and smiled.

Richard started talking to Sheena, much to Kay's relief. She would be so embarrassed if Ed had overheard Sheena's comments. Kay's thoughts turned to her ex Harry and how different the two men were. How could she be attracted to two men who were poles apart in looks and temperament? She was lost in thought about what Sheena had said when Ed turned back to her.

'A kiss for your thoughts,' he laughed at her.

'Huh? You wouldn't dare,' she giggled, shocked by his suggestion.

With that, Ed pulled her towards him and gave her a firm

kiss on her lips, much to the delight of the cheering guests. Kay blushed furiously, as the staff grinned from ear to ear at the boss and his out of character behaviour.

Sheena was the first to clap and mouth, 'I told you so.'

'Don't ever dare me, young lady, it's the one thing I always react to,' Ed said in a voice that all could hear. 'Now, what were you thinking about before I interrupted you?' he asked.

'How irritating you are,' Kay joked, staring into his smiling grey eyes.

'Really? Well at least you were thinking about me.'

Before he could add anything further, the staff arrived dressed in their native costumes and proceeded to dance and sing for the visitors.

Zumbe left the group of dancers and going over to Ed, he put his hand on his shoulder.

'Come, do the war dance with us,' he shouted over all the noise.

Ed immediately got up, as if he had been waiting for that moment. He followed Zumbe back to the other dancers, as they all started the yodelling sound of native warriors. Ed joined in, high-kicking one leg and then the other in time to Zumbe's steps. The guests sat enraptured by the wonderful display.

Kay couldn't hide her amazement at his antics and clapped along with the others in time to the singing.

After the dancing finished, they all agreed it was a superb evening and one they would remember long after they got home. Ed seemed happier than he had since her arrival at the lodge, Kay thought, as he told them all that it was time to pack up.

Back at the lodge, tired, but happy, Kay smiled as the guests hugged first her and then Ed, thanking them again for their perfect day. They departed to their respective rooms leaving Ed and Kay alone in the lounge.

'How about a night cap, Kay?'

'If you're having one, then I'd love an Amarula please,' Kay replied, stifling a yawn as she followed Ed to the bar. She sat on one of the cream high stools, watching as he poured their drinks. Coming back to the other side of the bar he sat next to her and handed her the Amarula in a small silver goblet. His hand grazed hers and she felt an electric current course through her skin.

They looked at each other, surprised. His grey eyes held her gaze. Her heart pounded against her ribcage, as his hand moved across and taking the large clip holding her hair in a ponytail, he undid it, watching as her hair cascaded like a sheet of silk on to her shoulders. Ed ran his fingers through the strands as he looked deeper into her eyes. She was mesmerised by obvious longing, her breathing laboured, willing him to kiss her.

'I've waited for this moment since I first set eyes on you,' he said softly.

Encouraged by his honesty and tenderness, she whispered, 'So have I. I never imagined you felt the same way.'

'When I thought you were attracted to Frank, it tore me

apart. I don't know what you've done to me. I vowed never to get involved with a member of staff and then you came along.'

They both looked up as the barman returned to the bar and began collecting glasses.

'I can't allow them see me breaking all my own rules,' Ed whispered. 'Let's get out of here. I'll see you back to your room, if that's okay?'

Kay nodded and then finishing her drink she took his hand. He led her out of the lodge, unaware of eyes watching them from the staff kitchen.

Ed waved the night porter away as he made his way towards them with a torch, signalling that he was not needed. As they moved away from the light of the surrounding rooms, Ed put his arm around Kay's shoulders. They reached her bedroom door and Ed pulled her into his arms kissing her with a passion that took her breath away.

Eventually, he moved back breaking the spell. 'I want you so much,' he whispered.

'And me, you,' Kay admitted.

He looked nervous for a moment and then said, 'To hell with the rules. Come home with me?'

'What, now?' She hoped he meant what she was thinking. He did.

'Yes. Pack a few things, toothbrush and clothes for tomorrow and we can go to my private lodge. We won't be disturbed there.'

It took her less than a second to agree. Her head spinning, Kay unlocked her bedroom door and went inside, hurriedly gathering a few things together. Ed waited silently, looking at the framed photos she had placed on a small round table.

'Are you sure you want to do this?' she asked halfway through packing her bag. 'After all, it's you who made the rules. What will people think if I'm seen going to your cottage and staying the night?'

'They can think what they like,' he said. 'If anyone does see us they'll know that I'm serious about you. After all, this isn't something I've done before. It's up to you. If you're happy to come with me…' Ed took her in his arms again. Kay wasn't sure if he was trying to persuade her to go with him, he did not have to, she was already happy to spend the night with him.

He kissed her more gently this time, as she groaned while returning his kisses with a passion she had never felt before, for any man. She melted into him.

'Come, let me take that bag and let's get out of here,' Ed said, picking up her holdall and opening the door with his free hand.

Kay locked the door behind her, before taking his outstretched hand and following Ed along the path to the garages where his pickup was parked. As they reached the kitchen block, someone came out of the dark towards them. Kay gasped and instinctively moved closer to Ed.

They fell silent, waiting to see who was about to appear. Ed put his arms around her and held her tightly.

'Frank?' Ed said in a relieved voice, as he came into the light.

'You're a hypocritical bastard,' Frank yelled, glaring at Ed. 'You give me a bollocking for kissing her and now you're taking her home with you?'

'This is nothing like your mauling of Kay last night,' Ed argued. 'And who the hell do you think you're talking to?' he added, furious. 'Come on, Kay, let's get away from this idiot. He's had a little too much to drink, by the look of things.' He walked past Frank holding Kay's hand, her overnight bag slung over his shoulder.

Frank grabbed Kay's other hand jarring her arm. She tried to tug it away from his grip. 'You're a prick tease, that's what you are.' He narrowed his eyes and glared at Ed. 'Think she fancies you, Ed, the big boss? Well let me tell you she'll dump you just like she did me. Collecting heads for her belt she is. It'll be the rangers next,' Frank shouted as spittle flew from his lips in rage.

'Let go of her, now,' Ed said, his nose almost touching Frank's and his voice so low and threatening even Kay was taken aback.

Frank released his hold on her. Shocked, Kay tried to swallow the tears of embarrassment and anger threatening to escape. She took her hand from Ed's and turned to Frank, slapping him hard across his face.

He raised his arm, balling his fist, about to hit her, but before she knew what was happening, Ed pushed her aside and grabbed Frank in a vice like grip.

'Don't even think about it,' Ed hissed through gritted teeth. 'You ever hit her, or any member of my staff, and you're out of here, do you understand me?' Frank's eyes widened, he seemed confused.

Ed let go of him. 'What the hell's happened to you, Frank? I heard how you tried to force yourself on Kay when you walked her back to her room. What would you have done if I hadn't sent a member of staff to find you?' Ed asked, shaking his head.

'I don't know,' Frank slurred. 'Leave me alone.' He sneered at them both before turning and staggering back the way he had come.

Kay let the tears fall and Ed hugged her tightly. She sobbed against his chest, hearing his rapid heartbeat and realising how angry he was at the unjustified attack.

'Hey, it's fine now,' Ed soothed. 'I'll make sure he's never alone with you again.' As she looked up at him, he wiped her tears away with his thumb. 'In all the years I've known him, I've never seen Frank in such a white-hot rage.' She only realised Ed had dropped her bag when he bent to pick it up. 'Come on,' he said, still holding her hand. 'I think there's more going on with him than meets the eye. I've had an uneasy feeling about his mood swings for a while. Either he's sickening for something, or there's something worrying him,' Ed said thoughtfully. 'Not that there's any excuse for his behaviour towards you.'

Kay stopped walking. Ed turned around, surprised.

'I don't know if we should be doing this, Ed,' she said. 'I feel nervous now, with Frank having seen us together. There's no knowing what he will do to cause you trouble. He's spoilt our evening now, anyway. Why don't I go back to my room and you go home? It's already very late.'

'If that's what you want, then of course that's fine,' he said. 'But do you really want that fool's behaviour to come between us?' Ed asked, the concern in his voice obvious as he waited for her answer.

'No, I haven't changed my mind. It's just that I am now worried that you'll have to deal with all sorts of problems tomorrow if Frank tells tales to the other staff about us.'

'Exactly,' he agreed.

Kay felt puzzled by his remark and raised her eyebrows in question.

'That's tomorrow, and if he does say something I'll deal with it then. Tonight, I want to be with you and if you're still happy to come home with me, then there's nothing I'd like more.'

Despite Ed's smiles in her direction, Kay was aware that he was still fuming as they drove away from the lodge. His hands gripped the steering wheel so tight his knuckles were white. She let out a long sigh to release some of the tension in her body that had built up over the altercation with Frank.

'I wanted to share with you that I don't made a habit of doing this,' Ed said in a serious voice.

'Even if you had, Ed, it really is none of my business who you entertain, or where,' she said. 'Thanks for telling me though, I'm honoured to be the first woman to visit your private domain,' she teased, smiling when he glanced at her to try and gauge if she was joking or not. 'Alice told me, that not many people even know you have your own place. You keep your private life to yourself and I like that.'

'When we all work so closely, I think it's good to keep

some things to yourself,' he said, squinting at the road ahead.

Kay felt comforted that he was always careful to look out for the wildlife. Ed's love and protection of the animals living on the land he looked after was a huge part of what she loved about him. 'How long have you lived down in this amazing valley?' she asked as he drove further away from the lodge. 'Doesn't it worry you to be alone out here when there are so many predators?' Kay questioned as they made their way into a clearing and she saw the outline of a rustic building.

He was so focused on where he was going, he didn't answer for a moment. 'Here we are,' he said. 'My humble abode.'

'If you didn't know it was here, I don't reckon too many people would find it,' she said.

'Good. It's not even in the reserve. The original owners used it as their getaway cottage,' Ed announced as he came to a halt next to the covered veranda of the cottage.

'You've no security, by the look of things,' she said. 'Only your firearms and a radio. Do you even get an internet signal down here?'

'No, thankfully,' he smiled, helping her out of the pickup and leading her to the front door.

Kay walked inside. There were no lights in Ed's cottage. The only glimmer came from the gas lamps hanging from the rafters. Kay couldn't believe her eyes as she looked around at his fascinating home. Brightly coloured cushions and throws make a kaleidoscope of colour in the lounge. The huge veranda looked well used, with old couches and pine tables on which stood two iron oil lamps. On a dresser were a group of candles. Ed explained that the skins on the stone floors were from animals that had been culled by the lodge. 'I never allow anyone to kill a healthy animal. I believe we're here to protect then, not cause them pain or suffering.'

Kay nodded her agreement. She was glad he felt the same way she did about the animals they worked near to each day.

Once all the lamps and candles were lit, and she had been shown around, Ed pulled Kay into his arms and kissed her. She relaxed against him, their tongues exploring each other's mouths. Her heart rate soared, and his passion made her body quiver with excitement.

As suddenly as he started, Ed stopped kissing her. She was about to complain, when he said, 'Damn, I haven't got any protection. We can't do this.'

Relieved, Kay said, 'It's fine, I'm on the pill.'

Smiling at her, he picked her up, carrying her to his bedroom. Kay had never been carried by a man before and felt as light as a feather in this wonderful man's arms, as he gently lay her down on the bed. Her body trembled in anticipation of what it would be like to have another man other than Harry make love to her. She realised she was about to find out.

Gently laying her on the bed, he proceeded to pull her shirt over her head. Then unbuttoning her jeans, pulled them down and threw them onto the floor. Expertly undoing her bra, he cupped her breasts in his large hands. She felt the rough calluses as Ed caressed her skin. Shocks of delight permeated her as he took each nipple in turn into his mouth and sucked hard, continuing down her body as he explored it with his kisses and gentle touch.

'I want you,' she murmured as her body squirmed upwards towards his. She didn't care if he thought her forward.

'You're so much more beautiful than I could ever have imagined,' Ed said tearing off his clothes. Naked, he stood looking down at her.

She felt no embarrassment as she studied his bronzed body. 'I promise I won't hurt you, Kay.'

With one swift movement, Ed lowered himself onto her, parting her legs and after a moment's hesitation when he looked at her checking one last time that she was happy for him to do so, he entered her.

Kay sighed, moving slowly at first as he held her hips, thrusting upward into her. Then when she was just about to scream with pleasure, he flipped her over so that she was on top of him.

'Now you're in charge,' he said, in a teasing voice, as she rained kisses on his face, neck and then slowly moving downwards to his chest, all the time moving on top of him. She moaned with pleasure as they moved in unison melting into the moment of ecstasy, as they climaxed together.

'You are incredible,' Ed said, slightly breathless. 'Now that I've found you, I have no intention of letting you go,' he added gathering her into his arms and covering their naked bodies with a sheet.

The last thing Kay membered before falling into an exhausted sleep, was Ed running his fingers through her hair, and kissing her neck.

Chapter Ten

Kay was woken the following morning by the chattering of a group of monkeys who were running across the roof of Ed's veranda. She slowly opened her eyes, realising she was not in her own room and momentarily couldn't place where she was. Recalling her blissful night with Ed, she turned her head and saw that she was alone. She heard sounds coming from a kitchen and the smell of coffee filled her nostrils. Kay stretched. The feeling of being alive sexually after the long months of abstinence was overwhelming. This handsome, virile man had opened her heart. He had made her feel sexy and attractive again.

She ran into the bathroom to take a shower. Towelling herself dry and wrapping herself in a white towelling robe that hung behind the door, Kay made her way to where she could hear Ed whistling a tune from the music they had danced to that night at the main lodge.

'Breakfast is ready, sleepy head,' came his cheerful voice as she joined him in the kitchen.

He was in just a pair of shorts, his tanned body, his hair still wet from his shower, curling at the nape of his neck. Her heart skipped a beat as she watched him setting eggs, bacon, sausage and tomatoes onto two plates. Toast sat in the silver toast rack.

'I'm impressed. Who taught you to be so efficient in the kitchen department?' Kay asked with a nervous giggle, as she pulled the bathrobe tighter around her, feeling a little shy in the light of day.

'My mother made my brothers and me have cooking lessons. She didn't think any woman would want to live with us, so it was a case of putting her mind at rest. Of course, we could all do a braai, and I can cook reasonably well, and enjoy doing so, especially this morning when I have a gorgeous girl to feed.' He placed her food in front of her. 'Now eat, before it gets cold. I need to get you back before the rest of the staff find out that you spent the night here with me.'

Stung by the thought he wanted to keep what had happened between them a secret, Kay glared at him.

'Don't look at me like that, Kay, I have no regrets. I just don't want you having a tough time from any of them.' He smiled and sat opposite her. 'I have no intention of this being a one-night stand, but I'm aware they will find it easier to have a go at you, rather than me. I'm just being cautious.'

They ate in silence, the noise of the Egyptian geese interrupting the peace of the dawn with their loud calls to each other.

Once breakfast was finished, Kay cleared the table as Ed stacked the dishes in the sink ready for when the cleaners arrived.

'You go and get dressed while I finish up here,' Ed told her.

'All right. I won't be long,' Kay replied as she hurried towards the bedroom. It didn't take her long to dress and tie her hair into a ponytail. She picked up her overnight bag and turned to leave the room, when Ed knocked at the door before entering.

He pulled her into his arms in a sudden movement that left Kay's head spinning. Kissing her passionately, Kay clung to him her arms snaking up around his neck as she pushed herself into him.

'Stop, I can't stand it!' Kay groaned, pulling away. 'We must get to the lodge, or they'll all know I spent the night here,' Kay said, as she kissed him quickly. He pulled her shirt over her head and undid her bra, his head moving down her neck, over her firm breasts as his fingers played with the one nipple, his hot lips and tongue teasing the other one, Kay gave a gasp of pure pleasure and in a moment was naked and lying on the bed. She watched as Ed tore off his shorts and joined her. Their lovemaking was fierce with longing, and as they climaxed together he held her tightly and shouted, 'You're amazing, I can't get enough of you.'

Kay felt as if her heart would burst with happiness. He was a wonderful lover, one she had no intention of letting get away from her. She was falling in love with this man of so many different moods. Not sure she would ever be able to fathom the depth of his mind, she was just happy that they shared the same passion. For now, that was all that mattered to her.

She felt herself being lifted off the bed, as Ed picked her up in his strong arms and took her with him into the large shower room. Putting her down gently, he turned on the taps and picking up a bar of soap washed her with such tenderness as he rained kisses over her body, she tingled with delight.

They took turns rinsing the lather off their bodies. Once out of the shower, Ed grabbed two huge bath towels and wrapped one around her, before kissing her. They dried and hurriedly dressed and were ready to leave.

'I enjoyed myself with you,' she admitted, standing on tiptoe to give him a peck on his perfect mouth.

'Me too and I live in anticipation of your next visit,' Ed said, smiling at her as he walked towards the door. He picked up her little overnight bag, his rifle and binoculars and holding open the door of the people carrier waited for her to get in.

Kay gazed at him as he drove, aware that she had never felt happier. This was the life she felt totally at home in, especially with Ed by her side. If only she didn't have to return to Durban and her commitments there, she thought. Was it time to tell Ed that she would be leaving the lodge just as soon as her leave was due? She was about to discuss it with him when he braked hard giving her a shock.

'Sorry, look over there,' he said pointing to an old buffalo wandering towards them.

'I want you to remember that chap, Kay. He's not from this area, but occasionally passes through. He's a vicious bugger; about a year ago he killed one of our trackers. Gored him to death, and because our guy had gone on a walk about without telling anyone where he was going, nobody was with him. One of my rules is that no ranger or tracker goes into the bush alone, or without a radio and rifle and of course the binoculars.'

'I'm surprised he wasn't shot, if he killed a human?' Kay questioned.

'Well nobody actually saw it happen, but one of the other rangers noticed that bull earlier in the day, and said he thought he was trouble, and not one of ours. We've kept a wary eye on him since then, whenever he comes our way.'

Ed turned the vehicle and moved off towards the lodge, where he dropped Kay off at her room and went to his office.

Kay was changing into her work clothes, as she relived her time with Ed. She hugged herself with pleasure and smiled as her thoughts took flight until a knock on the door brought her back to reality.

'Kay, are you there? Can I come in?' Alice asked while giving the door a harder knock.

Kay opened the door with a flourish and a huge grin on her face. 'Come in. I've got something I'm dying to tell you, but you mustn't breathe a word to any of the other staff.'

'I came to check you were okay, because you didn't come back last night,' Alice laughed. 'But by your dazzling smile, I presume it must be something very special.'

Kay proceeded to tell her all about the night she had spent with Ed in his cottage down in the valley. 'He was just so divine and not at all like he is at work. I wish I could have stayed with him forever, he really did amaze me, Alice,' Kay said as she finished brushing her hair.

'Bloody hell, you can't be serious, going to the boss's house? He made the rule of no shenanigans with staff, and he's broken the golden rule himself. For goodness' sake, don't let any of the staff hear about it, or you'll have major problems,' Alice said, frowning. 'Right, we'd better get going, or the boss will have my guts for garters.'

'Yes, we're having some VIP guests in for lunch today. Who's going to be their ranger? Have you any idea, Alice?' Kay asked, as they left the room and walked towards the lodge.

Hearing a commotion coming from the direction of the kitchens, Alice sighed. 'Sounds like Chef has lost the plot again. He's had so many warnings from Ed to stop his nonsense,' Alice grumbled, just as Ed came out of the kitchen and noticed the girls.

'I need to have a word with all the rangers and trackers, in my office immediately after breakfast,' Ed said, giving Kay a secret smile as Alice peered into the kitchen area, before walking on.

Alice hurriedly contacted all the staff on her radio, advising them of the meeting.

A grim-faced Ed waited for the staff to finish organising chairs in a semicircle around his office. Kay and Alice grabbed a seat together near the desk, ready with notebook and pen. Tom and the trackers arranged themselves next to each other. Ed looked around the room at each one in turn.

'Where's Frank?' Ed asked Tom.

'Don't know. He hasn't been seen all morning,' Tom

said. 'Shall I get him on the radio?'

'No, leave him. It must be important if he's missing a meeting. He knows what it's about, so let's get on with it, shall we?' Ed glanced at his watch before opening his folder and scowling at whatever was inside.

'I want you all to know that the poachers have been at it again. Kruger Park has sent me a memo saying that they've been having more rhino slayings.' He shook his head. 'It's getting very serious. They've also killed one of the Kruger Park's top trackers.' Several of the staff whispered as others gasped at the news. 'He was on his way home and became suspicious when he saw new tracks across unauthorised land. So, he went to investigate. Looks like they found another mother who was in calf.' Kay could see Ed was trying to keep his anger from showing too much. 'The tracker managed to radio before he died,' Ed added. 'They found the rhino in a bad way. The vets are trying to save her, but her injury is devastating. I have photos here to show you.'

With that he held up a picture of the rhino whose horns had been hacked off. Another was of the vets having darted her, filling the wound with creams and a gauze dressing.

'The bullet that was supposed to kill her missed all the vital organs and merely stunned her. With a bit of luck, they'll save her and her unborn calf,' Ed explained as they passed the pictures around.

When Alice saw the picture, she started to heave, and quickly got up and ran out of the office.

'Go after her, Tom, and check she's alright,' Ed said. 'No need for her to come back, but you must, I need you here as soon as possible. Tell Alice to get herself a cuppa and wait until we finish,' Ed said as he looked back down at his folder.

'That's terrible,' Kay said, unable to keep the trembling out of her voice. 'Why hasn't anyone caught these vile men?'

'There's a large syndicate of them,' Ed said. 'The noose is closing in, though, and we'll get these bastards before long. A couple of black rhino have been spotted just outside our area and look as if they're heading this way. We all know they're more aggressive than the white rhino, so I don't want any of you getting too close to them – if you're fortunate enough to come across them.'

'What if we're with a group of visitors when we see them,' asked Ben.

Ed shrugged. 'Simply tell them about the animal, like you would any other. Point out the differences between the black and white rhinoceros.' Ed looked across to where Kay was sitting and gave her a smile, as if to say he was aware she knew this. 'Both have the grey keratin horns, which are the same material as hooves, fingernails and hair. The white rhino has a square lip and are larger animals than the black, and they are not so aggressive by nature. Tell people that sort of thing,' he said. 'They are always impressed to discover how heavy these animals are.' He stared at Ben. 'How heavy are they?'

Ben thought for a moment. 'I think they can weigh up to two thousand, seven hundred kilograms.'

'That's right,' Ed said. 'What else?'

'They can live up to fifty years, whereas the black rhino only lives between thirty to thirty-five years,' Ben said, thinking for a few seconds. Kay could tell he was enjoying impressing Ed with his knowledge. 'With both, the calves live with their mothers from between two and four years, before moving on and finding a mate.'

Kay noticed Ed take out a piece of paper from his pocket, read it and tear it up before dropping it onto a nearby bin. He looked at her and then when Ben stopped talking turned his attention back to him.

'That's right,' Ed said. 'Well done, you're building your knowledge and that's what I need to see from you all. Remember, if we seldom come across the black variety, then imagine how exciting it will be for the guests. Be ready to answer their questions. I need you all to remember the correct information,' Ed added with a grin.

Kay watched as Ed proceeded to speak in Shangaan for the sake of the trackers whose grasp of the English language was not so good.

'Just as a matter of interest,' asked one of the newer rangers, who Kay noticed was making notes. 'Is the black rhino also semi-aquatic and do they also digest their food during the day and be able to walk thirty kilometres an hour?'

'Yep that's right,' replied Ed. 'Right, that's all for now, guys. Off you go.'

Kay got up to leave with the others when Tom walked back into the office.

'How's Alice doing?' Ed asked.

'She's in the kitchen and the nurse has given her something to calm her stomach. Good thing she's not a ranger with her fragile constitution,' Tom said.

Kay felt sorry for Alice. She remembered only too well how devastated she had been to see what the poachers did to the animals, still was upset, she mused. Cruelty was not something you could get used to, she decided.

Ed and Tom passed her in the corridor. Both had serious expressions on their faces as they ran to the people carrier and sped away in a cloud of dust. She had an uneasy feeling in the pit of her stomach. She worried in case they came across the poachers. She went to find Alice and hoped that the vets would save the rhino and her unborn calf.

Alice was sitting on the veranda outside the kitchen as Kay approached and waved. Alice beckoned her over. When Kay reached her, she could see that her friend had indeed been crying. She gave Alice a hug, as her friend rose to greet her.

'I'm sorry you're so upset. Don't feel badly, we all feel the same. It's just none of us dare show any sign of weakness in front of Ed, or he'll have us off our jobs,' Kay confided.

'I know. To tell you the truth, Kay, I've seen Ed with his head in his hands many a time as he sits at his desk. I've often stopped from going into the office when that happens. Poor bloke must look so macho in front of the staff, but he has a soft heart and only wants to catch the people behind all the slaughter. I don't know what will happen if those awful people aren't caught,' Alice said with a sigh.

'I was worried about Ed and Tom driving off like that,' Kay said crossing her arms across her chest. 'My stomach went into a knot for the first time. Something seemed off.

Did you see Ben putting a note on Tom's desk just before the meeting started?' Kay added, raising her eyebrows in question.

'No, I didn't. Why is that strange anyway? I often see either Ben or one of the trackers giving messages to Ed. Never thought much about it before you mentioned it,' Alice said.

'It was the way Ed looked around to see if any of us had noticed,' Kay said, lowering her voice in case anyone was nearby. 'He immediately put it into his pocket. Then when Ben was telling us something, Ed surreptitiously withdrew it and had a quick glance before tearing it up and dropping it into the waste basket.'

'Really?'

'Yes. He called an end to the meeting and had a quiet word with Tom before they rushed off.'

Alice rolled her eyes heavenward and sat back. 'I think you're letting your imagination run a bit wild. These chaps are always rushing off as if their life depends on it. Gives me some peace to catch up with all my paperwork when our boss buggers off,' Alice laughed.

Kay and Alice sat in silence as Kay's thoughts went back to the meeting. She remembered how Ed had given her a wink after he had read the note. Why would he do that when he caught her looking at his scowling face? His smile had been forced or was Alice right and her imagination was playing tricks on her. She turned to her friend.

'I think I'll go and freshen up now, I feel grubby from the heat. See you later for lunch,' Kay said, as she left Alice and went to her room.

'Thanks for stopping to take my mind off all the drama, Kay. I'd better go and sort out my desk before Ed and Tom get back, or Ed won't be pleased, especially after my dramatics earlier. He thinks women have no place in the bush as it is,' Alice moaned.

Kay now knew Ed well enough to believe it wasn't that they were female, but that Ed was protective and as the manager felt it was his duty to protect all his staff. She told Alice what she was thinking.

'Maybe. He is a good guy,' Alice agreed. 'I suppose it's just because we're not physically as strong as them that worries him.'

'I think so,' Kay said. 'He probably feels he has to protect us from some of the more imperious blokes that work here. I know that I'm as good as any of them in the field.'

'Yes, you are,' Alice said, patting her on the arm. 'And I've heard Ed telling people that many a time.' Kay saw her friend frown thoughtfully, before adding, 'I think he's falling for you, Kay. Just a word of warning, my friend. He's such a terrific guy, and we're all very fond of him. He's had a shit life, so if you're not interested, which I doubt, please don't break his heart.'

Kay was stunned by her friend's outburst, although she liked that she was so concerned about Ed's wellbeing. 'I didn't come here looking for romance,' she said. 'This thing, whatever it is that Ed and I feel for each other, well it's early days and I intend taking it one step at a time. I don't know where it's heading. He's a difficult man to read. One minute he's very business-like and brusque, and the next he's gentle and sweet.'

Alice smiled at Kay and stood up to leave. When Kay went to stand, Alice gave her a brief hug. 'I know you wouldn't intentionally hurt him, you're far too nice for that.'

They parted ways and Kay went to her room for a rest. She was pleased to have time to herself. The things Alice had said made her re-evaluate her feelings for Ed. Was he falling for her, really? Or was he lonely and just using her for company? No, she thought, his love-making had been far too passionate for it not to have been real, and she felt the same. When they were together the electricity between them was tangible, she recalled. She felt a tightness in her stomach and longed to feel his muscular arms around her, and his mouth on hers. She gave herself a mental shake. 'For goodness' sake, pull yourself together,' she said aloud.

After a quick shower and change of clothing, Kay made her way to the office where she knew Alice would have the list of all the new arrivals. As she got there, Frank's vehicle arrived in a cloud of dust. He leapt down and rushed towards her just as she reached the office.

'Hello, gorgeous, you looking for me?' he asked as if nothing nasty had happened between them. 'Where's lover boy this fine day? Hear he and Tom left after the meeting I forgot about. Any idea where they were going?'

'Hello to you too, Frank,' she said, relieved that he had cheered up a bit, but nervous to be alone with him. 'I've no idea, but I presume they went to find the injured rhino and her calf.' Unable to resist, she added, 'Where have you been? We missed you this morning.'

'Just had a few things to do over at the main lodge.'

Kay continued on her way to the office and was a little disconcerted when he followed her there. Alice was hard at work. She looked up as they entered, giving Kay a scowl when she saw Frank had put his arm around her waist.

Kay wriggled free. 'Please don't do that,' she said, walking over to Alice and taking the list from her.

'Remember what I mentioned this morning. Don't trust that one,' Alice whispered to Kay.

'Right, Alice, give me my list and stop gossiping, or I'll be forced to give you a kiss,' Frank said, snatching his list out of her hand and turning to Kay.

'What you girls need, is to get out of this place before something unpleasant happens to you. If it does, don't say I didn't warn you. This isn't a place for women,' he yelled over his shoulder as he left the girls staring after him.

'What an arrogant prick,' Alice snapped, furious.

Kay could not understand what Ed saw in Frank and why he let him keep his job when he was so difficult to work with. 'Did you see the look of rage on his face, Alice? Frank seemed so charming when I first arrived, but now he's like a different person. I wonder why?'

'I reckon he thought he could charm you, until Ed showed an interest and that's what's turned him. He really fancied you, Kay, and I thought you liked him. That is until he cornered you,' Alice said.

'He gives me an uneasy feeling now, although I can't put my finger on why,' Kay replied.

'Have you heard that Sally has taken a week off as from today?' Kay shook her head. 'She's with that American who comes to see her at the lodge every couple of months,' Alice said.

'Really?' Kay asked, wishing she could go away for a week of privacy with Ed.

'Yes, she's a lucky mare, having a whole week off. Apparently, he's taking her to that expensive thatched lodge, forgotten the name, but it's close to Marloth Park, along the Crocodile River. He's paying for her time away with the company's vehicle, as it's a long drive with some difficult terrain to negotiate, especially if they're driving through the Sabie Sands area.'

'He must be incredibly wealthy to be able to come and go all the way across the world so often,' Kay mused. 'How did she meet him? Shouldn't think they met here at the beauty salon, or did they?'

'No, her ladyship was dressed to kill and sitting at the cocktail bar in the evenings, just hoping and planning on meeting some unattached wealthy male, who'd fall in love with her.'

Kay shook her head and wondered why anyone could be bothered to do such a thing. 'But I assumed she was involved with someone?'

Alice nodded. 'Sally told me in confidence, that they are engaged, but as neither of them earn enough to get married, she is putting herself out there to get some poor unsuspecting visitor to give her lots of money. How she imagines she can entice him to part with his money, I've no idea. I did tell the silly mare I thought she was playing with fire, but she just laughed at me.' Alice grimaced. 'She thinks

I'm very dull and unadventurous, but she's bound to end up in trouble if she plays games with the male visitors. They might be wealthy but they're not stupid. She's very immature in some ways, although she looks and acts like she's conquered the world,' Alice said, shaking her head. 'She certainly has this guy hooked though.'

'Maybe they'll get together one day,' Kay said. 'He must fancy her if he keeps visiting every few months and is taking her on holiday with him, for all to see.'

'Yes, well he's a long way from home, and no doubt his fiancée in the States won't know what he's up to in SA,' Alice added.

Kay realised she had been chatting for far too long. 'I'll leave you to your office work now and go find Ben. We're planning a route for our next lot of visitors. We get bored traversing the same ones and need to be a little more adventurous,' Kay said, making a move towards the group of trackers chatting nearby.

'See you later,' Alice shouted. 'Be careful.'

Chapter Eleven

Ed drove north, in the direction where the shooting of the rhino had taken place. He hoped to find some clues that would lead him to the poachers. Turning into a sharp bend, a pair of zebra charged across the road. Ed had to brake hard to avoid a collision. Tom braced himself against the dashboard, as Ed veered down a rarely used shortcut which he hoped would shave miles off their drive.

'Hell, that was a close shave, my friend. Sorry for the erratic driving,' Ed panted.

'Why the hurry?'

'I've got a meeting with Fanalapie, one of my informers,' Ed said, wiping his forehead with the back of his hand. 'He's cultivated friendships with some of the tribesmen, at my suggestion. I supply him with tobacco and he pays them with it, so they pass on any information they might have gleaned. It amazes me how the underground works in the bush. It's as if the ground has ears.'

'Surely that's dangerous for Fanalapie, Ed?' Tom asked.

'It is, and that worries me, but he's as desperate as we are to find these poachers and volunteered to do it for me. I have to be sure that nobody finds out about my meeting, because if this knowledge falls into the wrong hands Fanalapie's life could be in danger.'

'Rather him than me,' Tom said.

'He gives me information. I inform the Parks Board and Kruger guys. Nobody asks questions how I obtain my information,' Ed said focusing on the road ahead.

'Does Frank or Dexter know this Fanalapie chap?' Tom asked.

'I haven't mentioned him to either of them, because both have a loose tongue when they've had a few. I'm not prepared to take the risk. Too many lives would be put in danger if anyone was to discover who the informers were. Even the other trackers and their families who are attached to the tribe would be targeted. I feel a bit disloyal to my staff at times, but the fewer people who know about this, the better,' Ed explained.

They motored on in silence, until Tom had another question.

'No problem if you can't tell me, mate, but how the hell do you get info from this chap when nobody sees him?'

'Here's the thing, Tom. Fanalapie gets his info from his contacts and sends me a message to meet him in our chosen location, through one of my trackers. You can probably guess it's Tsepho, my tracker, but Ben is also one of my informers. Neither knowing about the other, as once again, the less one tells each of them the better for their own safety.'

'It's a bit like being a spy in the Cold War,' Tom said, eyes wide.

'I don't know about that,' Ed said frowning. 'I'm just sorry not to be able to share this with Frank. We go back a long way and have been friends for years. Earlier, just as the meeting began, I saw a note had been left on my desk by Tsepho. All it said was to meet him at same place.'

'Where are we going, Ed?' Tom asked, scanning the area they were driving through. 'I've never been this way before. It's out of our concession isn't it?'

'It is,' Ed took his eyes off the road for a moment and stared at Tom. 'I trust you not to mention this to anyone, okay?'

'Yeah, of course,' Tom assured him.

'Good. I can usually arrange to meet my informant after hours, so that he doesn't become jittery. He'll be pissed off when he sees I'm not alone, so you'll just have to stay in the vehicle and keep a lookout in case he's been followed without realising it. I'll find out why he wanted to see me so urgently.'

Ed slowed the vehicle down slightly. 'We're nearly there. It's an old trading store that's been derelict for decades, but at the back there's a room that Fanalapie uses as a meeting place from time to time.' Ed smiled, picturing the tins of provisions. 'It's sometimes difficult for me to get away unnoticed. Hidden from view by thick bush, at the outskirts of the reserve, nobody would give a second thought to a derelict building, if they came this way though.'

'Bloody hell, man, it sounds like cops and robbers. You sure we should be doing this?' Tom asked tapping the dashboard absentmindedly.

'We have no choice if we're to outsmart these bastards, Tom. They're desecrating our rhino and elephants. We have no idea what's going on behind the scenes, and who is behind the killings. All for the millions they're being paid by other countries.'

Ed knew he was ranting and that it was not Tom's fault this poaching issue angered him so deeply. But he could not help himself and added, 'It makes one sick to know that we probably socialise with some of the bastards behind this. There's one heck of a lot going on with people watching everything, and I hate that we don't know who they are. I got a tip-off that some were staying at our main lodge only a couple of weeks ago,' Ed admitted.

They reached the derelict stone building after a few more near misses with wandering animals, who would suddenly appear as if from nowhere. Luckily, they had not met any other vehicles on the roads. Ed had managed to avoid the main paths the rangers used. It looked deserted as he pulled up behind the building out of sight of anyone passing. There was no sign of his informer, or the old battered bakkie he usually drove.

Ed could hear Tom breathing hard. He picked up his rifle, keeping it at the ready.

'Tom, put that thing away and calm down. He's here even though we can't see him,' Ed whispered.

Leaping out of his vehicle and taking his gun out of the holster, Ed ran across to the closed door of the building and looked around. He was feeling uneasy. Standing with his back to the door, Ed looked around and whistled softly into the breeze, knowing the person it was intended for would know it was him.

This place had not been chosen by chance. Ed thought of the months it had taken before he and Fanalapie were happy with their meeting place. They were both aware that they had to be extra careful with Fanalapie's people. He had explained several times to Ed that many of his own were in the pay of the poachers at one time or another.

Ed had his own key to the room. Entering, he looked around at the tattered ceiling where the thatch was full of cobwebs and what looked like moss. It smelt of mould, and mildew. Ed studied the cramped space. Fanalapie had sectioned off one corner of the room as a kitchen, which was equipped with an old iron kettle and some metal braai forks. An iron bed with an old hair mattress, looking like it had seen better days, was half covered by a crochet blanket. Ed left the room, locking it again.

Pushing his way through the thick bush, Ed was horrified to see Fanalapie on the people carrier with an arm around Tom's chest, holding a long panga across his throat.

'Fan, for fuck's sake what are you doing?' Ed shouted, running to Tom's rescue.

Fanalapie lowered the panga and reluctantly released his hold on Tom. 'Why you bring this man, boss? He bad luck. I don't like,' he scowled.

'Where the hell did you get to?' Tom asked, rubbing his neck. 'This bloody fool was about to cut my throat.'

'I told you he wouldn't be happy to see you,' Ed laughed, slapping his informer friend on the back.

'Where were you when we arrived, Fan? Were you hiding?' Ed asked.

'I hide. Bad things happening I hear. We must talk quick. I must get back before I am missed. One of my brothers is coming from Kruger Park with more news. We must meet here again after dark tonight. This time you bring big gun and small ones. Big poaching people are coming. Maybe bring him,' Fan replied as he pointed a finger at Tom.

'Thanks a bunch,' Tom smiled.

I'll do that, Fan. But why all the mystery? Is something big going down tonight?'

'I hear many bad men coming. Big money paid for horns. Some big white man coming. He the bad man with the money to pay for horn. We catch him tonight?'

'If that happens, Fan, you will be very well rewarded, my friend. We couldn't do this without your help. What time tonight?' Ed asked.

'I bring my brother here at twelve tonight. We meet and then and I'll have all the news for you.'

'Thanks, Fan, I'd better get back before too many questions get asked about where we've been,' Ed said, as he shook his friend's hand in the customary way of the tribe.

Within a second, Fanalapie had disappeared into the bush, without a backward glance.

Ed jumped into the driving seat and started the engine. He couldn't let Tom know how worried he'd been to see his informer about to slit Tom's throat. Thank heavens he arrived before something terrible had happened.

'Ed, you haven't heard a word I've just said,' Tom

chuckled some time later.

'Sorry, I was thinking of Fan and what he may have found out for us tonight.'

'I dread to think,' Tom frowned. 'I was telling you how bloody scared I was when he suddenly came from nowhere and attacked me,' Tom said.

'Why didn't you call me? I'd have heard you,' Ed said with a smile to try and make light of what happened.

'It was too late, when the huge sword was at my throat, and he said, don't move or shout.'

'He's suspicious of people, that's all. And with good reason,' Ed said thinking of all the people he didn't trust in his life. 'However, it's a good thing I arrived back when I did, or you may not be here to tell the tale,' Ed tried to sound light-hearted to hide his anxiousness.

Tom gave Ed an apologetic look. 'You're on your own tonight my friend. I'm not letting that bugger near me again. He may trust you, but he sure as hell doesn't me,' Tom grumbled.

'Seriously, Tom, I need you, and probably could do with Frank, but as he's behaving rather strangely of late, I fear he's been hitting the bottle, so unfortunately he's out. We must keep our wits about us, if were coming back in the dark. It's a dangerous game meeting up with an informer, never mind running into the poachers. That's far too big for us to handle by ourselves.' Ed rubbed his tired eyes. 'We'll have to inform the Parks Board police if we hear of an organised attack. It's our job to find out when and where. We'll leave the rest to them.'

Tom visibly relaxed. 'So, it won't be us trying to capture them then?'

'We will be involved, but hopefully the backup will do the main work.' Ed thought of Kay and added, 'Don't let Kay hear about this either, Tom. I don't want her to get involved in any way. This is far too dangerous even to know about our meetings. Mum's the word mate, okay?'

'I'm not going to tell a soul,' Tom assured him.

They drove on in silence, both absorbed in their own thoughts. Ed's turned immediately to the wonderful night he had enjoyed getting to know Kay better. It was a night he would never forget. It dawned on him that he had already fallen in love with her. He felt lucky she had come into his life, just when he had given up trying to find a woman who would be able to fill his wonderful Claire's shoes. Ed took a deep breath. He would never forget the short but happy time he and his late wife had shared. Giving himself a mental shake, he realised it was time to let the past go. His memories were locked in his heart and he knew Claire would want him to be happy. He was certain she would have liked Kay.

'I know that look, Ed,' Tom said sympathetically. 'You're thinking about Claire again, aren't you? Time to let the past go, my friend. Time to find yourself a woman who can make you smile again. It's been a long time for you to be on your own. Tell me to mind my own business, but you know I'm right,' Tom said.

Ed appreciated Tom's concern for him. They had worked together nearly as long as he and Frank had done. 'I hear you. I'll let you into a little secret, if nothing else but to make you shut up and stop bossing me around about my private life,' Ed laughed.

When Ed had finished telling Tom about how he and Kay were becoming close, Tom stared at him.

'Bloody hell, mate, you've just broken all the rules. No fraternising with the staff while at the lodge. Who made those rules?' putting his finger to his temple, he smiled. 'Let me think,' he said, laughing. 'I'm happy for you. Kay's a lovely girl. Hard worker, too, and she's a good ranger.'

'Well I have to admit I don't know where this is going, she seems hung up on some chap she was engaged to in Durban. Not sure what happened, but I reckon that's what brought her to the bush,' Ed confided.

'Getting over a broken heart d'you reckon?' Tom asked.

'Mmm, too early to broach that subject yet, but hey let's not worry about my love life right now. We've much more important and life-threatening things to think about.'

As Ed turned the final bend towards the lodge, they spotted the injured pregnant rhino, with a calf at her side. Ed slowed, stopping at a safe distance before he turned off his engine and radioed the other lodges.

He whispered to Tom, 'Get my bag from under your seat. I'm going to dart her before she moves off. Poor girl looks ready to collapse.' His heart contracted at the sight of the hurt animal. 'I reckon she's come close to camp so that we can look after her and her youngster. You call in and let the guys know what's going on and ask for the vet. She's not going to make it if that bullet is still inside her.'

Tom called in, just as Ed had requested.

Ed prepared the dart gun. 'Just look what those bastards have done to the poor beast. If we can't save her, I hope we can at least save the youngster. I'll dart him too. He must have run away when the poachers found them, his little horn is still intact.' Spotting blood on the calf's head, Ed peered at him and added. Looks like he got a bullet though. His ear is damaged.'

When the vet, rangers and trackers arrived on the scene, it was clear that the mother was beyond help. Ed swallowed the lump in his throat as the vet euthanised the magnificent creature. They loaded the mother and calf with some difficulty onto the back of the trailer which the rangers had driven and one of the trackers was sent with the vet to the clinic to try and save him.

Everyone was in very low spirits as they made their way back to camp.

Chapter Twelve

Kay walked to the swimming pool where she sat looking out towards the dam at a lone elephant splashing and rolling in the mud. She breathed in the scent of manure that filled the air, as the sun beat down on her bare arms. It reminded her of the times she spent in the bush with her parents when she was young. She was so grateful for those memories.

Her mind drifted on to Harry. She couldn't help imagining what her life would have been like had she married him and stayed in Durban. Fate had brought her to this place, and she would be forever grateful. She had toughened up and learnt so much. She felt rejuvenated as she thought of Ed and how close they were becoming. If only she had a little time for her art, life would be perfect. She realised that she missed the smell of her oil paints and turps.

Kay snapped out of her revelry at the sound of an engine coming towards the lodge. Her heart skipped a beat as she realised it was Ed and Tom returning.

Running back to the office, she was panting as she quickly told a surprised Alice they were back. They were trying hard to look business-like, talking about the new guest arrivals, when the two men walked in.

'Good to see you girls hard at work in my absence,' Ed remarked, smiling.

Kay could not help thinking how tired he looked.

'Where have you been?' Alice asked. 'Frank is in one of his strops again today and he's driving everyone nuts.'

'Get Frank on the radio and tell him I need to have a word, please, Alice.'

'Sure, will do,' Alice said, widening her eyes at Kay as she turned to call Frank.

'Why don't we all get an early bite of lunch, Ed, before things get busy with the new arrivals?' Tom suggested. 'I've got a safari outing arranged for this afternoon and I think you have too, don't you, Kay?'

'Good idea,' Ed said, looking a little happier. 'Let's meet in the dining room in half hour. Alice, you let the staff know we want to eat early. Kay, I need a word.'

'I can't get Frank to answer his radio,' Alice said, frowning.

Ed closed his eyes briefly. 'Don't worry about it.' He looked at Tom. 'Please try and get hold of Frank. What the hell can he be doing?'

'I saw him earlier,' Kay admitted. 'He said something about going to the main lodge.'

Tom went to the doorway. 'I need to go there to collect my guests later, but I'll pass by now to see if he's still be there. If so, I'll tell him to contact you. See you for lunch in a while,' Tom said, as he left the office.

Kay waited for Alice to follow Tom out of the room and

leant against the desk watching as Ed removed his ranger's cap and raked his fingers through his sun-bleached hair. She noticed his fringe appeared to be almost white against his tanned forehead. She felt an urge to do it for him. Kay realised he'd been talking to her.

'Sorry, Ed, I missed that,' she apologised.

He shook his head, his eyes twinkling, and she supposed he must have said something saucy that he had not expected to have to repeat. 'I said, I'd like to take you to my cottage right now and, well, I'm sure you can imagine the rest.'

Their eyes locked, and as she imagined what he might have said, Kay felt her face going red, and heart swell with longing for him.

'Even with everything going on here, I have to admit there's nothing I'd like more right now.' He cleared his throat and any amusement vanished from his face. 'I have to tell you something though, and then you'll understand why it's impossible for me to get romantically involved right now.'

She felt as if he had thrown a bucket of ice cold water over her. Her back stiffened and she turned away from him pretending to read some paper on the desk.

'I understand,' she replied without looking up.

'I don't think you do,' he said quietly. 'Will you please look at me?'

Kay felt humiliated and angry, unable to believe that she had misunderstood Ed's intentions towards their budding relationship. She gave Ed a stormy look.

'You do not owe me an explanation, Ed, just please forget

whatever it was we shared for one brief evening.'

She could feel the tears were ready to fall, as she turned to leave, but Ed grabbed her by the arm and swung her around to face him. Before she knew what was happening, she was being held in his arms and he kissed her with such force that her tooth cut into her lip. She tasted blood.

Ed moved away, his eyes widening in horror when he saw what he had done. 'Oh hell, Kay. I'm so sorry. You took what I was trying to say the wrong way. I can't stop thinking about you, but it's just not the time.' He rested the palms of his hands on his desk and closed his eyes. 'What I'm trying to say, is that there's a lot of bad stuff going on right now. I really must have my wits about me if I'm to be of any use to anyone. People's lives could well depend on me when the chips fall, and it looks like that's going to happen sooner rather than later.'

Kay retrieved a tissue from her trouser pocket and held it to her mouth. She felt a shot of anxiety rush through her body as she saw how stressed Ed looked. Something had happened since he and Tom went out earlier, she decided. She watched him silently as he paced the room, coming back to pull her into his arms once again.

'Can we put us on hold for just a little while longer, Kay?' he asked, a pleading look in his grey eyes. 'I have something I need to do tonight. If it ends how I hope it will, then we'll all come out of it unscathed. I don't want to involve you, and once this thing is sorted out, I'll be all yours. I promise I'll make it up to you.'

He looked deep into her eyes and she saw a love and

longing in his that matched her own. 'I'm sorry for the way I reacted,' she said not wishing to hurt him for a moment longer. 'But my trust in men was shattered when my fiancé betrayed me, and I made a decision to stay away from any involvement in a meaningful relationship. I wasn't expecting to fall for you and am a little unnerved.'

'Hey, you two,' Alice shouted passing on her way to the dining room. 'Lunch, remember?'

Kay felt a brief gentle kiss on her swollen lip, before Ed led the way out of his office. She knew she wouldn't rest until she found the underlying cause of his sudden change in behaviour. She just knew it was something to do with what had happened while he and Tom were out earlier. Her gut feeling was that Ed and Tom were plotting something big. It must be dangerous, she thought, or he would have told her about it. From the way he was behaving, she suspected it must be to do with the poachers. She wondered if Frank knew what it was and resolved to corner him later in the day after the evening drive, to glean more.

Her intuition was working overtime, as the feeling of fear permeated her mind. Something was very wrong. She intended to find out what. Especially as she had just found love again and had no intention of her lover getting into a situation that could harm him. The very thought of it made a shiver go down her spine.

After lunch, they were all about to go their separate ways, when Frank arrived.

'Why are you guys eating so early? You could have given me a call, I was only at the main lodge,' he grumbled.

'Is that so?' Tom admonished. 'I went looking for you before lunch and no one had seen you there, Tom admonished.

'Huh, shows how inconspicuous I am then. Hurts my ego that does,' Frank gave Tom a smile that Kay noticed didn't quite reach his eyes. 'There was no one in reception when I got there, so maybe that's why they hadn't seen me.'

'Who did you go to see?' Ed asked.

'Just one of the guests I know. Anyway, I'm starving, so I'll catch you once I've eaten,' Frank said, walking to the dining room without a backward glance as the rest of them stared after him in puzzlement.

'Great, I'll be in my office when you're ready,' Ed said, his irritation with Frank obvious. 'There's a few things we need to chat over.'

Kay had listened to the exchange of words between the men, felt uneasy, but couldn't put her finger on why. She caught up with Alice who was walking ahead to her room.

'Wait for me, I'm going the same way,' she called. 'I need to get my gear for the afternoon drive. I hope my new lot are interested in some of the small creatures, birds and trees instead of just the big five. Honestly, I spent such a long time going over and remembering all the different species, but mostly get asked details about the bigger animals. Have you any idea how many different frogs there are, Alice?'

'No, and unlike you, my friend, I hate frogs,' Alice laughed. 'By the way, what was all that about with you and gorgeous in the office before lunch? I heard you say, something having unnerved you. Or words to that effect.

You looked upset when I saw you.' She stared pointedly at Kay's lip. 'I notice you had blood on that tissue that you were holding to your lip.'

'How on earth did you manage to notice so much when you barely stopped to tell us lunch was ready?' Kay asked in surprise.

'Well, my friend, I also spotted the looks our boss gave you over lunch, and how he was gazing at that swollen lip of yours. No doubt in my mind who was the cause of that.'

'Alice, you really are a hoot,' Kay said, as she linked arms with her friend.

'So, tell me all.'

'I'm not really sure what to tell, as it's just my feelings working overtime. Ed did say there is something big going down and I think it's tonight, but he didn't confirm anything. I have an uneasy feeling that he's getting into something dangerous, but I'm only reading between the lines. Just between us, Alice, he asked if I minded if we put our relationship on hold for a while, because he needs his wits about him for whatever he's dealing with. I of course took it the wrong way, thinking he wanted to really cool off,' Kay explained.

Alice interrupted her. 'Blimey, I see now why you got such a passionate kiss from him. Worth having taken his chat the wrong way if you ask me,' Alice giggled.

'You're incorrigible,' Kay laughed. Then recalling what was happening, she added, 'I'm going to find Frank after dinner and try and find out if he knows what Ed and Tom are up to. Ed tells him everything, so he must be in it up to his eyeballs. Frank always likes to be the first with all the news, so it should please him to fill me in.'

'Not sure that's a good idea, Kay. What if he doesn't know, and you tip him off that something's going on? I heard from the main lodge that there were undercover Parks Board guys staying there and asking a hell of a lot of questions. Some of them about Frank.'

Kay was intrigued but listened as Alice continued.

'Haven't you noticed lately how weird he's behaving?' Alice asked. 'It's as if he's hiding something, rushing off all the time and not telling anyone where he's going. He was never like that until you arrived. I can't help putting it down to the fact that you've dented his huge ego, by not reciprocating his feelings for you. I know he tried to force himself on you and that is wholly unacceptable, but it's more than that. The night watchman told me that Frank watches you going to your room. The old man has been keeping an eye on you making certain you get to your room safely.'

Kay was horrified to think that she had not noticed anything unusual going on.

'Ed's instructions I gather,' Alice said. 'He wants to make sure Frank doesn't try any funny business again.'

'But I'm careful at all times,' Kay said, confused. 'I've never seen him lurking anywhere.'

Alice put her hands on her hips and nodded. 'He's been hiding behind the kitchen block. The crafty sod.'

'Oh hell. If that's the case, then he must have seen Ed walk me back a couple of times,' Kay said, wondering why that had not put Frank off from his night stalking. 'Mind you, Alice, he still chats to me in his flirty banter. Maybe you're right though, about not asking him questions. I'll think about it.'

'It's my afternoon off, Kay, so I've booked a spa treatment with Sally's replacement while she's away. I suspect Sally is the reason Frank goes to the main lodge so often.'

'Really?'

'Well that's what Zumbe told me. Apparently, Frank gets Zumbe to drop him off at the back of the salon building and then spends time chatting to her during her breaks. He insinuated there's more going on with our friend Sally Pope. And yes, she's engaged to some gorgeous but broke surfer. Given half a chance I reckon she'd dump him if she could snare her American lover, but he's engaged to a girl back home. I reckon he uses Sally while he stays at the lodge, when he comes to do business in Nelspruit every few months. I think he's a friend of the big boss, and that's why he visits,' Alice added.

'That wouldn't explain why nobody saw Frank at the lodge today when Tom went looking for him. Sally's not there.'

'I hadn't thought of that,' Alice said, frowning thoughtfully. 'Frank must have been in one of the guests' rooms then because that's the only other place he could have been, or he'd have been seen.'

'Maybe he's meeting one of those gorgeous models or one of the single women who've been staying?' Kay suggested in a hushed voice.

'You've got to be kidding? If that got around, he'd get the sack surely? Well nobody will hear a word from me,' Alice giggled.

'Nor me,' Kay agreed.

Reaching their respective rooms, they parted company and arranged to meet when Kay got back from her drive later that afternoon.

As Kay let the hot water of the shower beat down on her, she went over what Alice had told her. What Sally did was none of her business she thought, but Frank was another matter. He and Ed had been friends for years from what she understood, so how come Ed had no idea what Frank was getting up to by meeting Sally on the sly. Why didn't they come into the open with their relationship? Kay mused. Something was off, but try as she might, she couldn't come up with a reason for their behaviour.

Recalling the night at the bar, Frank had not even looked at Sally. She had not taken any notice of him either, which to Kay's mind was rather odd. She prided herself on the fact that she always picked up on couples, even when they were trying not to be noticed. It was how she had known her best friend was having an affair with Harry. That wound was beginning to heal though, she mused, thanks to Ed and his honesty and passion. She felt butterflies in the pit of her stomach as she thought of his kisses.

'Kay. You ready?' Alice shouted, knocking on the bedroom door. 'I've just seen your guests arriving early. Thought you'd like to know.'

Kay knew there was no time to continue dreaming about

Ed, or she would be late back to work.

'I'm on my way, thanks, Alice,' Kay yelled back as she hurriedly dressed.

Kay met her new guests and discovered they were all from Germany – two couples and a male friend on his own. They had never visited the bush before, so once introductions were made and they had been given afternoon tea, they set off. The group were very receptive to her talks about the different species of birds, especially the woman.

One of the visitors, a man called Gustave, wanted to know about the wild dogs, which he told Kay he had read up about before his trip. Kay was lucky enough to hear from one of the other rangers that they had spotted a female dog with her pups. It was half a mile away, so she didn't hang around to give them time to wander off and motored to where they told her the pups were. When she arrived, the other ranger moved off, and she was able to park very close to the pups, so that her guests could get excellent pictures. The mother looked like she'd just eaten and was relaxed enough not to bother taking notice of the humans as they clicked their cameras in delight.

After an afternoon seeing many animals, they stopped for sundowners before Kay took them back to the lodge. Her group were silent all the way back, each lost in their own thoughts and it gave Kay time to think of the evening ahead. She wished she could rid herself of the anxiety she felt whenever her thoughts turned to Ed and what was happening. The nagging dread had been on her mind all day. Earlier, as her guests had been taking photos of the cheetah she'd found sitting just above their heads in the branch of a tree, one man had been obviously annoyed when he had to ask her a question twice, as she had been miles away deep in thought. She really would have to get a grip, she silently admonished herself.

Arriving back at the lodge, Kay parked. Staff were handing out hot towels to the guests as they stepped down from the vehicle. Just the feel of wiping away the dust from her hands made Kay appreciate that extra touch that Ed had implemented when he took over as manager. He really was all about making every visitor feel important and that this really was a five-star trip that they had booked.

'Thank you, Ben and Kay,' they chorused as everyone parted company.

'Thanks, Ben,' Kay said. 'I think that turned out to be a good viewing. Pity we couldn't find a leopard though. This group are hell bent on seeing what they have on their list. Did you notice they were ticking off the animals as we found them?' Kay asked.

'The Germans always know what they want. I like that because we don't have to waste time finding things like the dung beetle,' Ben chuckled.

'See you tomorrow,' Kay said, yawning. 'I wonder how many of this group will be up for the early drive? Probably all of them,' she smiled.

'Yes, you're probably right. I've noticed that our German visitors are usually very organised and never miss any of our rides into the bush.'

'They really appreciated all we did for them this afternoon, too,' Kay added. 'Especially the way you set up some private place for the ladies to go to the lavatory,' Kay said patting her tracker on his arm. 'I must go and change before dinner.'

Kay came across Alice as she was leaving her room.

'Hi, Kay?' Alice said. 'I'm so glad I caught you. How did the drive go? Oh, I saw Frank while you were all out. When I returned to the office after lunch he was going through papers on Ed's desk. I asked him what he was looking for, but he gave me a frosty look and told me it was nothing to do with me. Bloody cheek. It sure is to do with me if the boss thinks I let Frank rummage through his private papers.' She frowned. 'He knew Ed was at a meeting, and probably didn't expect me back so soon. Anyway, I saw him putting a piece of paper into his pocket, but I've no idea what it was. He left without a word. Something had annoyed him, by the look on his face as he stormed out.'

Kay was horrified. 'Have you told Ed about this, Alice?'

'No, I haven't seen him, but I heard his bakkie return a few minutes ago. I just hope he's alone when I find him, so that I can let him know about what Frank's done.'

'Can you give me a couple of minutes to shower and change, and I'll come with you?' Kay asked. 'In fact, why don't you come in and have a glass of wine while I'm getting ready?'

'That's a great idea, and then we can both find Ed and let him know,' Alice smiled.

While Kay got ready, Alice read a magazine and drank her chilled Chenin blanc wine that her friend kept at the ready in her fridge.

'Remind me to restock my own fridge,' Alice said. 'I've been sitting on my veranda after you all go to bed and enjoying the sounds of the animals. Last night the lions were making a terrible din, enough to wake the entire Sabie Sands,' Alice laughed.

'I'm always too tired to do that, especially when I've got an early drive the next morning. Maybe when I have some time off I'll manage to stay awake and enjoy the solitude of the night. I love the sounds and smells of the bush. I envy you that time of solitude, Alice. It's something we should all be able to enjoy,' Kay said as she began to lather her hair with the fragrant shampoo.

She recalled the night drive when Ed took her to his cottage. That was phenomenal, she mused. To be out so late and hearing the calling of the lions to each other.

'I never realised before coming here, how it would all impact on my life,' she said, rinsing her hair. 'I wonder if I'll ever be able to leave this sort of life.'

'What about your life in Durbs?' Alice called. 'Surely you want to go back to that glamorous lifestyle, Kay? I know I could never settle permanently in the bush. What with the threat of malaria and the continual having to entertain the guests, not to mention this dry heat. Plays havoc on our skin, you know.'

Kay thought for a moment. Having finished washing her hair, she turned off the shower and stepped out, wrapping herself in the fluffy bath towel.

'I do miss my friends in the city,' she admitted. 'But I can't cope with the thought of bumping into Harry if I went back to teaching art. He's such a big name there. Everybody knows what he did to me, and my feelings are still a bit raw. I was so humiliated.' It was as if a big hand squeezed her heart as she thought of it. 'All the arty crowd felt sorry for me. I know, by the way they used to look at me and avoid me because they obviously didn't know what to say,' she added walking into the room and over to her wardrobe.

She grabbed some clothes and quickly dressed. Running the brush through her wet hair, Kay twisted it and clipped it up in an untidy bun. Touching up her make-up, she slipped on her shoes and smiled. 'Right, I'm ready to go.'

The girls left the room and linked arms as they made their way to the main bar where they knew Ed would be interacting with guests as usual.

Kay's spirits lifted when she thought of spending time with Ed, even if it was just to be in the same room as him while he spoke to others.

Chapter Thirteen

Ed was finding it incredibly difficult to concentrate on what people were saying. His mind was on what to do about later that evening and how he was going to get away without drawing attention to himself as he slipped away. He couldn't let any of the guests suspect what was going on.

The German visitors were busy regaling him with all the things that they had done before arriving at camp, and all the other places they had visited on their inclusive tour of South Africa. He half listened, so it was only when one of them mentioned Kay that his mind returned to pay attention to what was being said.

'You are so lucky to have such a knowledgeable girl working for you. We men were originally disappointed when we heard that we were to be given a female ranger. That was of course until we met her and discovered what an interesting person she was. She drove us over all those hills and gullies and was a fund of information. She certainly knows her job, which is why I wish to congratulate you on your very excellent young ranger, Ed,' Gustav announced in a loud voice.

His wife Greta gave Gustav a hard slap across the back of his head.

'What the hell was that for, woman?' he growled.

'That is for being so patronising about having a woman ranger. How dare you say such things to Kay's boss? You're an idiot sometimes, Gustav.'

'Don't be mad at him, I felt very uneasy when Kay first joined us. Being a woman in this business is not for the faint-hearted. Some of the native trackers were very unhappy,' Ed explained.

'You see, Greta my love, it is not only I that thought it surprising to have a woman ranger,' Gustav moaned as he rubbed the back of his head.

'I'm sure no man would have done better at having found that cheetah you men asked Kay to find,' said Greta in a heavy German accent.

'Did I hear someone mention my name?'

Ed's heart seemed to miss a beat when he heard Kay's voice. No woman had ever had that effect on him, he realised, even Claire who he had loved immensely. He turned to find amber eyes staring directly at him with what he took to be a questioning look.

'Ladies, what would you like to drink?' Ed asked, looking from Kay to Alice.

'Dry white for me please, and I'm sure Kay will have the same thanks, Ed,' Alice answered for them both as Kay nodded her head in agreement.

Ed was aware of Kay's eyes following his every move, and he was beginning to feel rather uncomfortable. She was looking around furtively as if she was waiting for someone or something. Whatever has gotten into her? he wondered. Alice was in deep conversation with the young handsome German who was on his own. This was his chance to get Kay on her own he decided.

'Can I have a quick word, Kay?' Ed said, as he picked up both their drinks and led her away from the others, to a small table in the corner.

Kay followed his loping strides as she tried to catch up. He pulled out a chair for her and as she sat down he became aware of her worried expression.

'Kay, what is it? You seem worried or annoyed or both? Please tell me what's the matter.'

Kay proceeded to tell Ed what Alice had told her about Frank rummaging through his private papers on his desk, and how he had put a paper into his pocket.

'I'm worried. He's up to something. Why would he go into your office?' Kay whispered. 'And what do you think he was looking for?'

'It's not the first time he's done that, Kay. I've caught him before now. When I questioned him the last time, he gave me some cock and bull story about having left something of his behind. He thinks I'm a bloody idiot,' Ed mumbled almost to himself. 'Frank has changed so much in the last six months. I thought he had a thing about you and was jealous of me, but it's more than that. When tonight is over, and I have more time, I plan to take him somewhere quiet for a drink and get him to talk to me like old times.'

'Do you think it has something to do with his being

involved with Sally Pope?' Kay asked.

'Sally? What the hell has she got to do with Frank?'

'Oh, you haven't heard,' Kay frowned. 'Frank's tracker told Alice that Frank makes him sit and wait for him when they stop at the back of the salon. Frank makes him keep a lookout and he has to hoot the horn if anyone comes near.'

Ed was feeling very uneasy as he listened to Kay. Something was seriously off, and he blamed himself for not having the time to focus more on what was going on at the lodges.

'It's times like these I wonder if it's my fault that Frank has gone off the rails,' Ed said. 'Maybe he's disgruntled that I was made manager when he's worked here longer than me. I was head-hunted by the team and it really did put poor Frank's nose out of joint at the time. Now I think about it, he was very sullen. I seem to recall he took a month off soon after. By the time he returned, I'd changed many rules and made new ones.'

As he spoke, Ed understood for the first time just how deeply Frank must have resented his promotion. 'He came back to new uniforms, I'd changed the timetable for the drives, and I even employed a new chef and head waiter. Maybe he needs more recognition for all he does around here?' he asked already aware of the answer. 'He's such a brilliant ranger. I need to sort this out with him. Thanks for bringing it to my attention, Kay,' he said placing his left hand on her arm. 'I'll get hold of head office and have a word.'

Ed studied the woman with the amber eyes and wanted

to take her in his arms. He resisted the urge, aware he would not want to stop once he started kissing those perfect inviting lips.

'We'd better join the others and get on with dinner,' he said. 'I'm just sorry I won't see you tonight. Perhaps we can make plans to go away for a night into Kruger? I know a perfect thatched hotel in the park. A friend of mine owns it. What do you say?' Ed asked.

Her eyes lit up and she beamed at him. 'I'd love that,' she said. 'You're the boss, so if you can arrange for me to have couple of days off, I'd be delighted to join you.'

Ed was aware of the effect he was having on Kay. He was mesmerised by her eyes, as they locked with his. Dinner was announced. They turned to go and join the group at the bar.

Just as they were about to start their first course of their meal, a screech of brakes and slamming door echoed around the building. Ed immediately sensed trouble and excused himself, quickly leaving the dining room. He could hear raised voices getting closer as he hurried to the outside bar area.

'Ben, Tsepho, what the hell is all the noise about? We have guests in the dining room for heaven's sake,' Ed said, furious.

A silence fell as Ben and Tsepho looked, both fidgeting in obvious agitation.

'Boss, it's Frank, he said he'd kill us if he finds out that we've told you,' Ben blurted out wringing his hands.

'Told me what? For God's sake, man, what the hell's going on?'

Ed could feel his anger rising, but knew he had to contain it or these men would clam up. He realised they didn't agree about whether to tell him. It dawned on him that if he had not heard their raised voices and come outside, he may have lost the opportunity to hear what Frank didn't want him to know.

'Right, you two, let's go to my office. We won't be disturbed there, then you can fill me in.' Ed led the way. They followed, still arguing in hushed voices. Try as he might, Ed couldn't make out what they were saying.

When Ed opened the office door and put on the light, he was horrified to see his desk had been ransacked. Papers from the filing cabinet were strewn all over the floor. His computer was on, too, despite him having turned it off before leaving. He ran his long fingers through his hair and turned to Ben.

'Quickly, go and get Alice and Kay. Tell them it's urgent but try not to let the others hear you.'

'Who on earth got into the office without anyone noticing, and what could they be looking for?' Ed asked in exasperation.

Running footsteps announced the women's arrival. They took one look at Ed's face, and then the mess in the office. Alice rolled her eyes heavenward at Ed.

'If you wanted to find something, you should have just called me,' she said picking up some papers and sounding cross.

'Don't be ridiculous, woman, I didn't make this mess. This is how I found it. I don't know what's going on, Alice, but there's something in this office that someone is intent on finding. Any ideas as to who that someone could be?' Ed asked, puzzled.

He watched as Alice opened her mouth to speak, but no words came out. He was worried she was about to cry, so he thought he had better calm down before everyone panicked. Turning to his computer, he tried to see what the perpetrator had hacked into. Moments later, he discovered that his private address book was what had been entered.

'Now why would anyone be interested in my address book?' Ed asked, looking at Alice.

'Maybe they were looking for the address of one of your guests? You have the guests' details on your computer. Don't you remember asking me to do a file for you? So that we could contact them when wanted to hold promotions?'

He nodded. 'I still can't work out who they would be interested in though. Any ideas?' Ed asked lowering his head into his hands and trying to think.

'Boss, that's what we wanted to tell you,' Tsepho, said. 'But Frank saw me watching him and when I went to find Ben, he followed me. He was red in the face with rage,' he added.

'What the hell do you mean, he followed you?'

'I saw Frank making this mess when I came back for my notes. I left them on Alice's desk. I pretended not to see what he was doing and quickly left, but of course he must have been worried I'd say something to you. He grabbed me and told me to keep my mouth shut, if I knew what was good for me.'

Furious that anyone had manhandled one of his staff, Ed asked, 'Did he have anything of mine with him when he was with you, do you know?'

'Boss, I was so frightened by his rage that I didn't notice. He could have put something in his pockets though. I went to find Ben, because he'd know what to do. Now he wants to tell you but then Frank will know it was me that told on him,' Tsepho moaned as he rubbed his hands across his face.

'Leave Frank to me. You two go and get on with what you were doing, and if you see him, don't mention that I know any of this. That goes for you girls also,' Ed added, glancing at Alice and Kay.

'What the hell's going on with Frank, do you think?' Alice asked, crossing her arms in front of her chest.

'If I knew, I'd tell you, but this is going too far. He seems to be having a breakdown. It's a pity I've got something on this evening, or I'd have it out with him. The heavy boozing is probably responsible for his behaviour,' Ed said. Turning his attention to his two trackers, he pushed his sun-bleached hair from his forehead in an exasperated movement, only for it to immediately flop right back. Ed could feel his temper simmering beneath the surface and knew he needed time alone to control himself.

He busied himself by picking up the papers that Frank had strewn over his desk and on the floor. Kay immediately started to help. Alice gazed at the chaos that Frank had caused. As Ben and Tsepho reached the door, Ed called after them.

'Don't forget our appointment later, and remind Tom

not to be late,' he said looking at Tsepho.

'Ok boss, see you later,' he replied.

'What are you doing later, Ed?' Alice as questioned, her voice trembling.

'Don't worry about that. You go back to our guests now, and not a word about this to anyone.'

'As if I need telling,' Alice sounded hurt as she turned to leave with a little smile at Kay.

'Well that went down like a ton of bricks,' Ed said, sitting back on his haunches as soon as he was alone with Kay.

'You know Alice is totally loyal to you, Ed,' she said, making him feel guilty. 'She'd never divulge any of your business to anyone else. I think you hurt her feelings by the look on her face as she left.'

He closed his eyes and felt weary as he thought about the night ahead and the dangers it could hold. After tonight, he vowed he would leave the poachers to the guys at the Parks Board and the Kruger staff; they could look out for them. He needed to focus more on the interests of the guests and staff that he was responsible for at the lodges. That was a mammoth enough task, not to mention the problem with Frank.

'What is it?' Kay asked. 'Please tell me what you're planning to do later tonight. I saw the look the boys gave you before they left. I know that whatever you're planning is dangerous. Please trust me enough to confide in me,' she pleaded.

Ed hugged her, kissing Kay on her forehead. He looked into her concerned face and but knew he couldn't divulge his plans to her. He also needed to be very persuasive if he was to put her off the scent. He managed a smile and tried to relax his jaw muscles.

'Nothing for you to worry about, my lovely Kay. I'm just having a meeting with the Parks Board guys later. None of us have enough free time during the day. We need to plan what to do about the poachers, but I can assure you there's no need for you to fret. Now why don't you go and entertain our guests, because I fear Alice is battling to cope after this break-in.'

'What are you going to do about Frank?'

'You leave Frank to me. I intend finding the underlying cause of this. He makes me so mad. It's totally out of character, but what the hell gives him the right to ransack my office, and again, what can he be looking for?'

'I'm so sorry. Let me clean this lot up while you check out your computer. You should be able to see what he's been into besides your address book.'

Aware she was not going to be persuaded to go that easily, he nodded and sat back down at his desk. 'That's a good idea. There must have been something important, and maybe he left the address book open as a red herring when Tsepho disturbed him.'

Ed and Kay got to work. It didn't take him long to fathom out exactly what Frank had been looking for. The file came up with his private letters between him and the Parks Board managers. One had been printed out, and as Ed read it he realised it was the letter where he had been informed that they were keeping tabs on some of his staff.

No names were mentioned, luckily, but Ed assumed that Frank was mad at him for keeping him out of the loop. Satisfied, he turned off his computer and turned to Kay.

'Well that explains it,' he said as Kay looked up at him.

'What does?'

'Frank wanted to read the letters I've been sending to the Parks Board guys. Maybe he thought they'd mention names, but all they did was advise me that they suspect some of my staff could be collaborating with the poachers and getting well paid for their information. Now, what would interest Frank in that? Unless he's just feeling left out and must have heard they're on to something, or someone.' He switched off the computer and took a deep breath before standing up. 'Right, let's get out of here, or they'll think I've run away with you.'

As they left the office, Ed made sure to lock the door behind him. His thoughts went back to Frank, as he accompanied Kay to the dining room. He didn't like to alarm her but had the feeling that Frank's intention was for them to have a show-down. The problem, Ed wondered, was why.

'You're deep in thought again,' Kay said, glancing at him.

'Take no notice of me, I'm still wondering what the devil Frank's up to. Maybe things will be clearer once tonight is over. I'm sure he'll turn up before too long.'

Ed tried to sound nonchalant but had a feeling of uneasiness in his gut. Something was going on, but he just couldn't think how it would involve Frank. He would be glad when his meeting with Fanalapie was over. Ed tried to put his thoughts aside and forced a smile on his face as he went to chat to the guests. It wouldn't do for them to pick up on his problems.

Chapter Fourteen

Kay spent time chatting with Alice, rehashing what they had seen in Ed's office. She confided that she was worried about Frank's behaviour.

'I think it's all because of you, that Franks got the zig with our gorgeous boss,' Alice said.

'Don't be crazy. I made it clear to him when I first arrived that I had no interest in the opposite sex. I think he gathered I had been upset by a prior relationship. When he saw Ed and I together, he was furious, I agree, but I think he's well over that now,' Kay said.

'You think what you like, but I've known Frank a long time, and he often gives me the creeps, despite his good looks and charming side when he wants to get his own way.'

Kay looked across the dining room at Ed, talking and laughing with the guests. He seemed back to his old self, but something told her he was putting on a good act. She would find out more later, she decided watching him looking towards the entrance, as if waiting for someone to appear? She knew the office situation had upset him more than he was letting on. She noticed how his jaw muscles clenched when he first saw the mess Frank had left. He had been furious, and she remembered how he had tried to make light of it because she was in the room. His eyes had been like cold hard steel. She shivered, as she remembered that look. She hoped never to have him look at her with that depth of fury in his eyes.

Ed must have felt her staring at him, because he suddenly turned. His eyes locked with hers. Kay's heart skipped a beat. Why had she thought she could avoid falling for this fascinating man? His sudden smile lit up his face, as he excused himself from his guests. Crossing the room in long strides towards her, he unexpectedly stopped. Kay followed his gaze and saw the night watchman wave from the doorway to catch Ed's attention.

Kay could feel her face fall with disappointment, as the spell between them was broken. She wondered if she would manage to get Ed on his own before he had to leave. She watched him go outside the door and could see he was obviously having a heated conversation as the other man jerked his arms around and pointed to the garages behind the building.

'Now what's going on?' Alice asked coming to stand by Kay.

'No idea,' she said honestly. 'Ed was making his way over here when he was called out. Do you think it's some news about the rhino, or the poachers?'

'Could be, let's go and find out before Ed does a disappearing act,' Alice suggested.

Just as the girls reached the doors, they bumped into a

worried looking Ed who was coming back in. He took one look at their faces and said, 'Yes, I know I have some explaining to do.'

He is not kidding, Kay thought, relieved that he seemed ready to confide in them.

'I'll make this brief,' he said keeping his voice low. 'The meeting I'm going to has been brought forward, so I need to leave in half an hour's time.'

Kay tried not to panic. She desperately wanted to ask if she could go with him, but the moment passed as Alice grabbed hold of Ed's arm.

'Who are you taking with you, Ed?' Alice demanded. 'I know you'll be armed, but make sure you're ready for anything, just in case you get into trouble. Don't forget what happened to Tom when they shot him,' Alice reminded him.

'For goodness' sake,' Ed said, looking exasperated, but also, Kay suspected, comforted by their concern for him. 'I've got no intention of going there alone. And don't breathe a word of my plans to anyone. That goes for Frank too, obviously. This is a highly confidential meeting and the fewer people that know about it the better. These tribesmen will kill one of their own if they think he's become a traitor. These informers risk their lives, which is why nobody must find out I'm going to meet mine.'

Just as Ed finished talking, Tom arrived. He greeted Alice and Kay with his usual casual air, and broad smile looking, Ed thought, very smart, dressed all in black.

'What's with the disguise?' Ed asked, pulling Tom to one side.

The women took their cue to leave Ed and Tom alone and returned to mix with the guests.

'We'll catch up with you tomorrow,' Ed said.

'Yes, and we should get back to our guests and be sociable, Alice,' Kay said. 'It's too early to go to bed.' The men left, and Kay added, 'I'll never sleep worrying about Ed and Tom. I have a funny feeling in the pit of my stomach, that we haven't been told what exactly is going on,' Kay whispered.

Kay heard Ed's vehicle revving. She walked over to the nearest window and peered out to where Ed was sitting in his pickup. He spotted her. Kay's heart leapt when he winked at her and then placing his finger to his lips to silence any goodbyes, he smiled before driving away.

Kay took a deep breath and tried not to worry. Ed knew what he was doing and she had to trust that he would be careful. She turned back to speak to Alice and said a silent prayer for his and Tom's safe return. Her German guests were in a great mood and made a big fuss of her when she returned them. Alice was flirting with the single man who seemed to be enjoying her company, Kay noticed. She wished Alice could find a man and fall in love. She tingled with the exciting thought of being back in Ed's arm very soon.

The staff were clearing away the remains of the evening festivities and some of the older members of Kay's group had gone to bed. Alice was yawning and looking very bleary eyed as she swallowed the last mouthful of her tequila.

'Hell, Kay, it's time we made our way to bed, or we'll

never be up for work in the morning. You've got an early drive with these guys,' Alice waved her arm towards the remainder of the guests.

'Yes, I have, but I'm not the one drinking copious glasses of tequila, am I?' Kay chuckled.

The two girls wished the remaining men a goodnight, and made their way to where a watchman was waiting with a torch to walk them to their rooms.

Kay couldn't sleep, so she picked up her night glasses and went and sat on her veranda, in the hope of seeing the lion she could hear roaring close by. Maybe he would come to drink in the dam, she thought hopefully.

The night had turned cold, so she wrapped herself in the warm blanket that she kept handy for nights like these when sleep evaded her. She was looking through her glasses just as a huge male lion arrived at the dam, followed by three females and two young cubs. This was a rare sighting, and one Kay had been wishing for ever since her arrival. She knew not many people got to see these animals so close to the lodge. She had seen lions in the bush when out with clients, but this was her first sighting at the lodge.

It was just before midnight when Kay eventually started to yawn. Her eyes ached with tiredness. She put down the glasses and went into her room. After a quick shower, she was just getting into bed, when there was a knock on her door. She grabbed her dressing gown, quickly opened the door thinking it must be Alice and froze to find Frank standing there. She tried to slam the door, but he placed his foot between it and the door frame.

'Please, Frank, go away or I'll call security.'

'Let me in, I need to talk to you urgently.'

She could not believe he had the nerve to ask her such a thing. 'You know I'm not going to do that.'

He lowered his head close to hers. 'If Ed means anything to you, you'll let me in,' he whispered through clenched teeth. 'This is serious, Kay, Ed could be in danger.'

Kay felt her stomach contract with worry. How did Frank know Ed was in danger? Her thoughts were running wild, as she opened the door to let him in.

'What's going on? What makes you think Ed's in danger? We know it was you who made that mess in his office, Tsepho saw you,' she said, instantly remembering that it was the wrong thing to do. 'I gather you didn't try to hide that fact either. And what were you looking for on his computer?'

Kay watched his face closely as a look of irritation crossed it, followed quickly by the usual smile, as he tried to make light of it all. She wasn't feeling very enlightened though and needed to be on her guard. It concerned her that Frank seemed to be acting rather strangely and kept pacing back and forth across her bedroom floor. He was making her nervous. Aware she needed to calm down to find out what he was up to, she took a steadying breath, just as he turned and grabbed her by the arm.

'Listen, why don't you get dressed and come with me?' he said. 'I'll explain everything on the way.'

'Frank, are you crazy? I'm not going out with you at this time of night, unless you explain exactly what the hell's going on.'

He glared at her for a moment and then shrugged. 'Fine. Ed is walking into a trap.' Kay gasped, covering her mouth with her hand. 'He thinks he's having a meeting with his informer.' He studied her face and when she didn't say anything, sneered and added, 'Ah, I see you know all about that.'

Kay's mind raced, and she had to focus on not panicking. What if Ed was in danger, she thought. Frank appeared to know all about the meeting Ed and Tom were going to. She stared into his eyes and saw a glint of pleasure as he looked back at her. Something about his smile made the hairs on her arms tingle, as if alarm bells were going off. Was it the drinks she had consumed earlier that was making her neurotic?

She could feel Frank's impatience as he stood waiting for her reply.

'Are you coming with me or not? I thought you'd want to warn lover boy, or at least pick up the pieces, of what's left of him if we are too late to warn him.'

Kay swallowed the lump in her throat. She had no intention of letting Frank see how terrified she was of anything bad happening to Ed. She picked up the clothes she had thrown on her chair and rushed into the bathroom to dress.

'Wait here while I change, and I'll come with you,' she said as she closed the bathroom door. She pulled on her clothes as quickly as possible and slid her handgun into the back of her trouser belt. Pulling on her fleece, she quickly checked herself in the mirror.

Frank was waiting at the open bedroom door, when Kay came out of the bathroom. She picked up her rifle on the way and joined him.

'I hope we won't be needing that, my girl,' he said with a frown.

A bleary-eyed Alice opened her door and looked at them in shock.

'What the hell's going on? Have you any idea of the time? I heard voices and I thought it was in my dream.'

'Go back to sleep,' Frank snapped.

Undeterred from his rudeness, Alice squinted at Kay. 'Are you okay?'

Kay nodded. 'I'm fine, thanks. Do as he says, it's late.'

'But why are you in your uniform, Kay?' she asked. 'And why is Frank here?'

Kay and Frank walked away from the rooms. Kay hoped Alice would be quiet and go back to bed, she didn't want anything to delay her reaching Ed.

'Oh my God, has something terrible happened,' Alice called. 'You both look very serious. I'll come with you, if you wait while I get dressed.'

Frank ran back to Alice and glowered at her. 'Shut the fuck up. And mind your own business, if you know what's good for you,' he said pushing Alice into her room and closing the door with a bang.

'Hey,' Kay shouted. 'You can't do that to her.'

He grabbed Kay's arm in a vice like grip and pulled her to the bakkie that he'd parked right outside the staff quarters. 'Get in, we've wasted enough time already. Things could have got out of hand in the time you took to make up your mind to come with me,' Frank growled.

He drove out of the camp at full speed, nearly knocking down the night watchman who was doing his rounds. Kay's knuckles were white as she held on to the dashboard.

'For heaven's sake, Frank, you'll get us killed. Slow down.'

'Did you know what Ed was up to?' he asked without taking his eyes off the road. 'Even before I logged into his computer I knew he's been having secret meetings with the poachers. He's behind the gang who've been terrorising our rhino and killing our staff. Bet he didn't tell you that now did he?'

Kay was horrified to hear Frank accuse Ed of such a vile thing. 'You're lying. Ed would never be a party to what you're suggesting.'

She felt sick with worry. One thing she was certain of was that she loved Ed and no way would she have feelings for someone who would be duplicitous enough to collude with poachers. Ed had asked her to trust him and that is what she would do. Maybe if she played along with Frank she could find out more, because he was talking as fast as he was driving. She knew it was imperative that she kept calm and didn't rile him, or they could end up in a ditch and then they would never get to Ed in time.

'Can you at least tell me where we're going?' she asked. 'Are you hoping to catch Ed with the poachers, Frank?' He didn't reply, so she added, 'I think we just left our lodge boundary and you know that's not permissible. Don't you think we should turn back and wait for Ed and Tom to return?'

'You do know more than you've let on,' Frank said. 'So, Tom is with Ed, is he? Now who told you that?'

'It's no secret that Tom and Ed left the camp together after dinner. They didn't mention where or what they were going to do, but it certainly seemed like a normal night drive to meet some of the Parks Board guys. Probably just checking fences, or something,' Kay said trying to sound nonchalant.

'Come off it, Kay, you can do better than that,' Frank sneered. 'Now be a good girl and shut up while I try and navigate this bloody donga.'

Kay was thrown backward as Frank drove up a steep bank and then roared down into a dry riverbed full of boulders. The bakkie tilted precariously on its side and for a split second it felt as if it would roll. Kay was shaking with fright as Frank managed to right the vehicle. He carried on, acting as if nothing untoward had happened.

Looking at her watch with the torch, Kay saw it was just after midnight and wished she was safely tucked up in bed. Why did Frank insist on having her with him? What did he hope to gain by insisting she accompanied him? She didn't dare ask for fear of annoying him further. She had never seen him crazier. Where was that charming funny guy she thought she could have feelings for when she had first arrived? She just hoped Ed and Tom were safely doing some routine job, and that Frank would soon realise he was on a wild goose chase. Somehow, she doubted it.

'I bet you're wondering where we're going and if you will get to see lover boy? Well there's one thing I'm certain about. You'll all be together in about half an hour from now. There's a flask under your seat, and some biscuits. You see, I've been very thoughtful, and you'll need a little nourishment for what you're about to discover about lover boy. Ed's got a lot to answer for, getting Tom involved in all this. It could get him killed if things go pear-shaped.'

Kay let him rant and rummaged around under the seat until she found the flask. Trying to keep her hands steady, she began to pour the coffee into the travel mugs.

'I'll have black with three sugars, and don't fill mine too much or I'll spill it trying to drive over this rough patch,' Frank said, sounding manic to Kay's ears.

'Could you please slow down a little while I pour the coffee, or it'll have it anywhere but in the mugs. Can't you find a less bumpy road?' Kay pleaded.

'Well for you, I'll oblige, but only while we have coffee. Don't suppose another ten minutes will change the outcome of tonight,' Frank laughed, sounding a little calmer.

Kay surreptitiously checked her gun was still in the waistband of her trousers despite feeling it digging into her waist, and then proceeded to pour the coffee and put the packet of biscuits on the dashboard, where Frank could reach them. Maybe the hot drink would calm her nerves, she thought as she rubbed her sweaty palms on her fleece. She looked at Frank and saw he was watching her.

'I can tell you're nervous,' he said. 'Nothing for you to worry about as long as you stay close to me. Being my girl will guarantee you'll be safe,' he added.

'This is beginning to sound very scary, Frank. Why would there be any danger for me if it's Ed who is meeting poachers?' she asked, wishing the nightmare was over. 'What do you intend doing if that is the case?'

'Stop asking so many damn questions and drink your coffee before it gets cold. You'll know soon enough.'

Kay wrapped her trembling hands around her coffee mug to stop them shaking. She didn't want to let Frank know how much he was frightening her. What was she going to do when they finally reached wherever they were going? She had no idea where they were, as it was way beyond any boundary that was her allocation to take guests. She would never find her way, so she knew she must bide her time until they reached Ed.

Kay was getting cold and extremely tired. She wondered what Alice had thought when Frank was so rough with her before they left.

Chapter Fifteen

Ed and Tom had made good time as they traversed across the paths leading to where they were to meet Fanalapie

'You haven't told me why you're dressed all in black,' Ed said, trying to lighten the atmosphere in the vehicle as he drove.

'I just thought as we're putting our heads on a block, the less conspicuous I am the less chance I'll be seen if the bullets start flying.'

'Sorry I made you come with me, Tom,' Ed said, guiltily. 'But, I trust you more than any of the others.'

'It's fine, I'm good,' Tom assured him.

'Fortunately, the moon is waning, so we won't be easily seen. This could be the night we find out who's behind all the big hits, too. I can't wait to uncover the bastard,' Ed fumed. 'I hope that Frank isn't involved in any of this,' he added.

'Shall I check we have plenty of ammunition?' Tom asked.

'It's a bit late for that,' Ed joked. 'Though seriously, it's fine. I've brought enough, as well as a full first aid box and plenty of water,' he said as they drove over a large bump which winded them slightly.

'Always prepared, hey boss?'

'Of course,' Ed could feel his shoulders tensing and tried to relax a little. He didn't mention to Tom that he had also hidden a sum of money well beneath the flairs they always carried in case they lost communication with the lodge during a drive.

'You ready, Ed?' Tom asked.

'Sure.'

'You never told me who we were meeting, Ed? Is it the chap we met last time?'

'The less you know the better it will be for you. Then if anyone asks, you can truthfully tell them it was just a case of being asked to accompany me because of the lodge rules saying that we have to go out in twos. It's bad enough to have you involved. I don't want the informers to see you or you to see them. They're always scared that someone will recognise them and be able to grass about them being an informer. If one of their own tribe find out they are working with us, they wouldn't live to tell the tale. If things go wrong, I'll need you to radio my contact at the Parks Board. There are a couple of guys waiting by the radio, so I can give them the go ahead when I find out who the guy is behind the organised poaching.'

'Are you worried about things turning nasty then?' Tom asked.

'Hell no, I'm just being careful. Don't want the same scenario happening as when you got shot. That's why I'm having this meeting. Fanalapie apparently knows who the perpetrator is. At last, we'll have a name.'

'How on earth did the guy get a name, Ed?'

Ed didn't hesitate to tell him. He trusted Tom and was glad to have him on his side. 'It was purely by accident that a cousin of his from the Marloth Park Reserve was approached to meet a man who said he'd pay him for tracking the rhinos so the poachers could move in and kill them. He works undercover for the Parks Board, to try and find out who's the big boss. By pretending to need work, the word gets around, and then it's a case of getting a name,' Ed explained.

'Is that why Frank was looking at your computer, do you think?'

'Yes, I do, because at the last meeting I had with the Department of Economic Affairs and Tourism, they were saying that the crime syndicates come mostly from Gauteng and Mpumalanga. Apparently, they plan to recruit an additional eighteen security personnel who'll be deployed in ten rhino reserves soon. They confirmed our discussions by email in the minutes that were taken.' Ed's fury with Frank increased. 'Frank knew about the meetings, but I kept him in the dark about what was being discussed and he was obviously pissed off.'

'So that's where Fan's cousin comes in? Just hope you get some useful info, Ed. Sounds all cloak and dagger to me,' Tom said, sounding nervous.

Ed had to slow down when the track took a sharp bend. 'Yes,' he said, speeding up again as it straightened enough for him to see a fair distance. His community resides near our wild life parks, they alert Fan's cousin, who in turn alerts the guys he works for in the Parks Board office. They then informed us, and so it goes on. The wheels that are turning now are well oiled, Tom.'

'Sounds like it,' he said. 'What's to stop his cousin from being involved with the poachers, and playing one off against the other?'

Ed had considered this scenario many times. 'It's possible, but if found guilty, he'd immediately be dismissed, ending up in jail with a criminal prosecution case brought against him. The law comes down very hard to set an example, as world exposure is such now that there's nowhere to hide. Far too many wealthy important people are involved,' Ed explained.

Had it been a bad idea to bring Tom along? Ed wondered. He felt the need to have someone with him to watch his back because he wasn't confident that his informer wouldn't double cross him. One of his best friends in the Kruger Park had been killed by the poachers, because he had been set up by his informer. Ed dare not tell Tom, as he realised his colleague was already jittery about being with him.

'I'm glad you didn't let Kay come along,' Tom said.

'I was tempted for a while, I have to admit. She's a top ranger and I know she gets upset with me when I don't treat her like you guys. There's no way I could put a woman in a dangerous situation like this, though. I couldn't stomach it if she was killed and it was my fault.'

'You mean I'm expendable?' Tom joked.

'No, but it is dangerous and who knows if I can trust the informers to keep their mouths shut,' Ed said, trying to distract Tom from his faux pas about Kay. 'Everyone knows we carry large sums of cash with us when they give us info and that we have to pay on the dot, otherwise they clam up. The only hope we have, is that we're paying the informer more than anyone else,' Ed laughed, trying not to let Tom think he was too worried.

Feeling the tension coming from Tom after his conversation, Ed thought he should have come on his own, after all. The one thing he didn't need was a guy who appeared nervous. Then he remembered that it was Tom who took a bullet the last time he got involved with poachers. Why hadn't he thought of that before setting off? Because his head was full of Kay most of his waking moments, he admonished himself. That was the reason he told her things had to cool between them. He must get this job over and done with and catch the perpetrators, so he could get on with his life with Kay. He couldn't wait to take their relationship to the next level, whatever that maybe. Tom was talking to him, so he quickly tuned in.

'I don't want to get involved, Ed. If it's okay with you. I'll stand lookout in the bakkie while you go and meet your friend.'

'Right mate, you do that,' Ed smiled.

His thoughts returned to Kay. Imagining her pretty face as she slept with her long chestnut hair fanning out over her pillow like a halo, as it had that night she stayed with him at the cottage. Was he in love with her, or was it just lust he felt? She was stunning, as well as intelligent and one of his top rangers. The guests loved her, and Ed wondered just how long he could keep her with him. It worried him that she had obviously been very hurt by that ex of hers. If only he could gauge how she really felt about him. It could be she saw him as someone to spend time with because they were stuck together in the bush. Time would tell, he told himself, hoping she felt as much for him as he did for her.

'Ed, you haven't heard a word I've said,' Tom grumbled.

'Sorry, what did you say?'

'I think I saw light up ahead, just over the ridge to our left,' Tom pointed in the direction as Ed slowed the vehicle. 'Did you see them? Could it be your chap arriving for the meeting do you think?'

'No, it wouldn't be Fan. He'd have driven without lights, because the moon would have been enough for him to see. I'll also turn off as we get closer, just in case anyone finds our meeting place. He insisted we do that which can be hairy when there's no moon. Hence me driving on side lights now.' Ed felt an adrenaline rush as they drew closer. 'We're nearly there. I wonder who'd be out this time of night? Maybe it's Kruger guys patrolling. Perhaps they've got wind of something big going down and are out in force. Could even be my friend, Paul and his security boys,' Ed suggested.

'Let's hope they are. I'd feel much happier if there were more good guys around, just in case. Have you got your handgun with you?' Tom asked. 'I didn't bring mine, but brought extra rifles instead and plenty of slugs. Watch out!' he yelled.

Ed suddenly noticed a huge bull elephant right in the middle of the road he was turning into. Tom's warning came just in time and Ed only just managed to steer his vehicle off the road, ending up in thick bush.

'Holly shit, that was a close call,' Tom said, his voice trembling in shock.

'No lie, mate, bloody animal is hard to see in this light. I could have hit him and then we'd have been in deep shit. Thank God you warned me in time.'

Reversing out of the bush, Ed felt a rush of exhilaration. Not long now and he would find out who was behind the latest rhino poaching. It must be someone who knew the area and had knowledge of how they kept track of the animals, he knew, so it must be an insider behind the whole thing.

Who could it be, and how had someone from the outside managed to infiltrate into the area to form a syndicate that was annihilating these powerful beasts? Whoever was behind these poachers, Ed thought, they had plenty of access to funds, which meant the horns were being shipped to somewhere like China. This was no little syndicate. These were big boys with guns and intent on using them if anyone got in their way. The sooner the night was over the happier he would be, Ed thought.

'We have to stop these bastards if these majestic beasts are to be saved from extinction, Ed,' Tom said needlessly. 'Thanks for including me in this meeting. I feel very strongly about our animals and the environment they live in. I admit I felt a bit apprehensive when we started out, probably because of the bullet I took before, but now I'm ready to get this show on the road. Just let me know what you need me to do.'

Ed's senses were on high alert as he turned towards the cabin hidden from view behind huge boulders and thick bush. Relief flooded him as Tom's words reverberated in his brain, knowing he had the old Tom back and not the nervous one he had been when they first set out tonight.

'How on earth did you guys find this place, Ed?' Tom asked.

'Fan uses it sometimes to stay in when he has to leave the area and travel long distances. He lives several miles away from here, so when he discovered it he set about fixing it up. Very few of us know about this place. In fact, only Frank and I have ever been here before, but since I've been meeting Fan on the quiet, Frank has probably forgotten all about it, as it's out of our concession for the lodge. We found it by a chance a couple of years ago when we were on our way to the Kruger gate at Crocodile River bridge. It's not an area we ever traverse as a rule.'

Ed thought back to Frank, hoping he'd not found the email from the Parks Board chap about their suspicions on the identity of the insider. Why was he worrying? he wondered. Just because Frank had been acting strangely of late, didn't have to mean he was involved with the poachers. It was time he got Frank alone and had it out with him. Yes, that's what he would do he decided, once tonight was over.

'Here we are, Tom, at last. Let's get on with it. You stay here and keep lookout, while I go and find Fanalapie.'

As Ed got out of the vehicle, he heard a gun being cocked, right behind him. He turned, as three men wearing balaclavas and carrying guns stepped out of the bushes. He was stunned and stared at each one in turn as they surrounded the pickup.

'Hands in the air, you two,' the tallest one ordered waving his gun at them.

'Do as they say,' Ed whispered to Tom. 'No sudden moves, or we'll be left for the buzzards.'

'No talking,' snapped the smaller of the men. He jabbed his rifle into Tom's ribs as he stepped forward onto the grass.

'That's enough of that,' Ed shouted as he watched what happened. 'Who are you guys and what do you want with us?'

'Why are you here?' the big one asked, looking at Ed. 'Are you meeting someone?'

'We're out looking for the black rhino that's on the way towards our lodge, and if you must know, I stopped for a pee. What the hell are you lot doing dressed in black and brandishing firearms at us? We're rangers and have every right to be here, which is more than I can say for you,' Ed growled, fury coursing through him. 'How did you get here? There's no sign of a vehicle, so did you walk?'

'Shut the fuck up and stop asking questions. Get inside,' the smaller man said, waving his gun in the direction of the building.

Turning to the other two, he spoke rapidly in Shangaan. Ed didn't want them to know he understood so stared at the ground. He was interested to learn that their boss would be very unhappy to find they had turned up on such an important night.

Whoever this boss man was, Ed couldn't wait to find out. He made eye contact with Tom as they entered the lantern lit room.

Once inside they were ordered to put their hands on their heads and turn to face the wall. Two of the three men were still outside and could be heard disagreeing about something, their voices getting louder. The one in charge was yelling about having let themselves be seen by the rangers and wondered if they had in fact only stopped for a pee. He fretted about being in serious trouble with their boss for blowing their cover. The small man who Ed assumed was the leader, pulled out his phone. It was obvious to Ed that he was talking to his boss, as he was blaming the other two for showing themselves and was assuring their boss it wasn't his fault. It then sounded to Ed as if he was being given orders by whoever was on the other end of the phone. He was now speaking to another person in English and walked out of the cabin to stop Ed from hearing the conversation.

'That will be the big boss,' Ed whispered to Tom.

'No talking,' shouted the taller of the two men, as the one from outside returned. He spoke to his comrades in such a low voice that Ed couldn't hear. Two of them left leaving one behind to hold the gun at them.

Then all went quiet, until the engine of the people carrier was started. Ed swung around to face the man guarding them, taking him by surprise.

'What are those bastards doing in my vehicle?' he

shouted. 'You can't take it and leave us stranded without our rifles and transport.'

'We need your wheels to get us to the village, where you can pick it up when you manage to free yourselves, which hopefully will take some time. Your rifles and a torch will be outside the door should you be able to open it,' said the large man in his broken English. 'If you run into us again, you will not live to tell the tale, so for your sakes this is goodbye. Do not move as we leave, or we will shoot. Do you understand?'

Tom turned and ran at the man as Ed tried to stop him, only to see Tom beaten with the butt of a rifle by the smaller of the two who had returned to the room. Blood gushed from a cut over Tom's eye as he collapsed on the floor.

'I warned you. Now we leave. Do not try again, or you die!' the big man shouted as he and his friend left the room slamming the door behind them and hammering bolts into place. Meanwhile the vehicle was being revved up into a frenzy, before racing away.

Ed tore off the bottom of his shirt and tied it around Tom's head, to stop the blood from getting into his eye.

'Hell, Ed, what are we going to do now? They've locked us in here and taken our transport. How the hell are we getting out?' Tom asked, wincing as Ed tied the material around his head.

'They never thought to take our phones, so guess what, this place is higher than the lodge, and if their phone worked, we should also get a signal.' Ed pulled his mobile phone out of his jacket inside pocket and held it up high to check connectivity. 'Yes,' he shouted to Tom.

There was a noise outside the door as if someone was trying to break the locks. Ed went over and put his ear close to the handle.

'Who's there? Anybody there? This is Ed Blake. Can you hear me?'

'It's me Fanalapie. I get you out soon, don't worry. I be quick.' With that there was a sound of breaking metal as the man outside cursed as he hammered. Eventually, the door swung open and Ed's informer smiled at him. 'I'm sorry, boss, I was waiting for you when these bad men were dropped off by a big four-by-four bakkie. I hid in the bushes way back in case they started to look around. I think they know this old trading store, because it had all new locks on the doors. They must meet here, so it will not be safe for us anymore.' Fanalapie looked over to where Tom stood, and asked, 'You bring him again? Again he's in trouble?'

'Don't worry, Fan, Tom knows why we're here and he's just as eager to find these bastards as we are. Now who were those men that left with my pickup? What the hell are we going to do? I'll try and call the lodge, but it'll take them at least forty minutes to get here, by which time those bastards will be long gone,' Ed said, furious at the unexpected turn of events.

'I can hear something,' Tom whispered. 'Maybe they've come back to finish us off.'

The three of them went to the cabin door to see who was approaching. Ed sprinted off to a huge cluster of boulders and shouted for Tom and Fanalapie to follow. He had no intention of being caught out by those three again. They crouched from view, waiting to find out who was approaching.

'It's time for these poachers to be taken down, Tom, before they kill or injure any more my staff. You've already been in their firing line, so we know they won't hesitate to shoot to kill. You were lucky to survive last time. We must alert all the other lodges and staff around this area as soon as we can,' he said, determined to sort this out. 'The Kruger has more manpower than us, and even they haven't been able to stop them. I was told they shot down a prize bull elephant last week for his tusks. It's got to stop, or these animals will be extinct by the time our kids have theirs.'

Ed watched, distracted as one of his vehicles from the lodge came into view. He couldn't believe his eyes when he recognised Frank, and with him, Kay. He glanced at his watch and saw that it was twelve-forty. Why would they be here? He signalled to Tom and Fan not to move or make a sound as they watched Frank and Kay leap out of the vehicle. Frank handed Kay a rifle and had his handgun at the ready. They watched silently as Frank pushed her behind him before rushing towards the cabin. Kay rushed to keep up with him. When they disappeared inside the building, Ed motioned for the others to follow him as he left their hiding place. He moved stealthily towards the cabin hearing voices as he reached the door.

'Why are we here, Frank?' Kay asked. 'You told me Ed and Tom were walking into a trap. If this is your idea of a joke, I'm not amused. I want to get back to the lodge.' Kay sounded near to tears.

'Calm down, woman. Let me think. Something's off. This is fresh blood,' Frank said crouching to touch the wet fluid before inspecting his finger.

'But it can't be anything to do with Ed, otherwise his people carrier would be here,' Kay answered. 'None of this is making any sense, Frank. Whose blood can that be?'

Ed had heard enough. He pushed open the door and strode in closely followed by Tom and Fanalapie. He watched Kay's face as she spun around and saw the three of them. Her hand went up to her mouth and her eyes widened as she stared at him. He noticed Frank's look of amazement to see him. Ed tried to recover his composure and control his thumping heart.

'Bloody hell, Ed, where's your vehicle and how in God's name did you get here?' Frank asked. 'What's he doing here?' He pointed to Fanalapie.

'What are you doing here, more to the point,' Ed asked glaring at Frank. 'That's what I'd like to know.'

'I heard there was a gang of poachers hitting on our area, both rhinos and elephants being targeted. Hell, man, what happened to you?' Frank asked noticing Tom's injuries.

'Long story, mate,' Tom replied, mopping the blood still trickling down his forehead.

'Why bring Kay into this, Frank? You knew this would be dangerous. How did you hear about all this anyway?' Ed didn't want to suspect his friend of being involved but seeing him gave him little option. 'Strange you know to come to this cabin, in my mind that can only mean one thing. You got a tip-off from one of the locals, or someone who's leaking info to the poachers. Which is it, Frank?'

'Okay, I can see how this looks, but it's a long story,' Frank assured him. 'And one we don't have time to get into right now. We need to get the hell out of here. Where are your wheels, Ed? Did you park some way off and walk? Bloody risky if you did,' Frank said without waiting for Ed to reply.

'You were right about one thing, Frank, we did walk into an ambush. They took our rifles and equipment and locked us in here. Thanks to Fan breaking the locks, we managed to get out, but Tom's losing a lot of blood,' he said glancing at Tom and seeing his head wound was still bleeding. 'We'd better get him to the hospital. Looks like he'll need stitches.'

'Do you want a lift, Fan?' Ed asked.

'No, I sleep here tonight and leave at first light. Those men won't come back tonight. They making plenty trouble for animals,' he said in his broken English.

'Okay. Be careful, my friend. Get a message to me and I'll meet you wherever you think will be safe. I reckon whoever those guys were, they've got a lot of explaining to do to the person who arranged to meet them here. They should never have blown their cover.'

'How do you know they were going to meet the big boss tonight, Ed?' Kay demanded.

'I'll fill you in on our way back. And what's more, I have a few questions of my own,' Ed replied angrily.

Ed, Tom and Kay, piled into Frank's vehicle. Ed's first thought was to get information to his friend at the Parks Board. He called in over Frank's radio and a sleepy voice answered.

'Have you got any idea what time it is? Can't a man get some shut eye around here?'

'It's Edward Blake,' he said.

'What the hell are you doing out at this time, Ed, or are you just having one of your no-can-sleep nights and want to piss someone else off,' the man laughed.

'Hi, to you too, Paul. You're not going to believe what just happened to us, but no time for that now. Just reporting that a gang of poachers have taken off with my vehicle and rifles and are heading into the Sabie area to meet more of them. They're after rhino and elephants. It's a big organised hit from what I've been told. Maybe your guys can see what they can do to find and stop them. Unfortunately, we need return to base as Tom got a smack over his head and needs medical attention. I'll get back to you once we're sorted and maybe start out again to lend a hand,' Ed explained.

'You get some sleep, Ed. We'll chat in the morning because my brain isn't in gear right now. Piss off and let me get some sleep, man,' Paul groaned.

As they drove back to camp, Ed told Kay and Frank what had happened, and why he had taken Tom along for the ride. After hearing why Frank had taken Kay with him and how he had thought Ed could be involved, Ed felt a little less angry. They all agreed to talk it all through in the morning as they were too tired to think clearly.

Chapter Sixteen

Kay was trying to stay awake to ponder on the goings on of the evening. How did she end up with this crazy bunch of men? Looking at Ed's strong profile in the moonlight, she realised there was nowhere else she would rather be. Danger or no danger.

'What are you going to do about Tom's head, Ed? He's bleeding badly, and looks like it's a very deep gash,' she said, concerned that Tom was looking very pale. 'We're too far away from the hospital, so I was wondering if I could do the honours once we get back to camp. I've done my first aid course and can close it with steri strips, Tom, if one of you can find the first aid kit?' Kay offered.

'It's all in my office,' Ed said, taking Kay's hand giving it a squeeze. 'Thanks. It'll save Tom a trip to the hospital, plus we all need to get some shut eye. Tomorrow will bring its own problems I'm sure.'

Frank drove on in silence as each of them were deep in thought. The moon was lighting the way back and the motion and hum of the engine seemed to have a calming effect on them.

Kay was worried about Tom and watched as he closed his eyes holding his head in his hands.

Ed stunned them all by swinging the huge night light over the road, as three lions crossing further along.

'Slow down, Frank,' Tom grimaced. 'We don't want to end up killing an animal. I know we all want to get back but take it easy, mate.'

Arriving back at the lodge, they went to Ed's office where he made coffee while Kay carefully sewed Tom's wound. She was relieved not to have ever been very squeamish and it was not as difficult as she had dreaded. By the time she had finished, it was after three.

Kay rubbed her tired eyes. She knew she had impressed them with how well she had coped with the dramas of the evening and stepping in to take care of Tom. She thought of Ed and how he was the most important person she was hoping to impress with her skills. He was one special man and he was beginning to take over her heart. If she wasn't careful, she would want him as a permanent fixture in her life. As her thoughts rambled on, she became aware of two pairs of eyes staring at her.

'What?' she asked, as they both smiled at each other.

'You're bloody amazing,' Frank said, going over to her and giving her a big hug.

'I was only doing my job,' she said sarcastically. 'I really do need to get some sleep now, Ed, or I won't be able to get up in the morning,' she added, stifling a yawn with the back of her hand.

'I think I know who's behind the poaching, Ed,' Frank announced.

'What did you say?' Ed's booming voice made Kay jump.

'No, this isn't the time to explain, and I may have my wires crossed,' Frank said thoughtfully. 'Let's see how tomorrow goes and see if my hunch is right.'

They all stared at Frank in astonishment.

'How can you make an announcement like that and then tell us to wait?' Ed shouted. 'For God's sake, man, tell us who you think is behind all this,' he demanded.

'Sorry I shouldn't have said anything yet, especially as I did suspect at one time that maybe it was you, my friend,' Frank said to Ed, who Kay noticed could not hide his surprise.

'Well, you're forgiven. I have to admit it had crossed my mind that it could be you, Frank,' Ed said. 'The crazy way you've been behaving of late, made me suspect you were up to no good. You and I need to have a good chat and come clean with each other – just as soon as this ring of evil is smashed.' He narrowed his eyes. 'Anyway, what the hell were you looking for in my office? And why did you tell my trackers not to tell me it was you? I don't understand.'

'Long story,' Frank said apologetically. 'I thought it would confirm my suspicions about you being involved. After all, you weren't telling me anything, but never mind that now, because I overheard a conversation that led me in an entirely different direction. That was how I knew you were being led into a trap,' Frank explained.

Ed rubbed his face and stretched. 'Right, everyone, let's call it a night. I'm knackered. We'll meet for breakfast and hear who Frank thinks is behind all this,' he announced.

Kay watched him as he rubbed his hand over his tired eyes. She wished she could kiss the look of concern from his face. What on earth made her think of kissing that mouth at a time like this, when she was almost asleep on her feet? she wondered.

'Kay? You look like you're in a trance, woman,' Tom whispered, nudging her.

She smiled at him reassuringly and tried to concentrate on what Ed was now saying.

'We've all got a long day ahead of us, as I'm sure Fanalapie will be getting a message to me. You stay here, Tom. I need someone capable in charge to run this place. There aren't any visitors booked in for a couple of days, so I'm just praying we get these poachers and finally be rid of these night missions. What do you think?' He looked at Tom. 'Why don't you get the keys for one of the guest rooms and sleep there?

'That suits me just fine, Ed. My head's really thumping now, so I'll take a couple of painkillers and get some shut eye. See you all in the morning.' Tom left the office and made his way to reception where the guest accommodation keys were hung.

'I think we should also sleep here tonight, Frank. That way we'll be on call should Paul need to contact us. Unfortunately, the signal at my cottage is terrible, plus it's on the other side of the ridge. Much quicker from here if we need to get going with little notice,' Ed said waiting for them all to leave the office before turning off the lights and following them out.

'I'll keep my radio on as well, then if they can't raise you they'll be able to make contact with me,' Frank said.

'Sure, mate, that's a good idea, but let's hope things stay quiet until daybreak,' Ed said hopefully.

'I'm going to see you safely to your room, Kay. You look about to collapse. Come on, let's get you out of here.' Ed took her by the elbow and led her away from the office.

She was relieved to be going to bed and alone with him for a few moments. Once on the path to her room, he pulled her close as she felt his hand slip around her waist. She lay her head on his shoulder as they walked to her room.

Ed waved the night porter away when he indicated that he could come with them to light the way. 'No need thanks, plenty of light,' Ed said, as he waved his free arm towards the moon.

She gave Ed her keys from her shaking hand and he opened her door. The shock of what she had experienced and her first efforts at stitching another human was beginning to kick in. Once inside the room, Ed immediately took her in his arms. Taking her face gently between his hands, he kissed her.

'Much as I would enjoy making love to you, I think you need to get some sleep.'

She could smell the bush and the smoke from the cabin on his clothes. Transfixed by his incredible lips moving as he spoke, she leant forward to kiss him. There was a loud knock on her door and they pulled apart. She watched as Ed went and opened the door. It was Frank.

'Sorry to interrupt, but while I was getting some things

out of my vehicle a call came through over my radio from your friend Paul. He wants to talk to you urgently, Ed,' said Frank, taking a step into the room. He gave Kay a brief nod. 'I'll be waiting for you outside,' Frank said as he turned leaving the room closing the door behind him.

'I'd better go and find out what that's all about,' Ed said, kissing her on the tip of her nose. 'Get some rest.'

Kay watched him go and without changing, lay on her bed and, hoping there would be no more drama during the night, fell asleep.

She seemed to have only just gone to sleep, when her alarm went off at six o'clock. Kay groaned into her pillow, remembering what had happened the night before. How was Ed? she wondered. Maybe she should go and see how Tom felt this morning. Thoughts were running through her mind as she slowly got out of bed and headed for the bathroom. The hot water of the shower helped to wake her, as it cascaded over her head while she shampooed her hair vigorously. She regretted not showering and changing into her pyjamas earlier.

Leaving her bathroom, with her towel wrapped around her body and another on her head like a turban, she went to make herself a strong cup of coffee. Everything came from the camping shop at the main lodge. The folding table she had in her room was covered with a colourful cloth depicting a guinea fowl and her mug was similar. It cheered up her room, she had decided after all other furnishings were in khaki or beiges.

She carried her coffee to the veranda, noticing an

envelope peeping from under the door. Balancing her drink, she bent to retrieve it. She couldn't remember having looked there the night before, and mail usually waited in the boxes at the entrance to the lodge.

Sitting on the veranda after taking a gulp of coffee, Kay opened the envelope, and read a card that fell onto her lap. It was from Harry. She could not understand why her ex-fiancé would be writing to her after all this time. The only thing on his card was one line written in his flowery hand as if he were painting. *I'm on my way. Please forgive me. I love you.*

With trembling hands, she turned it over to see the familiar logo, with his handsome face smiling up at her. *Harry Horncastle—Artist Extraordinaire.*

How on earth it had got to the lodge? There was no stamp or address. Just her name. Anger coursed through her. How dare he presume he could just pick up the shattered pieces of her heart and put it all back together again? She had managed to make a new life for herself away from Durban and all those humiliating memories. Kay had to admit she was curious to learn what had happened to her friend Jennifer, after she had slept with Harry. He was acting as if he still had some claim over her, which as far as she was concerned his wording on the card implied? If he thought she was about to fall into his arms, he had another thing coming.

Gulping down the remains of her coffee, Kay hurriedly got dressed and dried her hair, tying it back into a ponytail. She applied a little tinted factor fifteen moisturiser and darkened her eyelashes.

'Kay, you ready?' Alice's voice brought Kay out of her daydreaming. She rushed to open her door and found her friend looking very sullen.

'What's eating you?' Kay asked.

'I've been worried about you going off with that shitty Frank last night. I tried to stay awake to hear what happened but fell asleep. I want to hear all about it now though,' Alice said. She noticed the card lying on Kay's table. 'What's this? Handsome sod whoever he is,' Alice remarked picking up Harry's card. She read the message.

Kay didn't have to wait long for Alice to react.

'Bloody hell, Kay, lover boy is on his way. What're you going to do? Does Ed know?' She giggled and had obviously forgotten her annoyance with Frank. 'Two handsome hunks vying for your attention, and who to choose?'

'Do shut up, Alice.' Kay snatched the card out of her friend's hand and slipped it into her pocket. 'Sorry, my friend, but I'm furious with Harry for thinking he can just pitch up here. I honestly haven't decided what to do or say. I only saw the note this morning.'

Desperate to turn Alice's attention away from Harry, Kay added, 'Let's go and have breakfast. I'll fill you in on our horrendous drive and what followed last night. You're not going to believe it.'

Ed and Frank were having breakfast in the staff kitchen as the girls arrived. A very pale looking Tom followed them in. Kay noticed Ed looked stony-faced and wondered what had happened since she last spoke to him. He barely looked at her as she and Alice joined their table.

Frank was the first to speak. 'Well, Kay, tell us about your ex coming to visit then. I couldn't believe it when Ed told me just now.'

'How did you know?' Kay said glancing at Ed, her cheeks burning. 'Have you read the message he wrote? I'm so angry that he thinks he can just arrive here,' Kay fumed.

She watched Ed closely as his jaw muscles relaxed, and he started to grin at her. 'I think you'll have to miss our outing today, Kay, because your Harry is already here. That's to say he's staying at the main lodge.'

'Already?' She could not believe what she was hearing.

'He arrived late yesterday on the big boss's private jet. Apparently, he's done family portraits for him, and they were at school together. Just goes to show, there's no getting away from our past is there.' Ed patted her hand, but his eyes were unfathomable as they met hers.

'What's happening today?' she asked determined not to miss anything Ed had planned. 'I've got no intention of meeting Harry, so please count me in. Have you heard from your informer?'

'For goodness' sake, take a breath,' Frank moaned. 'Let Ed fill us in. He was just about to do it before we all got sidetracked.'

Kay sat quietly. She did not want to give Ed any more reason not to include her in the day's events.

Ed finished his coffee. 'After breakfast, Alice, I need you to stay in my office on radio contact. I received a message to say that those sods from last night are back for a big meeting with their boss who's the one organising everything. I intend being there in plenty of time to hide my vehicle and then I'll go on foot to the cabin. Fan will be waiting with a couple of his trusted locals, but we can't be careful enough. There's so much duplicity going on now that the Parks Board guys have warned me to take care. They suspect that one of the informers works for the poachers. They'll also be wondering how we got out when the doors were locked, and I don't want Fan implicated,' Ed said.

Alice cleared her throat before interrupting. 'I think you ought to have better backup, Ed. This whole poacher organisation is huge. Why don't you wait for the other lodges to send some of their rangers to help? What about helicopters like they have in other parts of Africa? Can't the Kruger Park organise something like that?'

He nodded thoughtfully. 'Yes, that's a possibility, but this has to be low key. I've been delegated to find out how this ring is worked because it was my informer who discovered what was going on, and he'll only deal with me as he trusts me because we've known each other since we were kids. Kruger is waiting to hear from me before charging in. They don't want to step in too soon and end up not catching the bastards. So, does that answer your question?' Ed winked at Kay before looking at Alice

'Yes, boss,' she smiled, pulling a face at him.

'Kay, so you're not included.' She went to argue, but he raised his hand to stop her. 'After what happened to Tom, I'm not taking any chances,' Ed said with a look that broached no argument.

Kay felt her anger rising as Ed's eyes locked with hers.

She was not about to let him see how furious she was, so lowered her eyes before they gave her away. How dare he presume to tell her she couldn't be included? Before she could argue with him, Frank started to speak.

'Ed, sorry, mate, but I've a meeting at the main lodge. If you go ahead to meet your chap, you should be fine, as you're only finding out what the poachers plans are, with a bit of luck. I'll follow on later if you intend going out of camp. You can let me know by radio if you need me. I'll ask Chef to pack us some food in case we have a long wait. You'll miss lunch as it is,' Frank added.

The receptionist came through and knocked lightly on the door.

'Yes, what is it?' Ed asked.

She glanced from Ed to Kay and then addressed Kay, saying, 'I've been asked to pass on a message to you from your ex-fiancé,' she said. 'He wants you to know that he will be coming over here shortly.'

Ed's shoulders visibly relaxed and Kay knew instantly that he was relieved that he had another reason not to take her out with him to meet his informer.

'You had better wait to see him, Kay,' Ed said, with a scowl.

'I may as well,' she snapped. 'It's not as if I have anything else you need me to do today.'

Ed glared at her and opened his mouth to argue, but as if on cue, a vehicle from the main lodge drove in to the car park in a cloud of dust. Ed peered out of the window.

'I think maybe your ex has arrived,' he said quietly.

Kay stood up and left the room. Not bothering to change out of her khaki, she went out to meet Harry. He had already got out of the car and was looking towards the dam where a huge bull elephant was rolling in the mud and showering himself with water. He was laughing as he turned to the driver and made some comment that Kay couldn't hear.

She walked towards him, her heart heavy, as Harry turned and saw her. He had lost weight but was still as handsome as ever with a smile that lit up his face and made his deep blue grey eyes crinkle at the corners, just as she remembered.

'Harry, what the hell are you doing here?' she asked, trying not to show her irritation.

His smile froze on his face and he walked towards her. Taking hold of her hand, he raised it to his lips for a kiss. He gazed deep into her eyes as if searching for something. Not finding it, he let go of her hand and stepped back.

'Is there somewhere we can talk in private, Kay?' he asked.

She looked over to where Ed, Frank and Tom had walked out of the dining room. They were watching Harry. None of the men were smiling and she could sense Harry's unease.

'You can call off your henchmen,' he sneered. 'I only want to talk to you. They're looking at me as if I'm about to abduct you, or something.' He lowered his voice. 'That tall fair-haired chap looks murderous, if you ask me,' he said in a low voice that only Kay could hear.

'Come on, I'd better introduce you.' Kay led the way to

where the three glowering men stood waiting.

'Ed, Tom, Frank, this is Harry, an old friend of mine from Durban,' Kay said as Harry followed with a hand outstretched. They all shook hands, but only Tom made an effort to be friendly, inviting Harry to join him for coffee.

Frank and Ed made their excuses and left without a backward glance. Kay followed Tom and Harry onto the veranda where the coffee and tea were ready for guests or staff to help themselves.

'Great place you have here,' Harry told Tom. 'Are you the manager?'

'I wish, mate. I'm not, Ed is. He's that big chap you just met. He's tops. Best you'll get too. A really good guy to all his staff. He wasn't pleased when he had to take on a woman though, was he, Kay?' Kay could not believe Tom was telling Harry this information. Tom gave her a wink, oblivious to her irritation with him. 'That's all changed now because Kay puts some of the guys to shame, and the guests love her. She's one of our top rangers. Did you know that?'

Kay saw Harry's look of amazement as Tom spoke.

'Hell no, I only ever knew Kay as a brilliant artist and teacher,' Harry said, as Tom poured the three of them coffees. 'That's how we met, through art. Your grandmother did tell me you were a ranger,' he said addressing her. 'But I just thought she'd got her story muddled. That's why I'm here actually, Kay, to get you back to Durban where you belong.'

'What?' Kay said, stunned by his cheek.

'Your grandmother gave me strict instructions not to

return without you,' Harry said.

Kay looked from one to the other of the men, realising by the look on Tom's face that he felt a little in the way. How dare Harry imply that her place was in Durban? Feeling her irritation mounting, she turned to him.

'When we've finished coffee, I think you and I should maybe move to Ed's office and have a good talk, Harry. If you'll excuse us, Tom?' she added, closing her eyes briefly.

'Sure thing, Kay, I have to go and collect a vehicle from the main lodge anyway. Nice to have met you, Harry. Will you be staying long?'

'That all depends on Kay,' Harry replied, as he followed her out.

Once in Ed's office, Kay quickly closed the door and turned to Harry. He started to speak before she could utter a word.

'Kay, I've come all this way because I hate the way we ended our engagement. I wanted to be face-to-face with you when I told you what a bloody idiot I've been. I was mortified about the way I let you down. Let us both down, in fact. It really was a one-night stand, but I know now that was no excuse and I'll have to live with what I did for the rest of my life. I don't expect you to take me back,' he said miserably. 'Can you please forgive me though? I'd like us to still be friends, if possible. I still love you and wish you'd come home to Durban with me.'

Kay couldn't believe his arrogance expecting her to pack up and leave with him simply because he asked. 'You can't seriously think I'll go with you, surely?'

'Your grandmother misses you, and I know she blames me for your sudden departure to the wilds,' he said. 'She worries about you living in the bush, and maybe catching malaria or getting hurt by an animal. She told me to bring you home.'

Kay could see he was determined to try everything to get her to go with him. She had never seen Harry looking so wretched or crushed.

'Don't look at me like that,' he pleaded. 'You and I can still find our way back to what we shared, Kay. I know you still love me. Don't you?'

Kay felt a stillness surround her, and all the hurt and upset she had been harbouring, seemed to melt away. Having Harry stand there declaring that he still loved her was just what she had fanaticised and prayed would happen all those weeks ago. Now that it had, was it really what she wanted any more? She had a strange feeling of being set free. Knowing her heart had been broken into a thousand pieces, to having it back together in the blink of an eye. What is happening? she thought. She had rehearsed what she would do if ever the chance came that Harry would apologise and ask her forgiveness. She had always thought they could make it work, just as he said.

'Darling, please look at me. You do still love me I know,' he said. 'Say you forgive me. Please,' Harry begged.

She wanted to leap for joy but couldn't imagine why. The dynamics had changed since spending time at Impangela Muzi and working with the incredible people at both lodges. Then there were her feelings for Ed. She pushed them to the back of her mind as she turned to Harry.

'Yes, Harry, I do still love you, but I can't rekindle what we once shared. Maybe it was a blessing in disguise that you slept with my best friend, because if it has taught me anything, it has been about myself. You see, I've changed so much since getting this opportunity to work as a ranger. The whole training experience has motivated me to be the best I can be.' She realised she was enjoying spelling everything out to him after all this time. 'Art is something I found easy and I just fell into teaching as you well know. I've now met dedicated people who put their lives on the line to protect the wildlife. I can't go back to Durban and a life of socialising and trying to impress others.' As she spoke it dawned on her how much she loved this new way of life.

'I don't think you realise what you're saying, Kay,' he argued, moving to take hold of her arms. Kay stepped back, and Harry's arms fell to his sides. 'I'm asking you to marry me. I've bought us a house on the Berea.' He smiled. 'It has the sea views you've always wanted. It's everything we've ever dreamt of. It even has a huge outside room that we can use as our studio. We can teach from home.' Harry pulled Kay into his arms, and before she knew what was happening he was kissing her as he held her tightly against him. To her horror she heard the office door open.

'Sorry to interrupt. I had no idea my office was being used for this happy reunion,' Ed fumed as he gave them a look of rage. Going to his desk he picked up some papers and stormed out, slamming the door behind him.

Kay pushed Harry away with force. She could feel her

cheeks burning in humiliation that Ed had walked in on such a scene. Looking at Harry and saw him looking smug.

'How dare you come here and expect me to fall into your arms, Harry Horncastle,' she fumed. 'I know exactly what you're saying and exactly what you expected, but let me tell you this, I'll never marry you. I thought I knew what love was when I agreed to marry you, and I'll probably always have those feeling for what we once meant to each other.' She pictured Ed's handsome face. 'I now know that I wasn't in love with you. You're a good person and easy to love but being in love and loving someone are two different things. Fortunately, I now know the difference.' She smiled happily. 'I'm sorry you came all this way to hear that, but it's the truth.'

'Kay, you can't mean that,' he said, his face crumbling. 'You'll never find another guy like me who loves you the way I do.'

'I already have, Harry.' Kay took a deep breath.

'Has it got something to do with that big guy who just stormed out of here? I saw the possessive way he looked at you. If looks could kill, I'd be a goner.' Harry studied her face for a few seconds, anger hardening his eyes. 'Son of a bitch has got his hooks into you, hasn't he? I knew something had changed when there was no response to my kiss. Well, if you can fall for someone like that I guess you're not the same girl I wanted to marry. You've changed from a sweet girl into someone I hardly recognise,' he said spitefully. 'This place has done you no favours, Kay.'

Kay recalled a time when Harry's nasty temper would

have devastated her, but this time she felt nothing at all. 'I'm sorry, Harry, I had no intention of hurting you, but your visit was unexpected and one I was ill prepared for. We have so much going on here now, and you appeared out of the blue. My grandmother had no right to encourage you to visit and I have no intention of returning to Durban other than to visit her.' She smoothed down her top. 'I suggest you get one of the rangers from the main camp to show you around while you're here, but as far as I'm concerned there is no "we" any more. I got used to that when you cheated on me.'

She walked to the door, opened it and waited for Harry to walk out of the office. 'I think your driver is still waiting, Harry, so I'll say goodbye. Give my love to my grandmother when you report back to her,' Kay said.

He marched out of the office and outside the building. Kay watched to make sure he went straight to the driver still waiting at the entrance. She saw Harry turn around as he got into the vehicle and wave. Kay waved back, relieved to see him leave.

Kay was trembling with the shock of seeing Harry again after all that time, but worse still was the image in her mind of Ed walking into the office when she was in Harry's arms. He had looked thunderous as he stormed out.

'No, no, no,' she said, sitting down in Ed's chair with her head in her hands. She jumped up, when the office door was flung open, relieved when Alice bounded in.

'Who was that gorgeous guy who just left, Kay? Kay, what's wrong?'

Kay sat down again tears welling up as Alice perched on the edge of Ed's desk.

'I've lost him, Alice,' Kay let the tears fall as her friend leapt off the desk and enveloped her in a bear like hug.

'Kay, I'm so sorry, and him so bloody handsome too. Shall I go after him and bring him back for you? The driver told me he had an important guest from the main lodge he had brought over to see you. Was that Harry?' Alice stared at her open-mouthed. 'Oh my God I don't believe that cool guy was your Harry?' Alice sounded amazed.

Kay couldn't help but be amused by Alice's ramblings. Drying her tears, she managed to smile at her friend.

'No, Alice, you've got it all wrong. I don't care about Harry any more. It's Ed I've lost. Harry did come all this way to tell me he's sorry for everything, which was nice, but he wanted a second chance. He asked me to marry him again. As if I'd be so stupid,' Kay sighed.

Kay told Alice how Ed had walked into the office and thought she and Harry were reconciled. 'I could have died of embarrassment. Honestly, Alice, I'll never forget the look on Ed's face when he stormed out and slammed the door. There's no way he'll believe I was taken by surprise at what Harry did. It was so sudden and unexpected. What shall I do?'

Alice looked puzzled. 'I wish I knew what to say to make you feel better, Kay, but Ed's such a proud guy, he'll not take kindly to seeing you in your ex-fiancé's arms, that's for sure. Let him calm down before you try to explain, or it could make matters worse. Anyway, he'll not be back until much later, so it gives you time to think how best to explain everything.'

'I do hope you're right, Alice,' Kay said miserably. 'I feel terrible. Even my wonderful grandmother is miffed with me because she seems to be behind Harry coming here to take me back. Maybe I should just go back to Durban and my old way of life. If Ed won't listen to me and I've lost him, then that's what I'll do. Not that I'd ever go back to Harry,' she added quickly before Alice misunderstood. 'I now realise the love we shared was incomparable to what I feel for Ed. Even if he doesn't reciprocate my feelings, I still can't settle for less.'

'For goodness' sake Kay, are you listening to yourself? I've seen you and Ed together and I have to admit that the way he looks at you makes me very jealous. Sally and I had our eye on him long before you came on the scene.'

Kay could not believe what Alice was telling her. 'Seriously?'

'Yes. If I hadn't liked you so much, I'd have hated you. Sally and I were having a competition to see who could get him first. Hell, he didn't even notice we fancied him,' Alice said grinning.

'I didn't realise,' Kay exclaimed.

'Good,' Alice smiled. 'Now it's up to you to find that boss of ours when he gets back and tell him how you feel about him before you lose your nerve. Can't say I envy you though, he's got a hot temper when crossed and won't be a pushover. You may well get a flea in your ear before you have time to explain,' Alice laughed.

'Very funny, not,' Kay said, grateful to her friend for trying to help her sort out her mess.

There was a sound coming from the radio and Alice tilted her head to hear.

'Hold on, Kay, that sounds like the boss on the radio.'

Kay felt a quiver of worry as she waited to hear what was being said. She moved closer to the radio to listen as Alice picked up the speaker and heard Tom's voice.

'Hi, Alice, can you hear me clearly?'

Kay's heart pounded willing Tom not to give them any bad news.

'Come in, Tom,' Alice said. 'Hearing you clearly.'

'Ed wants you to get hold of Frank and ask him to pack extra ammo just in case things get out of hand. He's heading to the other side of the ridge to pick up his tracker and then for some rendezvous Frank knows about. He wants them all to be prepared and doesn't want to be taken by surprise. Oh and, Alice, the dart gun as well. May need to tranquilise, or euthanise if we find one of the rhino they've butchered. You got all that?'

'Sure thing, Tom, I'll get on to it right away. Over and out.' Alice stared thoughtfully at Kay. 'That sounds very ominous. They must have had a tip-off to want more ammo. Sounds serious this time.'

'If you're busy I can go and give Frank Tom's message before he leaves,' Kay said, wanting to do something to help.

'That would be great.'

Kay tucked a stray strand of hair behind her right ear. 'I thought it was strange the way Ed was rushing around and eager to leave so early,' Kay said. 'He certainly means to be prepared. The strange thing is, he didn't know all this before he left, or he'd have taken the extras with them. Do you think he's already met his informer, Alice?'

'Sounds like it. Look, I still have these letters to finish. Thanks for the offer. I'd be grateful if you could get hold of Frank and tell him all that. If you're not too busy, that is?'

'No, I'll be glad to do it for you. It'll take my mind off my own worries. See you later,' Kay said as she left the office.

Frank was driving in as Kay reached the garages. He stopped when he saw her rushing towards his vehicle.

'Hi, you looking for me?' he yelled above the noise of the engine, seeing her waving at him.

She was thankful that he turned the engine off to hear her reply. She gave him the message and was surprised by Frank's reaction. There was something not quite gelling with her about the way he seemed so nonplussed about the whole thing.

'Now why are you bothering your head about things that don't concern you?' he asked. 'Ed told you clearly enough that he didn't want you involved with all this.'

'I came to find you to help Alice. The poor girl has loads of office work to catch up on,' Kay said, irritated with his condescending attitude towards her. 'I don't have any guests to look after today, so could come with you if you're going to follow Ed and whoever else he's with?' she suggested trying her best not to sound as if she was pleading with him.

'If you insist,' he said giving in far more easily than she had anticipated. 'I'll get sorted while you organise Chef with some food and drinks. Deal?'

'Absolutely, Frank,' Kay replied, delighted to be going with him.

'I need to make a couple of phone calls first and then I'll meet you back here in an hour. See you then.'

Kay watched as Frank hurried towards the lodge bar and wondered why he wasn't using the phone in the office. Her thoughts turned to the jobs at hand, just as the shrill call from a fish eagle filled the air. She smiled as she looked to the sky and watched the bird circling over the dam. She loved this place, far more than she could have ever explained to Harry.

Kay arrived at the vehicle first, closely followed by the porters helping her carry the full picnic hampers. Another man brought along a rifle and a box of ammunition, as well as another heavy looking bag which Kay knew contained the vet supplies Ed had ordered.

'Have you got your gun with you, Kay?' Frank asked when he joined her.

'Yes, I've put my rifle in your bakkie. I asked Chef to pack us some sandwiches and water, as it looks like we'll miss lunch. It's such a long drive to the cabin, if that's where we're heading?'

Kay watched as Frank loaded the extra things into the metal box at the back of his vehicle with the help of the staff. He looked troubled, she thought. He must know something he wasn't telling her. She decided to keep her ears and eyes open and her wits about her. She suddenly realised Frank wasn't taking his tracker with them but didn't like to annoy him by asking why.

'I still don't like the fact that you're coming with me. You could get hurt. To tell the truth, I'd never forgive myself if anything bad happened to you,' Frank said in a worried tone. 'Jump in if you're coming, and don't blame me for any mishaps.'

They were about to leave when a vehicle sped into the parking area. Frank gasped when Ed jumped out and, with his long stride, ran to speak to them.

'Where's lover boy?' Ed asked looking at Kay with eyes like cold granite.

'Not now, mate, leave that until later. Suffice to say he's no longer around, as beautiful here, sent him packing with his tail between his legs,' Frank laughed.

'Er, thank you,' said an indignant Kay. 'I am here, you know.'

'What are you doing back anyway?' Frank asked. 'We're just about to set off to join you.'

'Things have changed.' He stared at Kay. 'You are not coming with us. I told you plainly enough earlier that it's much too dangerous and I don't want you involved. Stay here and help Tom and Alice. There's plenty to occupy you.' Before Kay could argue, he turned away. 'I'm just getting something from my office, Frank, and then we can go.'

Kay felt humiliated. How dare he talk to her as if she wasn't capable of looking after herself? She was as qualified as any man. 'I'm coming with you, Frank,' she insisted. 'You said I could, I've had the same level of training as any of you guys. Please have a word with that chauvinistic boss of ours. Tell him you think I should be with you?'

'Shit, woman, you know what he's like when he makes

up his mind. He's the boss for goodness' sake.'

Not ready to give up, she gave him a pleading look. 'Please, Frank. Don't you think you owe me after all the crap you've put me through since I arrived?'

He scowled at her. 'I'm already skating on thin ice where he's concerned. Shush, here he comes. Leave this to me. Try not to look so murderous for heaven's sake, or anything I say will fall on deaf ears,' Frank whispered so that Ed couldn't hear as he joined them.

'Kay, I thought I told you to stay here?' Ed growled.

'Listen, mate, I'd said she could come with me and she's all prepared with guns, darting equipment, etc. just in case we find that injured animal they radioed us about. She won't get in your way, if that's what you're worried about,' Frank argued. 'Come on, Ed, we're wasting time. I'll dump her in the river if she gives us any trouble,' Frank said, as he gave Kay a wink.

'I don't have time to argue now, but if we run into any sort of trouble, I want you to keep out of the way. Do you understand me?' Ed glared at her as she lowered her eyes to hide her triumphant look.

They were interrupted by the biggest man Kay had ever seen arriving on a motorbike. Parking it under cover, he walked towards them.

'Here's my tracker,' Frank said, leaving to greet the huge man.

'Ed, this is Bear. Bear meet the boss of this lodge Edward Blake, and another ranger Kay Anderson. Don't underestimate her, she's as good as, if not better than the guys.'

'I'm delighted to make your acquaintance, Mr Blake and Miss Anderson. Please call me Bear,' he said in a public-school voice. 'I earned the nickname when I was playing rugby, and it stuck.' He shook hands with them both.

Kay watched Frank looking on in amusement at their shocked expressions.

'Well, Bear, I'm surprised Frank has brought you on board. He had better explain to me when we're on our way why your presence is needed instead of one of my own trackers,' Ed said turning to Frank and lowering his voice. 'Where the hell did you find him? He's not one of my staff.'

'I use him sometimes when I go out alone hunting the poachers. Don't worry, Ed, he's reliable and has a good eye. We were at college together, and he saved my butt a few times over the years. He's just returned from playing rugby overseas. I reckon we could do with his expertise. He knows the bush like the back of his hand. He's also been instrumental in raising money to save the rhino, while he's been travelling. Let's get moving,' Frank said as he motioned for the tracker to get onto the back seat.

He and Ed jumped into the front and Kay sat directly behind them. They set off in a cloud of dust with Frank at the wheel.

Why, she wondered, did she have an uneasy feeling in the pit of her stomach? Maybe it was the new tracker who she had not set eyes on before that afternoon, or it could just be the way Frank had looked at her when she arrived. She couldn't quite put her finger on it, but something was very amiss.

As they drove, Ed explained why he had returned to get backup. He then told them about the letter delivered to him by one of the Parks Board trackers who was often the go-between Paul and himself when they were unable to meet. They never discussed the poachers or their meetings over the radio, but he told them they had devised a code that when an urgent message had to get to Ed, he would know where to meet Paul's tracker. Which, Ed added, was why he had left in such a hurry earlier.

Kay listened and learned that the letter from Kruger was quite specific, telling Ed not to get too close as this was the gang that had been killing the rhinos in the park. It sounded like they were a very sophisticated group and well-armed. She knew that it was going to take them at least an hour to reach the area where they were last seen. Ed added that they planned to meet up with the men he had sent out earlier.

Ed turned to look at Kay, as his hand slid over the one she had holding on to the back of his seat.

'The only reason I've agreed to have you along today, Kay, is because we need another pair of eyes. I don't want you to think I'm not aware of your expertise as a ranger, but I'd never forgive myself if any harm came to you.'

She felt a shock as his hand gripped hers and was thrilled to see his eyes were no longer hard and cold as he looked over his shoulder at her, but back to their warmer grey. She began to hope that she had got him back after the awful debacle with Harry earlier. Ed gave her a wink as he turned back to Frank.

Ed looked over at Bear then at Kay, giving her a puzzled

look, which worried her a little. He obviously wasn't happy having a stranger tracker taking the helm.

Frank changed direction by swerving onto a little track. It was very rough terrain with thorn trees and shrubs brushing against the sides of the vehicle as it bumped from side to side as Frank tried to miss large boulders.

'What the hell are you doing, man?' Ed shouted. 'Where do you think you're going? This will lead us right into the path of the poachers, and we're supposed to be coming at them from the opposite direction. They'll hear us long before we get there at this rate.' Frank didn't slow down. Kay held her breath as Ed shouted, 'Frank, stop for God's sake, before you get us all killed.'

Kay had to hang onto the bar in front of her seat. She was being thrown from side.

'Shut the fuck up, Ed, you're not the boss any more. I am. Bear,' Frank shouted at the tracker.

Kay barely had time to think before the tracker swung his huge body around to point his rifle at Ed. Kay screamed before she could stop herself. Frank's arm swung with fury as the back of his hand connected with her face and knocked her sideways. Ed leant over to help her up.

'If either of you do anything stupid like that again, you won't live to see what I have in store for you both,' Frank sneered. 'Keep watching them, Bear. Shoot if I give you the command.'

'Frank, have you completely lost it?' Ed snapped. 'Is this a prank? If so it isn't funny. Get that bugger to put his rifle away before he shoots someone.'

'You're so full of your own importance, and looking down on the likes of me,' Frank screamed. 'Taking my girl from right under my nose with all your fancy talk. Well this is payback time and I'm having the girl, and you can have the pleasure of watching me before you both die.'

'Are you insane?' Ed bellowed 'You won't get away with this, Frank. Everyone at camp knows we all left together. How are you going to explain our disappearance to them?' Ed asked, reaching and taking Kay's shaking hand in his.

'Yes, please make the most of being lovey dovey, while you can, you patronising prick.' Frank shouted above the noise of the engine as he raced along the track.

Suddenly Bear shouted something Kay couldn't hear. They swung around a bend on a blind rise. There, in the middle of the road, stood a big male buffalo, who was so surprised to see them, and had such a fright, that before anyone knew what was happening, he charged straight for the tracker, who had jumped down from his seat and was running to Frank's side of the vehicle to get in. Frank stopped with a screech of brakes and jumped out to ward off the buffalo. He raised his rifle and fired, wounding the animal who was now moving too fast for Frank to reload.

Meanwhile, Ed saw his opportunity, and jumping into Frank's seat, started the engine and swung the vehicle sharply to the right, making the tracker lose his footing, but managing to hold on to the bar with his enormous hands.

Kay, seeing him still there, got her gun and started to beat at his hands until he bellowed and let go, falling face down into the veldt. She looked for Frank and saw that the buffalo had gored him in his abdomen and Bear was making a run for it.

She screamed when the buffalo noticed Bear and began to give chase, catching up with him when the tracker tripped over a small boulder. Kay watched in horror as the animal dug his horns into Bear and tossed him into the air, like a rag doll. The animal snorted, attacking him again as Bear hit the ground, pummelling with his head until the man lay still. Only then did the animal seem satisfied and slowly wander off over the hill and out of sight.

Ed had moved them far enough away, so they could watch until they were certain the buffalo had disappeared. Then Ed drove over to where Frank lay moaning on the ground. Blood poured out of the gaping hole in his stomach.

'Frank, can you hear me?' Ed shouted, stepping down from the four-by-four. 'I'm going to try and get you in the vehicle and take you to a doctor.' Kay helped as Ed carefully placed Frank into a sitting position.

'Kay, can you pick up his feet?' Ed asked, as he heaved an unconscious Frank up. 'Let's get him in before he comes around again.'

'Sure,' Kay said as she picked up the limp man's feet.

Between them they got Frank into the seat and covered him with a blanket.

'Keep an eye on him,' Ed said. 'I'm just going to see if Bear is still alive.'

Just as Ed was about to walk towards the still form of the tracker, a pride of young male lions appeared over the hill. The tracker moved and screamed in agony. Ed ran back and jumped into the vehicle, slamming the door and starting the engine.

'This is a bloody nightmare, I've got to save the poor sod before they spot him,' Ed said to Kay, slowly turning the vehicle to drive closer to Bear.

'I'm afraid you're too late,' Kay winced. 'They've seen him. Oh no, they're going for him,' she cried covering her eyes, as bile rose into her throat at the hideous sight.

Ed drove slowly forward until the vehicle stood between the injured man and the young lions. He raised his rifle into the air and let off a couple of rounds. Kay watched in relief as the startled animals turned and ran into the bush.

'Can you hear me, Bear?' Ed asked, leaning over as the injured man let out a groan.

Kay realised Frank was too silent and felt his wrist for a pulse. She found a very weak one. Her mind was racing; she tried to fathom what had just happened. In the space of no time, they had two men close to death.

'Kay, give me a hand, will you?' Ed shouted. 'I can't leave this guy for the buzzards and he weighs a ton.'

She watched Ed trying to heave the huge man off the ground. Much to her surprise Bear began to sit up and, hanging onto Ed's arm, managed to sit up. She jumped off the vehicle and rushed to help. Between them Bear managed to pull himself up and put his arms across both Ed and Kay's shoulders. She buckled under his weight but held on as they slowly walked him to the vehicle. Finding strength from somewhere, Bear pulled himself up and onto a front seat. Blood was pooling on the floor by his feet.

'Here's my scarf, Ed,' Kay said as she passed the long piece of material to Ed. 'We need to stop the bleeding, or he'll die,' she added, unsure how they were supposed to do such a thing when Bear's stomach and back seemed riddled with holes from the buffalo's long horns.

She and Ed wound the material tightly around his gaping wounds, as Bear lost consciousness and fell against the door.

Ed got into the driving seat and started the engine. 'Let's get the hell out of here before we have a death on our hands. Can you see how Frank's doing? We're not far from the cabin now, thanks to Frank taking that awful short cut,' Ed said, his voice weary. 'I still can't make out what got into him to turn on us like that.'

Tears filled her eyes as she looked at Frank's ashen face and wondered what could have happened to make him this evil. She was so preoccupied with Frank that she hadn't realised they had changed course and were now slowing down as the cabin came into view. She looked at Ed as he turned to see how she was coping.

'Well done, keep it up. We've got to save him. God knows what he's managed to get himself into, but I think we're about to find out. How the hell did they get here?' Ed said in a startled voice that made Kay look to see who he was looking at. Ed drew up outside the cabin.

Kay couldn't believe her eyes. There was Sally, grim-faced as she stood next to a tall good-looking man, both in handcuffs. Next to them were three Parks Board guys in uniform holding rifles at Sally and the man. Fanalapie walked out of the cabin, and spotting Ed, ran over to the vehicle.

'Boss, they said you were dead. I am so happy to see you and Miss Kay. This is one terrible day,' he said shaking his head.

Ed got out of the vehicle and placed his hand on Fanalapie's left shoulder. 'It's okay, Fan, calm down,' he said walking over to the men holding Sally and her friend hostage. 'What the hell's going on here, and why are you pointing rifles at these two, Paul?' Ed asked.

'This chap, my friend, is the American behind the poachers,' Paul said. 'We got a tip-off from Fanalapie. His cousin told him they were meeting here to pay everyone off as things were too hot for them at the moment. Everyone was then supposed to lay low until things cooled down a bit,' Paul added.

Kay jumped out of the vehicle and ran over to Sally, wondering how she could have been persuaded to become involved in the operation. Sally glared at her and then looked down, deliberately avoiding Kay's questioning look.

'Sally, please tell me what's going on,' Kay asked. 'Is he the American you told Alice and me about?' Before Sally could answer, Ed interrupted.

'Never mind that now, you guys. I've got Frank here and another chap who's probably going to die if we don't get them some urgent medical attention.

'Frank?' Sally screamed, rushed over and climbing into Ed's vehicle. She took one look at the state Frank was in and burst into tears, screaming for someone to help him.

Kay couldn't believe what she was witnessing. Sally became hysterical, screaming at the astonished men who quickly rushed over to help Frank.

Two men managed to lift the unconscious Bear out of the front seat and lay him on the grass, just as another land cruiser arrived with four rangers, who jumped out with guns at the ready.

'It's all my fault,' Sally cried. 'I got Frank involved. I'll never forgive myself if he dies, Ed,' Sally cried, tears coursing down her ashen face.

'What the hell do you mean?' Ed asked, helping Sally down from the vehicle to give the men room to attend to Frank.

'Ed, I've called in a helicopter to get these guys airlifted to hospital asap,' Paul shouted.

'Thanks, mate,' Ed gave Paul a thumbs up. Then he looked to those trying to lift Bear and Frank towards to cabin. 'Be careful how you move them, they've been badly hurt,' he said.

'Sure thing, Ed,' they replied in unison.

Kay walked over to where Ed was talking to Sally. She could not understand how her friend got involved with the poachers. As she joined them she noticed a look of defiance return to Sally's face as she glared at Ed.

'It's all right for you, Ed Blake. You're the big boss man around here and we're all the minions. Frank was very useful to us because he had access to your computer and until lately, you told him what was going on and how and when the Parks Board guys were infiltrating into the area to trap the poachers.'

Kay could not believe what she was hearing and by the

look on Ed's face, she realised he was equally as stunned.

'Ron, my American friend, is the one funding the organisation along with some other guy I don't know. Frank just helped us. Of course, you hadn't noticed that he'd begun using again.'

'What? Drugs?' Kay asked.

'Yes, drugs,' Sally spat. 'He needed the money. He was also very pissed off with you, Ed,' she said pushing Ed's shoulder, 'when missy here took a fancy to you.'

Kay had never seen such venom coming from someone, but after what Alice had told her earlier about her and Sally having feelings for Ed, she suspected this was why Sally's antagonism towards him was so filled with spite.

Sally sniffed and continued her rant. 'It was the last straw for Frank. Until then he tried hard not to get involved. Once you rejected him, Kay, he just seemed to give up on being the good guy. Mind you he was taking strain of late and the drugs were making him increasingly morose.' Sally's explanations were interrupted by the arrival of the helicopter landing in the clearing nearby.

Kay gave a sigh of relief as she watched Ed and Paul run over to where Bear and Frank had been laid down on blankets. The doctor and his assistant jumped out of the helicopter and ran towards them with stretchers. Sally and Kay joined them. With all the men helping, they managed to lift Bear.

Just as they lifted Frank onto the stretcher, he grabbed hold of Ed's arm, and pulled him closer, whispering, 'I'm a bloody idiot, mate, to get involved with this lot. Truth is, I needed the money.' He winced in pain as it momentarily took his breath away. 'I'd never have hurt you or Kay.'

Kay doubted him very much. Only an hour or so before he had threatened to kill them both.

'Take it easy,' Ed said. 'There'll be time for talking when you've been checked out at the hospital.'

'I'm so sorry. I let you down when you've been like a brother to me,' he gave a sob and passed out.

Kay looked at Ed and felt a pang of sadness. He looked shell-shocked by what his friend had done to them. She stood open-mouthed as he immediately recovered his composure and took charge of the situation, shouting orders to everyone present.

'Right, I'm heading back to camp with Kay now. What's going to happen to these two?' Ed asked, pointing to Sally and the American who hadn't uttered a word since they had arrived.

'We'll look after them, Ed,' Paul assured him. 'They'll both be delivered to the police at Hazy View. I'll let you know what happens to them afterwards.'

Kay and Ed watched as the two were led away. They waited until all the vehicles were out of sight before Ed pulled Kay into his arms in a hug that left her breathless.

'If anything had happened to you, I don't know how I'd have coped,' he murmured into her hair. 'Let's go get Fanalapie and lock up the cabin.'

Kay had completely forgotten Fanalapie until Ed mentioned his name. 'Where is he? I can't see him?'

'I asked him to take a rifle and keep a lookout for any

predators coming our way. He's on top of the ridge and would have fired a shot off if we needed to be warned of danger. He has excellent vision from there. Mind you with all the noise we've been making I doubt any animal would risk coming this way. That helicopter would have sent them off in different directions for starters,' he said giving a weary laugh.

'Can I do anything to help?' Kay asked as Ed walked towards the cabin having called to Fanalapie.

'No, I want you to take the rifles and get into the vehicle while I lock this place up. Then we'll head back. I'll drop Fanalapie off at his village on the way.'

Kay noticed the look of strain on Ed's face as he turned towards the cabin, and her thoughts turned to Frank. Would he have acted differently if she had not turned him down? she wondered. Or was that just an excuse? She hated to think that she could have been the cause behind any of this nightmare. Her thoughts were interrupted by Ed returning with the bike. She watched as he tied it onto the back of the vehicle before he and Fanalapie got in.

They were talking in a dialect she didn't understand, but gathered it was about the gang of poachers and the bad man behind the organisation.

They dropped Fan off at a nearby village and motored back to camp in silence, both exhausted and lost in their own thoughts. Occasionally Kay sensed Ed look at her, and then felt his hand resting on her leg as if to check she was still there. She felt totally traumatised by the events of the day and suspected he did too.

Chapter Seventeen

Only when they reached the lodge did Ed speak to her as he parked his people carrier under the carport.

'I don't think we should tell everyone about Frank's drug problem, Kay,' he said quietly. 'It'll be sufficient to say that he was injured and has been airlifted to hospital along with his friend from university.'

'Of course,' she agreed, happy not to have to try and explain anything that had happened to the others. She watched Tom and Alice rushing towards them as she and Ed collected their things.

'Bloody hell, Ed, we've been listening to the radio at the news. The big man behind the poaching syndicate has been arrested with none other that our Sally,' Tom shouted. 'Can you imagine prissy Sally being an accomplice to all this? Is it true?' Ed nodded. 'And what about two members of staff being taken to hospital?' he asked helping Ed unload the vehicle.

'For goodness' sake, you two,' Alice said, glancing from Ed to Kay questioningly, 'tell us what's going on before I pop with curiosity.'

Kay watched as Ed rubbed his temples and noticed how stressed he looked. He had dark rings around his eyes when he took off his sunglasses and pinched the top of his nose as if to relieve a headache. He turned and saw her staring at him and gave her a wink before addressing Tom and Alice.

'I'm ravenous, as I'm sure Kay is too. Let's sort our stuff out and get cleaned up before we tell you what happened. How about we meet on the veranda in half an hour and you can hear all the gory details?' Ed said, before retrieving more of his things from the vehicle.

Half an hour later, showered and feeling much calmer, Kay was delighted to join the others and find that they had organised for a buffet to be served in the shadow of the huge marula tree in the front garden. As she approached, her spirits lifted, and she heard Ed telling Alice that both Frank and Bear would make a full recovery but that it would take time.

He told them all that Frank had spoken to him before going in for surgery. 'He seems very remorseful,' Ed explained as Kay sat down next to him in the free seat.

'I should think so,' Alice mumbled.

'By the way,' Ed added. 'Paul got hold of me to say that Sally and her American friend are behind bars and awaiting trial,' Ed shook his head. Kay could see that he was having as much difficulty as her to come to terms with what Sally had done. 'It seems they'll be moved to a court in Pretoria. They've confessed to having dealings with another three accomplices who are being arrested as we speak. The

American refused to speak until his lawyer arrived from the States. Nasty business,' Ed added.

'I really didn't expect it of Frank,' Alice said miserably. 'He was always such a charmer with the ladies. Despite him being rough with me the other night, it makes me sad to think he's messed his life up so badly.'

'I feel much better knowing the main perpetrators are being rounded up,' Tom said. 'I know he could be a bit annoying,' Tom said, 'but I will miss having Frank around. He was a good friend to me.'

The rest of the afternoon passed quickly for Kay. Just before they left to go their own ways, Ed pulled her aside and whispered that he wanted to meet her back at the marula tree for a sundowner before dinner.

She was feeling a little apprehensive as she made her way to her room. Why had he sounded so serious? Maybe she should have made the decision to return to Durban and her darling grandmother, and this could be the opportunity she had been waiting for to break the news to Ed. It would probably save him having to ask her to leave, she decided, aware that it was her insistence on accompanying Frank that had caused Ed to fret about her.

He was never happy to have a woman ranger in the first place and obviously worried needlessly about her, despite her proving her worth repeatedly. Kay couldn't bear to think that some of the stress Ed was under was directly linked to her. Remembering how he had looked at her when they first arrived back at the camp earlier that day, it didn't surprise her that he would no longer want her around. She was in love with him but if nothing else, she would always be grateful that she experienced being made love to by Ed in the way she had never known before.

'Kay, wait for me,' she heard Alice yelling. She stopped and looked over to her friend. 'Bloody hell, you take such long strides I battled to catch up with you,' Alice moaned, as she reached Kay panting for breath.

'Sorry, I was miles away. It's been such a roller coaster of a week and with this latest thing with Sally, I'm feeling a little traumatised. And relieved that the gang have been caught at last,' she said shrugging. Kay linked her arm through her friend's as they continued to their rooms.

'Ed's the one I'm worried about,' Alice confided. 'I've never known him to take things so badly. He really feels let down by Frank.'

'Wow, that's quite a mouthful,' Kay laughed, raising her eyebrows in surprise.

'Those are Ed's words, not mine. Did you think I'd suddenly swallowed a dictionary?' Alice asked, grinning. 'Come, let's sit on my veranda and relax. You can tell me why you were looking so sad when I caught up with you. I'll make us a coffee, and you can tell all,' Alice said, as they reached their rooms.

'I had intended to do just that when we got a chance. Now's as good a time as any I guess,' Kay answered.

Once coffee was made and they had settled down, Kay filled Alice in on her plans to save Ed the embarrassment of asking her to leave. Much to her surprise, Alice jumped to her feet spilling her coffee over her shorts as she did so.

'Are you out of your tiny mind? You can't leave him. He's madly in love with you for heaven's sake.' Kay opened her mouth to speak but Alice wasn't finished. 'Kay, you've got to be joking? You absolutely cannot break that man's heart, especially now he's lost his best friend,' Alice insisted, sounding very agitated.

'Do calm down, Alice, you'll give yourself a heart attack if you carry on like that. Ed wants me to meet him for a talk later,' she said. 'By the look on his face when he asked me, I can only deduce that he's had enough of having me on his team. I'm not taking it personally; I now see how dangerous it can be. I was only ever concerned with the wildlife. I never realised the dangers that poachers could bring to this job,' Kay explained.

Alice sat down heavily on her chair. 'Please, do me a favour and don't say a word about your plans to leave until he's had his say. I've a feeling you're barking up the wrong tree,' Alice said.

'Talking of trees, it's the marula tree that I'm to meet him under,' Kay smiled.

'You must let me know what he wanted after your meeting, Kay. I'm going to ask the kitchen to send me a meal here on my veranda. After fretting about you lot all day, I can't face having to go to the dining room.' Kay didn't blame her and knew she would have probably opted to do the same thing if she wasn't meeting Ed.

'I'll knock on your door when I get back,' Kay said.

'Do, and don't worry how late it is,' Alice said, leaning

back in her chair. 'I want no excuses from you why you can't tell me everything.'

'You're so bossy,' Kay said, getting up to leave.

Alice nodded. 'I know,' she said giving her a thumbs-up before Kay left.

Going to her own room, Kay showered and changed into her skinny jeans and a crisp white shirt. She shook her hair loose and liked the way it felt as it hit her shoulders. Checking her face in the mirror, she noticed tiny lines around her eyes, but apart from that she was happy with the tan. If she was going to leave, she would like Ed to remember her as an attractive woman rather than an unwanted ranger, she decided.

The lump in her throat as she thought about leaving was beginning to hurt. 'Pull yourself together,' she told her reflection. Adding mascara and a little lipstick, Kay picked up her bag and left the room.

As she approached their meeting point, she saw Ed was speaking to one of the staff who was placing a tray down on the table under the huge marula tree. She would miss the deep timbre of his voice and the way he kept pushing the hair off his forehead. Kay felt the knot in her stomach and pushed away the thought of how empty her future would seem without this sometimes-impossible man as part of it.

She watched as he left the shadow of the tree and walked to meet her with a look on his face she had never seen before. Something must have happened to Frank or Bear, she thought. Ed looked almost nervous as he reached her and took her hand in his, silently leading her back into the shadow of the tree and sitting her down on the chair next to him.

'What's the matter, Ed?' she asked nervously, having felt a quiver go through him as he had taken her hand in his. 'Has something happened to Frank? If this is a bad time for us to chat, I'm happy to meet another time.'

'Will you stop fussing while I organise our sundowners,' he said, his voice gentle, but filled with emotion. 'Just look at the colour of that sun. Nowhere is it better than in the bush. I've asked Tom to take a picture of us together as it sets, and the orange glow lights up the sky.'

Kay was confused. Could Alice be right, when she assumed Kay had misunderstood Ed's invitation to meet him? She decided to try and just relax, as she prepared herself for whatever he was going to say or do.

'Now, Kay, I want to ask you something,' Ed said, his hand trembling slightly. It was so out of character that Kay kept quiet and simply nodded.

Kay sat in the shadows, hoping Ed couldn't see her expressions as she contemplated what he was about to tell her. She could feel the beating of her heart against her ribcage and watched him fiddle with his watch before running his hand through his hair again.

He was obviously agitated and finding it difficult to tell her she was no longer needed at the lodge and the photo must be a goodbye gift for her to take with her. She opened her mouth to speak, closing it when Ed continued.

'Firstly, Kay, I want to thank you for all your help and ability to stay calm in that fiasco earlier. Secondly, I have something I very much want you to agree to. I don't expect an answer right away, but if you'll bear with me until I finish I'll give you the reason I need you to hear me out.'

Certain now that she had been right in her thinking, and before she could stop herself, Kay said, 'Edward Blake, I am fully aware that you never wanted a woman on your team. Even though you have been very kind and considerate to me since my arrival here. It has been an amazing experience, and one that I'll never forget.' She knew she was rushing her words but needed to tell him. 'The intermittent times we've spent together will be forever in my heart. I felt I had to make a concerted effort to work harder than the men to prove I could hold my own with my guests on the drives.'

He looked stunned, and opened his mouth to speak, but Kay, determined to have her say before he had a chance to fire her, continued. 'You don't have to ask me to leave, I've already arranged to return to Durban and my grandmother's cottage,' she fibbed, aware that her grandmother would welcome her home in a heartbeat. Kay took a deep breath as her eyes filled with tears at the look of astonishment on Ed's face.

'If you've quite finished telling me what I was about to say, would you do me a favour and let me speak?' he asked. 'Talk about getting the wrong end of the stick.'

Through her tears she saw Ed take a huge stride towards her. He pulled her into his arms and engulfed her in an embrace that took her breath away. He kissed her tears away, and then kissed her with such passion, her mind reeled. She pushed him away as she caught her breath. Looking up into his face, she watched as his smile reached his warm blue-grey eyes.

'I don't understand,' she stuttered.

'My wonderful girl, if you think you're leaving me for Durban, you can think again. Now can you just wait while I speak? Let's sit while I try to explain,' Ed said as he pulled his chair closer to her and took her hand in his.

'I've been offered a job that I applied for months ago. The boss has opened a game lodge in Tanzania, and they want me to manage it and to train the rangers. I'm having to recruit a couple of staff from here, ones I trust and who know the ropes. That's where you come in. Would you join me and become my assistant manager?'

Startled by what he had asked, Kay took a moment to react. 'But Ed,' she said.

'I'm not finished yet,' Ed laughed. 'I want you to join me there, as my wife.' He took a deep breath. 'There, I've said it.'

'I, I didn't expect that,' she said, wanting to laugh and cry at the same time. 'It's the very last thing I thought you'd be telling me. I don't think I can take it all in.' She laughed and covered her face for a few seconds. 'Was that a proposal?'

Ed laughed, lifting her into his arms. 'Let me try again,' he said, holding her at arm's length. 'My amazing and beautiful Kay, will you do me the honour of becoming my wife and business partner for as long as we both shall live?'

Kay threw her head back and laughed, as relief and delight coursed through her. She didn't need to consider this question. 'I will,' she said kissing him. 'My goodness I really can't believe this is happening to me. I was so sure you were going to ask me to leave. I'll have to call my grandmother,' Kay hugged him tightly, as Alice joined them.

'What's all the excitement, guys?' she giggled. 'I was waiting for you, Kay, but you've been ages, so I got fed up and thought I'd come and find you.' She frowned and studied Ed and then Kay's faces. 'What's going on with you two? Look, here comes Linzie with a bucket of champagne. What are we celebrating, Ed?' Alice asked, eyes wide with excitement.

'Well, as you're here, I guess we'll have to tell you,' Ed gave Kay a questioning look. She nodded in agreement. Tom arrived with a camera.

'You did it, mate,' Tom smiled at Ed, patting him on the back. 'I knew you didn't have to work yourself up worrying like you did.'

'Did what? Alice asked.

'Kay has agreed to become my wife. I've just plucked up the courage to propose, Alice,' Ed explained, looking happier than Kay had ever seen him before. Her heart swelled with love for the man who had helped change her life.

Alice shrieked and hugged them both, as Tom shook hands with Ed and gave Kay a kiss on her cheek. Tom then popped the cork on the champagne, and more glasses were brought.

Tom made a short speech and he and Alice raised glasses to the newly engaged couple.

Alice interrupted the proceedings. 'Where's the ring, Ed?'

'With all that's happened,' he said nervously. 'I haven't had a chance to buy a ring but in the circumstances, hope you don't mind me using my grandmother's for now.'

Alice pulled a face at Kay, as they watched Ed rummage in his pocket and pull out a velvet box. Getting down on one knee, Alice gasped, as he looked up into Kay's eyes.

'My sweet, brilliant and wonderful Kay. Will you please agree to marry me again, this time in front of witnesses,' Ed laughed opening the little box to reveal a large white diamond, surrounded by smaller yellow diamonds.

Both Alice and Kay let out a gasp simultaneously when they saw the stunning ring.

'Darling Ed, I'd love to marry you. But that ring is utterly amazing,' Kay said as Ed slipped it onto her finger. 'I'm more than happy to keep this one, especially as it has so much sentimental meaning for you.'

'Bloody hell, mate, what a rock,' Tom yelled.

'The yellow diamonds are the reflection I see when I look into your amber eyes,' Ed said quietly, pulling her into a kiss as Alice and Tom cheered and clapped.

'Now, if you two would give me a moment with my fiancée,' he said, putting his arm around Kay's shoulders, 'come back when the sun is setting, Tom, so that you can take our photo, please, then we'll meet you for dinner and tell you the rest of our plans,' Ed said, waving them away.

Once alone, Ed couldn't take his eyes off Kay. She felt her heart was finally healed after all the upset with Harry. She knew that her new-found love would never let her down. As she gazed into his eyes, any notion of leaving the lodge vanished. Even in the shadow of the marula tree, the diamonds sparkled sending shafts of light across the grass. Kay gave a deep sigh of utter contentment.

Also by Green Shutter Books

Broken Faces

The Boardwalk by the Sea Series:
Summer Sundaes, book 1

Printed in Great Britain
by Amazon